# And Then Spring Comes

## Jean Rover

Blue Agate Press

This is a work of fiction. Names, characters, places, and incidents either are products of the author's imagination or are used fictitiously and are not to be construed as real. Any resemblance to actual events, locales, organizations, business establishments, or persons living or dead, is entirely coincidental.

**And Then Spring Comes**
Copyright 2024 by Jean Rover
Blue Agate Press, Salem Oregon

All rights reserved.



ISBN: 978-0-9967130-5-4 (Blue Agate Press)
978-0-9967130-6-1 (eBook)
Library of Congress Control Number: 2024917245

Cover design: designpointinc.com
Back cover photo: Lois Rosen

Manufactured in the United States of America

The author is grateful to the editors of the following publications in which versions of these stories first appeared: *The Saturday Evening Post's Great American Fiction Contest* anthology, "The Day Truman Ruined Our Jam"; *Short Story America* anthology, "Fog"; *Short Story Me*, "Have You Ever Been In Love?"; *Literary Yard*, "On Edge"; *Freshwater Literary*, "Smart This, Smart That"; *Evening Street Review*, "Cliff Hanger"; *Propertius Press*, "And Then Spring Comes"; *Potato Soup Literary Journal*, "One Last Shout"; *Beneath the Boughs Unseen* anthology, "The Promise" & "Mildred's Secret"; *Helix Literary Magazine*, "The Invitation"; *Paper Tape Magazine*, "The Lie"; *Gold Man Review*, "Walk to the Gym" & "Reading Lillie," *Rose Red Review*, "One Kind Thing"; *Blue Cubicle Press* & *Work Literary Journal*, "Epiphany"; *Linden Avenue Literary Journal*, "Addie of the Strawberry Fields," *Liars League, London England,* "Strange Heart"; & *Liars League, Portland, Oregon,* "Secrets."

Thanks also to the following for recognizing my work: *Writer's Digest Annual Writing Competition,* "Stalked"; *Oregon Writers Colony,* "Addie of the Strawberry Fields," and *Willamette Writers,* "The Bridge."

## Also by Jean Rover

Touch the Sky

Ready or Not

Beneath the Boughs Unseen

# Contents

*If we had no winter, the spring would not be so pleasant: If we did not sometimes taste of adversity, prosperity would not be so welcome.*
**Anne Bradstreet, The Works of Anne Bradstreet**


*Sitting quietly doing nothing, Spring comes, and the grass grows by itself.*
**Matsuo Basho**

# And Then Spring Comes

J ulie Minotti had all the fans in the house going full blast but could hardly feel the blowing air. She stared at her face in the bathroom mirror. Beet red. Her hand clutched her stomach to hold off the nausea, but there was no stopping it. She puked into the toilet for the second time that morning.

Being ill in August was a double whammy. It was as if the hot weather joined forces with a virus and slugged her in the gut. Her head hung over the bowl while another nauseous wave hit. This time it was an agonizing dry retch. She rested on the edge of the tub, ran her fingers through her sweat-soaked brown hair, and covered her face with a wet cloth. When she pulled it away, the room started spinning.

Randy said she probably had a case of Delhi belly. "That spicy stir fry you had last night at the Indian restaurant must've been a real gut bomb. There were lots of hot peppers and curry in that thing. I mean who gets the flu in summer?" He grabbed his backpack.

"Maybe we could get one of those window air conditioner thingies," Julie suggested.

"What? For the ten days or less that we have sweltering heat in Oregon?" He slipped the straps over his shoulders. "You gotta be kidding." With that, he headed off to his university job in an air-conditioned chemistry lab.

Julie gathered crumpled towels from the bathroom floor and tossed them in the hamper. You'd think he could have picked up after his shower.

Maybe she should have gone to work, too. Her office building would be cool, but the thought of shuffling papers in her cubicle didn't help her queasiness, and if she had a virus she didn't want to spread it.

In the kitchen, she grabbed ice cubes from the fridge, tossed them in a glass, and doused them with ginger ale. The phone rang just as she finished pinning her long hair into a bun.

"If you can't keep anything down, suck on the ice cubes so you don't get dehydrated," her mother advised in her matter-of-fact way from Pennsylvania. "Don't you have air conditioning out there?" Louise didn't wait for an answer. Her motherly voice turned thin. "The test came back. That lump in my armpit...they say it's cancer."

Stunned, Julie watched the ice melt in her glass. "Oh no, oh no. Mom—"

"I'll have to have chemotherapy and radiation. The oncologist said it's the fast-growing kind." Louise's voice cracked. "I'll lose my hair."

The achy feeling in Julie's head spread to her chest. By the time she hung up, all the fizz had gone out of the untouched ginger ale. The big round thermometer on the patio said 104 degrees for the third day in a row.

The sickness in her stomach lingered. So did the dull chest pain.

Two days later, Julie found herself babbling to the nurse practitioner at her company's wellness clinic. "I can't seem to shake this."

After she peed in a cup, had a blood test, and a pelvic exam, Julie sat up on the examining table while the nurse moved the stethoscope over her chest.

"First, I thought it was the heat. Then I learned my mother has breast cancer. I mean I'm here. She's there. I'm her only child." Her voice cracked.

"Sorry to hear about your mother. Take another deep breath," the nurse said.

"The rest of the family all moved away from that small town. Who's going to take care of her? My breasts hurt. Maybe I should have another mammogram. Maybe Mom should move to assisted living, only I don't know if they take people with cancer. Things are really hectic at work. I think I'm getting an ulcer."

The nurse smiled. "Julie, you're pregnant."

***

She and Randy had tried to have a child for twelve years. Well, *tried* was probably not the right word. No, it was more like if *it* happened, they would go through with it. If it didn't, well that was okay. Now, the day of reckoning had come. She should be jumping for joy, but she was not. To be pregnant at thirty-eight was a scary thing, and there was her paralegal job at the law firm. A baby, when you're pushing forty? What about plans, like going back to school for a JD or taking that vacation to Sorrento, Italy? And, how the fuck could you water ski with breast milk dripping all over? And, what about Mom? Was it normal to feel this way? Maybe knitting tiny hats would help. Wait. She didn't know how to knit.

***

"Mom says she's going to come out here and stay awhile after the baby is born. I think she should come now," she told Randy who'd already begun patting Julie's stomach, happily calling it Junior. "I don't know how much time she's got. We should get her moved before I'm too far along, or she's too ill. And…she wants to know *when* the wedding is."

Randy had taken the news of Julie's pregnancy well, but he didn't seem a bit enthused about getting married or having a visit from Louise. "Whoa. Let's take this slow." He took a deep swallow. "Like, one day at a time."

For some reason, they'd never gotten around to doing the marriage thing. Julie remembered meeting Randy during a heavy December snowstorm years before. Major snow was as rare in Oregon as extreme heat and no one, not even the weatherman, was expecting it. The day had started out overcast and rainy. By mid-morning a few flakes sailed to the ground; by noon, everything was white. Schools closed and businesses dismissed their employees early. Julie, brown eyes wide and clutching the steering wheel, was relieved to have made it home. She was about to drive her red Mustang into the apartment parking lot when it got stuck in a snow drift that had accumulated at the entrance.

Now what? She looked through the snowflakes gathering on her windshield and spotted that good looking hunk who lived above her in 302, looking out his window. What an opportunity. She stepped on the gas causing the engine to whine and the tires to spin. She waited. Oh goody, all six feet two of Mr. Handsome was heading toward her.

She rolled down the window and looked into his smiling gray eyes. "I guess I'm stuck," she said, playing the damsel in distress.

Snowflakes collected on his blue wool hat and locks of curly black hair that escaped beneath the hat on the front and sides. A few flakes stuck in his dark mustache. "Quite a hot rod you've got here," he said, patting a fender. He squinted into the falling snow. "You steer, I'll push."

Once he rescued her, she planted a grateful peck on his cheek. Three days later, after the snow had turned to muddy slush, he invited her to a movie. Soon, they began spending weekends together. He gave up his apartment and moved into hers, and the months turned into years. They always said they would tie the knot when Julie got pregnant, but that never seemed to happen, even after they bought a nifty little craftsman house together on Warner Street with a big leaf maple tree out front.

A distraught Louise had claimed Julie's infertility was because they were living in sin. Julie came from a pious and fertile Italian Catholic family. All her cousins married young, had several children, produced numerous grandchildren, and even a few great-grandchildren.

"You have two extra bedrooms and nothing to fill them?" Louise had asked, upset.

"We're thinking about getting a dog," Julie said, hoping to distract her. "A pit bull, maybe."

The dog comment went right over Louise's head. "He's just taking advantage of you. You know what they say, 'Why buy a cow when the milk is free.'"

"Mom, stop."

"What? You're not good enough for him. Don't let him use you like that. Leave."

"He's *not* using me. I have a job that pays well. I don't *need* to be a kept married bitch."

"We sent you to a fine Catholic school, and you talk like that. Good thing your father's not alive."

***

Louise was always in a slump after their noisy holiday gatherings back in Pennsylvania, complete with jillions of cousins, a new baby to pass around, and someone in tent-sized maternity clothes. Along with the meatballs and manicotti came the questions: "When are you guys going to get started?" "Have you thought about wearing looser underwear?" Sometimes, after enough wine flowed, she heard the whispers. "He must be shooting blanks."

"I don't know what I did to get cut off like that," Louise would wail to Julie, her hands cutting the air in classic Italian fashion. She turned her eyes, behind oversized glasses, toward the heavens, and clutched her forehead. "Who's going to take care of you when you get old?" Saint Louise was aching to be a grandmother and for her daughter to be *legally* married, even though she was never particularly fond of Randy whom she still called *what's his name*.

"Whee-jums is the only one with a barren daughter," Randy teased.

"Who says *I'm* the problem," Julie shot back. They'd never bothered to see a fertility specialist.

***

"I want to be there when you have that kid," Louise said over the phone, not caring that her cancer treatment was taking its toll. "I told my oncologist, I'm going out there to see my grandbaby, if it's the last thing I do."

"Did he think that was a good idea?" Julie asked. "I mean with your—"

"Doctors. Harumph." Louise lowered her voice to mimic his. "'Or-eh-GONE is a long way from Pennsylvania, and babies still take nine months.' The ol' sourpuss reminded me of my next chemo session. I don't care what he says. I want to come to the wedding, too. I bought a new wig."

*Jeez. The wedding?* Julie didn't respond. *Get over it, Mom.*

"You there?"

"Uh-huh."

"Marriage protects a woman. Don't let anyone tell you it doesn't. You don't want your baby to be born a bastard. You make God mad, and you could lose that baby. Try to reason with *what's his name.*"

*Mothers.* Julie twisted her hair around her fingers. "That was then, this is now. Today, singles outnumber married people," she said.

"Oh my dear God. Your father is spinning in his grave. I'm coming out there."

***

"Whee-jums? Coming for a wedding?" Randy slapped his forehead with his hand when Julie told him about her conversation with her mother. "Jesus. That woman has a one-track mind. I like sleeping in on Sundays, and I sure as hell don't want to hear her lectures about fire and brimstone. Shit, she can't even call me by my right name," he said, discounting his own nickname for Louise. "Christ, it was your mother's marriage-and-babies phobia that drove you to run away to college in Oregon."

Randy wasn't letting go. "We've come this far. There's no sense rushing things." His own parents split up when he was nine, leaving him devastated as a child and leery as an adult. "Knots," he said with a pained expression, "aren't necessary, and they can end up choking you. We're probably common law anyway."

"You *better* get married," Louise fretted whenever she and Julie talked. "Settle down."

At times, Julie wished she wasn't pregnant. She couldn't help feeling like it was a mistake. Shouldn't she have maternal urges? She hated the idea of getting fat and ugly, and she worried about Randy who recently turned forty. Did he realize how having a baby at their age would change things? Plus, it was so hard to have two major events going on in her life—the birth of a child and her mother wasting away day-by-day.

How could she share her feelings with Randy? Especially after he came home from work clutching a toy football he bought on his lunch hour so he could teach "The Boy" the basics. Julie didn't even want to know the sex of the baby.

While Julie prepared a salad for dinner, he stood in the kitchen tossing the little ball in the air until his thought processes changed lanes.

"You remember Phil from work?" He snuck a cherry tomato and stuffed it in his mouth.

"Yeah," Julie said. She added dressing and began tossing the salad greens. "Tall, thin, blond, pimply face. About thirty-five. Races cars?"

"He just became a father for the first time."

She stopped. "Well, there goes the race car." She cut cubes of cheese.

"No kidding." Randy snitched a cheese cube and popped it into his mouth. "Phil was in the delivery room, and man, he said giving birth was like shitting a watermelon."

Julie shuddered. Images of blood and pain fogged her mind. She touched her stomach. There was a little being growing in there. Why did he have to put it that way?

***

After a long and splendid Indian summer, the November sky had changed to a cobalt blue. A windstorm chased the last leaves from the maple tree and left them in dull brown heaps on the ground. Julie was in her fourth month, constantly suffering from fatigue. Sometimes her blood pressure shot way up. She craved chocolate ice cream, egg salad sandwiches, and pickled things, even though they made her stomach lurch.

"Quit that job," Louise advised each time she called Julie from Pennsylvania. "Let *what's his name* step up to the plate and support *you* for once."

Julie had seriously considered her mother's advice, but put off discussing it with Randy, who now was fighting a severe bout of flu. He had a high fever, his body ached, and he felt weak all over. When the weakness lingered, his doctor said they needed to do more tests. Randy didn't have much of an appetite and his weight dropped ten pounds. The laundry piled up, the house needed cleaning, and bunches of maple leaves rotted on the lawn. Thanksgiving was just around the corner, but neither felt like going out for groceries let alone cooking.

Julie cried the night Randy decided to call Louise. "We need you to come...for Julie's sake," his voice cracked. "The doctors say I have leukemia. I could...I don't know how long I have. We need to talk."

***

Being needed was like an infusion to Louise's cancer-ridden body. She hopped on the next plane and arrived wearing a cheap, brown wig that hung too low on her forehead. Coupled with her big glasses with rhinestone-studded frames, she looked like the notorious Bad Hair Bandit wanted for a series of bank heists.

At first, doctors gave Randy a fifty percent chance for recovery, but then adjusted the diagnosis, calling his case acute. His need for blood transfusions increased from two to three times a week. Sadly, his immune system weakened until he became bedridden.

Louise walked to church on the next street every day to pray for Randy, and she made batches of her Stracciatella comfort soup—hot chicken broth into which she dropped a paste of beaten egg and Parmesan cheese and swirled it in the hot broth making shreds. "Eat, eat," she said, when it was done, "Shredded soup makes everything better. I dropped in three eggs." She held a spoon of the golden broth to his mouth. Randy, in his weakened state, didn't resist, even though his intense chemo treatments diminished his enthusiasm for food.

It made Julie happy to see Louise caring for Randy like he was her own child and Randy letting her do it. She remembered her mother feeding her the same delicious soup when she was a little girl, sitting by her bed when she was ill. Louise believed soup and a slathering of Vicks VapoRub could cure anything. In spite of her strong opinions, she was a good mom and Julie loved her for it.

In the evening while Randy slept, Louise relaxed in the recliner, watched Jeopardy, and worked on a quilt for the baby. "Get married before it's too late," Louise advised Julie. "I know Father Donahue would gladly come over here. *What's his*...Randy could at least do that for you."

"I can't do that to *him*. You bring a priest here, he'll think it's for last rites. Can't you see he's skin and bones?"

"Think about the baby. I'll make you a dress."

"For Christ sakes, Mom. A dress isn't going to fix a damn thing."

"Such language." Louise went back to her quilt.

***

December came and went. Christmas was a blur. Randy's health continued to decline. After a serious infection set in, he contracted pneumonia. When he struggled to breathe, Julie dialed 911. An ambulance moved Randy to the hospital, where he drifted in and out of consciousness.

After more tests and a series of examinations, doctors placed a *Do Not Resuscitate* order in his chart notes. Julie wanted to call Louise, but decided not to for fear she'd say something that would upset her more. She tried calling Randy's father, but there was no answer.

She finally reached his mother, who was obviously intoxicated. Her words slurred. "I can't come now. I'd like to, but I can't. You'll let me know? I can't—"

"Yeah," said Julie disgusted. Poor Randy. It was up to her. She never left his bedside.

"Take care of Randy Jr.," he said, during a lucid moment. He grasped her hand. "You...you'll give him the football?"

"Sure," she said squeezing his hand to reassure him. "You bet."

"Get hold of Vinny in HR. He'll know about my benefits. I got life insurance and a 401(k)."

"You're going to be all right," she lied.

"I should have married you."

"Shhh," she said. She swallowed, fighting back tears. She didn't want him to see her cry. She touched her fingers to her mouth and then to his lips. "In our hearts we're joined. That's all that matters."

That night, after calling Louise with a status report, she tried to get comfortable in a chair near Randy's bed, a daunting task with her pregnancy bump. After shifting several times, she finally settled down listening to hospital sounds—beeping noises from the equipment hooked up to Randy, ringing telephones, distant conversations, footsteps in the hall. Exhausted, she started to doze but jumped up when she heard moaning. She rushed to Randy's bedside but couldn't tell if he recognized her.

She patted his cheek. "Do you know who I am?" she asked repeatedly. He blinked his eyes but didn't focus. Julie pressed the nurse-call button to summon help.

A short, round nurse bustled in. She grasped Randy's wrist, feeling for a pulse. "I think he's leaving us," she said. "Our instructions are not to resuscitate. I'm so sorry."

"Don't say that," Julie pleaded. "He can still hear." She grabbed his hand.

Randy gave a final gasp and lay still.

"I'm sure you want a few minutes," the nurse said. She patted Julie's shoulder. "Stay as long as you need."

In the dim light, Julie leaned over the bed and kissed Randy's cheek and a tuft of hair on his bald head. "Goodbye," she said. There was nothing else to do.

Randy died on a cold, snowy day in January when Julie was in her sixth month. Five inches of snow covered the ground before the thermometer hit bottom, turning it to ice. The leafless maple tree in the front yard loomed like a dark skeleton against the gray sky. Grief welled inside, but Julie was unable to cry.

Julie and Louise arranged for a private, brief graveside service. Randy's father and his mostly sober mother joined them. They arrived separately from the Midwest, she with a hint of brandy on her breath.

Julie's doctor didn't want her to stay out in the cold too long. The added stress took its toll on Louise, too. As they huddled before the casket, Julie, clutching Randy's toy football, remembered the snowy day when she first met him, his warm touch, and how during tender moments, he called her his "snow bunny." The tears finally came. Slow at first and then racking sobs. The wind blew sleet under the canopy. "Damn this weather—why can't it stop? Why can't it just stop?" Julie cried.

Her mother put her thin arm around her. "It'll pass, honey," she said. "It'll pass."

At home, Louise made hot tea and toast while Julie, nauseous and exhausted, rested on the couch with a heating pad. "Drink this slowly," Louise said, handing her a cup of chamomile. She sat at the end rubbing Julie's feet, trying to help warm her.

Louise's awkward wig, too full for a woman her age, overpowered her now fragile and pale face. "When I was young, I had big dreams. I wanted it all, marriage, a large family. Instead, I got two miscarriages. Then you came along." She smiled. "You grew up, moved away. Life went on until your father died. After that, I just wanted to wrap my arms around a grandchild." She paused, tugging at her chin. "Will you give the baby our last name or Randy's? Otherwise, you'll have two different last names. You don't want that."

"Don't rub so hard. My feet hurt," Julie said, not wanting to engage.

*Why didn't she just quit?*

After the thaw, on a bright February morning, they had a small memorial service for Randy attended by co-workers and a few friends. Julie sat in the chapel with her hands on her swollen stomach. *If this baby is ever born, it's going to be the saddest creature in the universe, because there hasn't been a happy moment in my life since I've been carrying it.* She heard Louise softly praying for a few more months of life.

***

March, true to its nature, roared like a lion. There were days of wind and pelting rain. Louise's health took a turn for the worse. The cancer that seemed to be in remission outwitted her treatments and spread to her lungs and liver. Julie struggled to take care of her mother and herself. She was eight months pregnant, and the doctors cautioned her to stay in bed or she could lose the baby. Those eight months had seemed like years to Julie. More gray cropped up in her dark hair, but she didn't have the desire or the strength to keep hair appointments. Finally, she used some of Randy's life insurance money to hire a housekeeper.

On a cold, rainy day, two days before spring officially arrived, Louise died. No ambulance, no fire truck, no flashing lights, or sirens ushered her out—she was at home with only Julie and the hospice nurse in attendance.

During those final moments, Louise reached for Julie's hand. "I'll never get to see the baby." Tears glistened in her eyes and spilled into the deep wrinkles below them.

"You can feel it," Julie said. She lifted her top and held her mother's gnarled hand against her bare stomach. "Did you feel it kick? The baby knows you're here." They both cried. It would be as close as Louise would ever come to her grandchild.

After Louise's private funeral, Julie's doctor confined her to bed. "Be careful. Be very careful," he warned. "We don't want to lose this one in the home stretch."

***

Eventually, spring mellowed into daffodils, hyacinths, and violets blooming everywhere. The maple tree came to life again with massive green leaves and creamy yellow flowers. Children played outside. People planted sweet-faced pansies in window boxes, and the robins were back.

Julie actually grinned that sunny morning in late April, standing over the graves. The air picked up the woodsy scent from the stand of tall firs nearby. A blue jay, pecking the grass, cocked its head and looked at her curiously before flying away. The cemetery was empty, except for a lone worker trimming a hedge.

It was the first time Julie had been to the cemetery since her mother passed, but she felt compelled to come. She hardly had time to grieve for Randy before her mother's health deteriorated. They were all she had, and she needed to connect with them—even if it was this way. She squatted awkwardly on the cool grass and placed bunches of yellow tulips by each of the markers, patting Louise's and smiling again. I wonder what Randy would think about Louise resting right next to him. She managed a giggle. She's probably telling *what's his name,* he should have married me.

The grievance counselor who'd come to her home advised her to take it slow. "Go through the sorrowful phases, the sadness, the anger, whatever. Take little steps," she'd said.

Julie's eyes teared. "I don't know. I feel abandoned. I wake up tired. I go to bed sad, and I don't sleep."

For Julie, coming to the cemetery was one of those little steps. A start. But, let go? Move on? How did people do that? What if they couldn't? She thought back to that hot day in August when *it* first showed up. How would she raise a child alone? She'd have to return to work. Who'd take care of the baby? It was hard for her to focus, so she hadn't given a lot of thought to finances. She had a mortgage, bills, and a small savings account. She could never go back to Pennsylvania. Randy's parents offered help, but they lived in Iowa in different cities, struggling with their own lives. Louise left only a couple of certificates of deposit. Did Oregon recognize common law marriages? She hadn't taken time to pursue it.

Sometimes, she secretly hoped she would miscarry, so she could feel normal again. Sometimes, she felt like everything around her was dying or that she should just find a bridge and jump. It always ended with guilt.

Julie glanced at the headstones again. She patted her stomach, now the size of a beach ball. "The two people that mattered most to me will never get to meet you." When she tried to stand up, she could feel something wasn't right. First, it was a twinge, a cramping followed by a series of sharp pains.

She massaged her temples. "Why did I come here? Cemeteries are pastures of death. I should not have risked it," she said to her belly, as if the baby could hear. A warm trickle, then a gush dripped from between her legs. She dropped to the ground. "Help me," she screamed. "Please, somebody help me."

The groundskeeper dropped his hedge trimmer and rushed to her side.

Her body twisted in agony. She felt scared. Alone. Surrounded by death.

"Relax ma'am. Try to relax," the groundskeeper said. He kneeled next to her, wiping sweat from his brow. "I called them. They're coming. Just hang on. Please, just hang on."

Her gut tensed. She thought she heard Louise's voice. "Trouble always comes in threes," her mother would say after a third relative or neighbor passed away. Sometimes she included celebrities in her count. "If you make God mad, you could lose that baby…"

Once the ambulance arrived, the EMTs loaded her onto a gurney. Julie cried out as another wave of pain shot through her abdomen. "Breathe," they told her, "breathe." She tried, but in the yellow haze that clouded her vision, she saw another funeral and people, strange people, carrying a tiny, white casket. "No! No!" she pleaded to the serious, hazel eyes of an EMT before losing consciousness.

***

"You look better today." The nurse smiled and pulled open the drapes. The sun streamed in, making a bright rectangle on the green tile floor.

Julie pushed the button that elevated her bed. She could hear the sound of a lawn mower in the distance.

The nurse placed a pillow across Julie's lap and handed her the baby. "Just touch her upper lip to your nipple, honey. Pull her onto your breast when she opens her mouth."

Julie stared at the little nursing bundle. She was actually holding the child that Randy was so certain would be a boy. She searched for signs of him. That was Randy's curly dark hair wasn't it? She gently fingered the small clenched fist with paper-thin nails that seemed to belong to Louise. And that nose, that was hers. All of us together packed into that tiny body. At least, it seemed so. Maybe she would name the baby Randi Louise. If only they could be here to see this precious being.

"I see your daughter arrived on April 22. That's Earth Day you know." The nurse lingered by the window. "Everything's so green out there. It's going to be a beautiful day. I'm a gardener myself. Can't wait to get outside and dig in the dirt."

Julie's throat tightened. Her counselor's words echoed: *Tuck your loved ones in a special corner of your heart...and go on.*

*Go on. Go on. Go on.* She needed to. God, she wanted to.

Julie lean over and kissed the baby's soft cheek, drinking in its sweet newborn smell. *Me and you against the world, little one.* The baby's eyes flicked open.

The nurse poured a fresh glass of water and set it on the bed stand. "Have you decided on a name yet?"

"April," Julie said, without hesitating. "Her name is April."

# The Day Truman Ruined Our Jam

I stood on a wooden stool next to the kitchen sink wrapped in an oversized apron plucking stems from strawberries with a dull paring knife. Mom rinsed what I hulled and crushed them with a potato masher, until she had enough to dump into the speckled blue pot on the stove. The sweet summery fragrance of cooking strawberries overpowered the lingering smell of our breakfast bacon. A line of Ball jars with open mouths waited on the counter.

A fly buzzed at the window, rubbing its hairy black legs together probably licking his chops. Maybe he really wasn't a fly. Maybe he was a prince under the spell of some wicked witch waiting for my kiss to release him, so he could carry me away to a magical land, a special place where dreams come true, and there are sparkles on everything. Castles, carriages, white horses—

Wop! Mom smacked him with a rolled up newspaper. "How'd he get in here?" she asked.

Now, with my dark-winged prince squished on the sill, there was no one to rescue me from all these berries.

"Keep hulling, Cassie," Mom said. "Today's a two-batch day." She winked at me. "I declare, for a seven-year-old, you do as good a job as those cannery ladies."

Maybe so, but I didn't want to be a cannery lady and plucking all those hulls made my shoulder ache. I snitched a fat strawberry and squished it in my mouth. Its sweetness tingled on my tongue, but the berry was so big, juice dribbled down my chin. I spit the hull into the sink and wiped my mouth on my shirt sleeve.

The screen door slammed. "Hurry," Daddy said, his gray eyes round. "Get the kids. The President of the whole United States is going to pass through Rivers on the train."

Mom continued to stir. "Really? President Truman? In Oregon? In June? Can that be?"

"He came to see the Vanport flood damage. Afterwards, he's coming through *here*," Daddy went on. "Not many people know his train's coming through Rivers. Al down at the Chevron station told me when I filled up. There wasn't time to put anything about it in the *Rivers Signal*."

Al was a big man with a mustache like a squirrel's tail. He knew a lot because he ran the gas station and went to most of the "doings" in town. Out in the country, we pretty much kept to ourselves, except for church.

"He's getting in some campaigning," Daddy said. "Probably going up against Dewey. He's making some stops on the way from Portland, heading to K-falls."

Mom smoothed her thin, cotton housedress, lines forming between her brows. "I've got some jam going here." She pointed to the big pot of berries bubbling on top of our Universal stove, gave the pot a healthy stir, and then banged her wooden spoon against its rim. "You and the kids go."

Daddy switched the knob on the stove to off and jerked the wooden spoon from her hand. "You can always make jam," he said, setting the spoon on the counter. "Can't always see a real live President." He stood there with his arms folded over his chest, his jaws clamped together, his steel-toed boot tapping impatiently on the linoleum. Whenever Daddy got like that, you knew you'd better get hopping.

"Okay, then," she muttered, "but I already dumped in the sugar and stirred in lemon juice."

We'd been listening to Arthur Godfrey on our small, white Philco radio that sat on top of the fridge. "Go get yourself some Lipton Tea," Godfrey said, just as Mom reached for the dial and snapped him off. Her lips pursed. On top of ruining a batch of jam, I could see she wasn't happy about missing her favorite program.

"Where's Rodney?" Daddy asked.

I knew where he was. After finishing his morning chores, he went outside to our dandelion-pocked yard dressed in his Roy Rogers shirt and black cowboy hat to shoot outlaws with his cap gun.

"Cassie, go get your brother," Mom said.

I hopped off the stool and undid my apron. Daddy followed me out the door, probably knowing Rodney never did anything I said, him being two years older than me.

Sure enough, Rodney wasn't budging. He peeked around the skinny trunk of a filbert tree, our black dog, Trigger, at his feet. We'd named him after Roy Rogers' horse.

"Reach for the sky, mop head," he said, pointing his gun at me, making fun of my unruly brown curls. "I'm takin' you in."

"Quit your nonsense," Daddy ordered.

"Can't," Rodney said his gray eyes serious. "They're after me."

"Git," Daddy said. "We're going to town to see the President."

Rodney dug in. "Not without Trigger."

Daddy narrowed his eyes. "Harry Truman is President of the United States. Dogs aren't interested in that."

Rodney's mouth scrunched into a pout. "Trigger's my horse," he insisted. He brushed a wedge of brown hair from his face.

"No he ain't," I said, "He's a dog. You don't have a horse."

Daddy pointed a thick finger at Rodney "Git movin'. Right now."

I gave Rodney a big "gotcha last" grin. He stuck out his tongue.

Daddy herded us all into our tan Dodge coupe, Rodney sitting in the middle; me on Mom's lap, since our car only had one seat.

The train depot was a low, tan clapboard building. Daddy parked in a lot across the street and hurried us to the side facing the tracks. There weren't many folks there—the Ridgeways, with their two boys, and Margaret Skinner all gussied up in a pink summer dress. She stood next to her lawyer daddy who wore a suit. Snooty Margaret always had her nose high in the air because she lived in town and got store-bought dresses at Bessie's. Me and Mom shopped for fabric at Della's Variety and Dime. I kinda enjoyed sorting through all the patterns and watching the lady at the cutting table measure the material with a neat machine that figured costs.

There was a bunch of other people at the depot I didn't know. One lady held a bawling baby. Then, there was us—Mom still in her apron; Daddy, standing there in his faded shirt trying to smooth his thick, dark hair, Rodney armed with his cap gun, and me in my overalls and scuffed, brown oxfords with the toes cut out. I hoped no one noticed the red smear on my shirt sleeve.

"Here it comes," Daddy shouted. The blast of the train horn almost popped my eardrums. Its big wheels clanked on the tracks; the brakes hissed as it slowed. The flashing red dinger that warned drivers at the intersection up the street waved back and forth. I was never that close to a train before.

Two men stood on the rear platform behind a railing of what looked like a big, fancy caboose. President Truman, I guessed, was the one doing all the waving. I thought someone that important would be the size of Paul Bunyan or at least as tall as Daddy. What I saw was a white-haired, old man in a suit. With his glasses, Truman looked more like Grampa Owen than a President. Only Grandpa hardly every wore a suit.

Mr. Truman had a big smile on his face, as if passing through our town was special. He gave us all a big wave, and we waved back. Especially Daddy. I thought maybe his arm would jerk off.

"Give 'em hell, Harry," he shouted. It didn't seem like he should talk that way to the President, but the man grinned real big when Daddy yelled that. He glanced over at Daddy and pointed. The other grownups cheered. All except Margaret Skinner's dad. He stood there with his arms folded, looking like he just bit into a sour apple.

Rodney aimed his cap gun. Pop! Pop! No one much noticed, except me. I mean with the clapping and all.

The train never really stopped, just slowed. In a matter of seconds, it moved down the tracks, and the waving Truman shrunk to the size of an ant.

"You'd think they'd of stopped the train and let him say something," Mom said. "Especially, with that big flood we had in May. All those poor folks that helped build ships during the war flooded out when the dike gave way. Left with nothing."

"Probably already talked about that up in Portland," Daddy said. "He's only stopping in cities on the way south. Salem, Eugene. Places like that. He's gonna save his wind for then."

"Mom," I said, pulling on her dress. "Rodney shot at the President."

"I didn't neither," he blurted. "I saved him from those gunslingin' outlaws hanging on the train." He pointed his cap gun at the tracks. "I only pop off outlaws."

Mom's hands flew to her hips. "Put that thing away. Next time, we'll leave you two home."

"Next time. Next time," Daddy said, not hearing the whole conversation. "There's not gonna be a next time. It's not every day a President of the United States rolls through Rivers."

Mom reached into her purse for a hanky and wiped her nose. "I don't know if it was worth losing a pot of jam."

"You can reheat it," Daddy said.

"No." She sighed. "It'll be all rubbery. Spent all my egg money for the sugar. Dumped in four whole cups."

"Slop for the pigs, now," Rodney said.

Mom glared at him. "Not with the cost of sugar. Maybe we can use it on pancakes or to flavor a cake."

Rodney made a face. "I'm not eatin' anything that's turned to rubber."

"We'll use it one way or another," Daddy said, his voice gruff. "We'll make do." Then he grinned at us. "So," he said, "now you can tell all the kids you saw a real live President of the United States."

"I wonder," Mom said, as we headed toward the car, "what he thought, me standing there in my stained apron. My hair not even combed." She had a head of brown curls like me, which she tried to tame with her fingers.

"He's the *President*," Daddy said. "He's probably seen it all. If we waited till we got all prettied up, we'da missed him."

Rodney shrugged. "Butch's daddy says Dewey is gonna whip his butt."

Butch Skinner was Margaret's brother.

"Don't you talk that way," Mom said. "What do we send you to church for?" She curled her index finger against her thumb and thumped Rodney on the neck.

I gave Rodney an ear-to-ear smirk. He didn't dare punch me with Daddy so close.

"Aw, Dewey hasn't done nothin' for the workingman," Daddy said, frowning. "And, Truman could a done even more if it wasn't for that 'Do Nothing Congress.'"

***

That night, Mom sat on my bed tucking me in. "Does Mr. Truman really care for us like Daddy said?" I asked.

"I think so, honey." She handed me, Annie, my ragdoll. I can't sleep without Annie. Mom made her especially for me outa one of Daddy's ol' wool socks.

"President Truman's done a lot for us common folks. Someday you'll understand."

"Do you think he really saw me?"

"Well, he saw us all standing there supporting him, so in a way, yes."

I thought about my fly-prince lying belly up on the windowsill and what could've been if Mom didn't swat him, and he turned out to be real. "Mom, when I grow up, I don't want to be *common*."

"You can be anything you want, dear. President Truman is just trying to make sure you get the chance."

"Mom."

"Now what?"

"Will you check under the bed before you turn out the light?"

"Cassie, sweetheart," she said, ruffling my hair. "There's no need for that anymore. Boogeymen don't dare hide under the bed of a little girl that's seen a real live President of the United States."

I slept really well that night, knowing Mr. Truman was out there. I even forgave him for ruining our jam.

# Fog

Clement Diddle used to have a job in a book bindery. That was before the fog came and he quit, or maybe he was asked to leave. He couldn't remember which. Just that he wasn't able to concentrate and went out on disability. That's where the checks came from.

At the book bindery, all those clunking machines talked to him at once. It was better now because he only had Izzy and those little blue pills. People didn't understand. He had this gift. He could hear voices that they couldn't. At first he thought the voices were from his neighbor's TV coming through their shared wall, kind of like a swarm of bees nesting in the plaster, but then the pulsing water in the shower talked to him, too. People were so one dimensional.

Clement lived in an efficiency unit on the second story of *The Beverly*, an older brick apartment building off Cliff Street. His place was at the very end, next to the stairs, so he could come and go without running into other tenants. Those people that always smiled and said, "How ya doin'?" They didn't care and he didn't know.

His little space was his world, and it had everything he needed—a tiny bathroom, a couch that opened to a bed, one brown Naugahyde recliner, a refrigerator, kitchen sink, a two-plate stove, and a table for his computer and precious printer. Clement had always lived alone, but not lately because Izzy, his ink-jet printer talked to him: "Go there. Go there. Do it. Do it."

Having a printer was expensive because it required reams of paper to keep it talking, and it couldn't be any ol' paper. It had to be smooth, bright white, and just the right weight. Clement liked to rub the paper against his cheek before he loaded the tray. He always typed in the same thing—*Talk to me. Talk to me, Talk to me*—in fourteen point Times Roman. No printer would take his message seriously if he used say, Comic Sans or BaaBookHmk. And why were there so many fonts anyway? It was confusing and the world didn't need them.

Once he hit file, print, he'd close his eyes and listen to the chugging sound. It was like music. The printer fired up and calm swept over him. "Good job. Good job," Izzy said.

Having a printer was a job-and-a-half because once Izzy spoke, Clement had to shred all that paper. He couldn't dump Izzy's droppings—they might contain a secret message or could bring him bad luck. Fortunately, his shredder didn't talk, it just murmured *whirrrrrrrrr* as it chewed the sheets and spit out strips.

Before his fog worsened, Clement had belonged to an online chat group. He'd struck up a conversation with a woman named Butterfly who suggested they meet for coffee since they both liked the same things: corn curls and Snickers bars.

Clement opted out because he knew she wouldn't be interested in him as a person. No woman ever was. And the picture he'd posted online wasn't really him. Clement was a hulking, overweight middle-aged man with reddish, balding hair, freckles, and beefy arms. A pair of vertical lines ran up his forehead almost to his receding hairline. His gray, dead eyes stared out over a button nose and knob-like chin  He always wore black slacks and a black T-shirt. Colors didn't do anything for him, and besides, too much color made him anxious.

Butterfly devoured romance novels and chatted about them non-stop, which baffled Clement. Why would anybody read those things? He never read books because when he did, the print ran together making him reach for another pill. His favorite reads were those chocolate candies that had little messages inside their wrappers which he saved and comic books, especially ones about Batman or monsters from outer space. Those things were straight forward, easy to follow, and made sense. The world needed sense.

Besides he never trusted women. Not really. He even asked Izzy if he should hook up with Butterfly and she said, "Don't go. Don't go." Computers, especially ones with printers, were like windows—you could see the world, but you didn't have to go out into it. He liked it that way.

Clement Diddle. Clammy Clem. Fiddle Diddle. None of it was his fault. In grade school, the kids used to tease him about his name. Gray mixed with rocks in the head, like a big cement mixer they said, taunting him. What kind of a chance did he have with a name like that? Shiddie Diddie, Shidiot, Piddle Diddle, they called him. His mother said to pay them no mind. He was different, special even. And that's all he can remember of his childhood. The rest of it was haze.

Clement always parked his blue Toyota pickup in a particular spot even though the spaces at his apartment weren't reserved. He had to have that same spot, the one over by the oak tree with its thick trunk and sprawling branches that seemed to reach for him. He loved that tree, and it helped him remember where he left his vehicle. Anxiety kicked in whenever he had to park anywhere else, leaving large wet spots under his armpits.

Emery, that skinny, snot-nosed thirteen-year old, never failed to park his mountain bike in Clement's spot. The little dipstick left it there while he ran up to his apartment somewhere in the complex, never in a hurry to move it. That meant Clement had to get out of his pickup and shove the blasted thing aside before he could drive in.

The damn brat. He does that on purpose. And who names a kid Emery? What do the kids call him? Em? Emmy? A friggin' sissy name. Besides that, the little weasel had zits all over his pinched face and dark-framed know-it-all glasses. Clement never much trusted kids—especially ones with pimples and egghead specs.

One day, after returning from the drugstore, Clement had had it. He refused to jump out and move the bike. Instead, he blasted his pickup right into it, crushing the front wheel and its fender. Afterward, Clement tossed the bike as hard as he could onto the sidewalk. *That'll teach the little shit.* There was no one around to see what he'd done, so he clumped up to his apartment and typed as fast as he could. *Talk to me. Talk to me.* He ordered ten copies and clicked file, print. The printer cranked up, chuntering, "Deny it. Deny it."

Clement spent the rest of the morning filing candy wrapper messages, until his stomach growled. Ah, yes, he needed to go to the grocery store, although he hated going there. Too many people, and all those squawking brats with their dirty shoes and diapered butts riding in the carts like monkeys. That's why, for the most part, he went late at night. Unfortunately, he was all out of apricots and almonds, another of his favorite things next to corn curls and candy bars. Just the thought of pressing an almond into a soft apricot and slowly chewing was orgasmic.

He grabbed his black hat and hopped into his pickup. He had to laugh. The bike was gone, except for one bolt lying there on the asphalt. Too bad. So sad. He would've loved to see Emery's face when he discovered his precious bike was a heap of metal. Twit, twit, twit.

Satisfied, Clement gunned his engine and drove off to Big Mike's Market down the street. He went there because he loved looking at the bulk food bins all lined up in neat, gleaming rows: beans, spices, rice, cereal, flour, all kinds of noodles, tea, piles of candy, and things he never heard of like quinoa and anise seed. He could find almost anything he wanted in the bins. It was like Christmas year round.

***

Clement grabbed a cart. He picked out a gallon of milk and a couple loaves of bread before hurrying toward the bins. Wheeee. He filled a bag with almonds, listening to the whooshing sound they made as they tumbled into his plastic bag. He tied it off and wrote down the bin number. Now, onto the apricots.

A small boy, with dirty blond hair, opened the lids of various fruit bins with his chubby hand and watched them slam shut. Every time a dropping lid made a bang, he'd giggle.

"Ricky, come here," his mother called. Ricky didn't listen. "Rickeee don't do that," she said again, her voice rising. The boy ignored her.

Clement towered over the boy and watched the little chub wipe his nose on the back of his hand. In his other one, the kid carried a small, red toy car. "Whroom, Whroom," he said, as he drove it on top of a bin lid.

"Get away, listen to your ol' lady," Clement said in a gruff voice. Ricky paid him no heed. He lifted the lid of the apricot bin and let it fall. That infuriated Clement. Apricots were sacred. When the kid's mother went around the corner to look at cereal, the little snot stuck his tongue out at Clement. Then he opened the bin and reached in with his hand. The same one he's used to swipe his snotty nose.

*Oh, dear God. Who'd want to eat those apricots now?* How dare that little shit defile his precious apricots? Then, the darn kid did the unthinkable. He dropped his toy car inside and looked up at Clement with a wide grin. "Car gone," he said.

That did it. Clement grabbed the kid by the arm and smacked him hard on the bottom.

Ricky wailed and took off in the direction of his mom. "That bad man hit me," he yelled, sobbing.

"What man?" He heard the woman say.

*Run!*

Clement disappeared through the work area where the staff unpacked boxes and headed out fast to the dock. *Phew no one was there.* He jumped down and huffed and puffed his way back to his apartment. He didn't even stop to get his pickup. Even Clement knew you never touch somebody else's kid. The police would be after him.

His heart beat was chaotic like that time he'd had a panic attack. Oh, God, he needed Izzy. Once home, he turned on his computer and with shaky hands typed, *Please Izzy. Talk to me. Talk to me. Talk to m e.* File. Print. He waited. Izzy said, "Bad move. Bad move. Hide out. Hide out."

Clement hunkered down in his apartment. He couldn't sleep. What if the store had cameras? There were cameras all over these days. He tossed. He turned. He didn't have a TV. Watching things moving on screens freaked him. And how did he know that the TV wasn't watching him?

The next morning, Clement snuck out and swiped the landlord's newspaper from his door step. Back in his apartment, he flipped through the pages. *Oh, no! There it was.* A small story. Police were looking for or seeking information on a man who assaulted a four-year-old child at Big Mike's Market. No description. The little boy said the man was "big and mean looking." His mother claimed "the brute" left a handprint on little Ricky's bottom.

The article warned the public to be on the lookout. What was worse, it said what the penalty was for felony child abuse—jail time and a fine of over $6,000!

Relieved they had no description of him, Clement tossed down the paper and pulled the drapes.

Mid-morning there was a knock on the door. *Who could that be?* Clement peeked through the drape covering his side window. Yikes. He spotted a police cruiser parked on his street.

His shirt stuck to his back. He could feel his face flush. *What to do? What to do?* He rushed to his computer and sent a document to his Izzy. The paper jammed. "Shit. Please Izzy, please."

The knocking got louder. Clement tugged at the jammed paper, clearing the roller. He tried again. Finally, the printer kicked in, "Don't talk. Don't talk."

Clement wiped perspiration from his forehead with his sleeve, took a deep breath, and opened the door. "Yes," he said, in his most innocent voice.

The officer looked him over. "You Clem Diddle?"

"That's Clement Diddle. Nobody calls me Clem."

"Clement then. Folks at the Big Mike's found a vehicle left in the parking lot. It's registered to you." He pulled a note pad from his pocket.

*Oh, no. My pickup.* Clement scratched his head. He remembered what Izzy had said, "Don't talk. Don't Talk."

*Think.*

"I, uh, I'm diabetic, something I got from my mother. Got shaky, so I didn't feel like driving. Afraid I'd pass out. Low blood sugar makes you crazy. So I wandered a bit. Sat down, ate a candy bar, came home, crashed. Wanted to get the pickup, but haven't been feeling well. Still feel weak."

"I see," said the officer. He scribbled on his pad.

"Heh, heh," said Clement. "Thought I was dying."

"Did you go into the store, Clem?"

"That's Clement."

"Uh-huh. So did you? Go into the store?"

*Is he trying to trip me up?* "Nah, nah. Wanted to, but I was wobbly. Just sat there. Didn't want to chance drivin'.'"

The officer's eyes narrowed. "So, you were in the parking lot?"

"Yeah, sure."

"You see anyone running from the store?"

Clement swallowed hard. "Nah. I always park in the back. Less hassle and I was pretty lightheaded." His legs trembled like Jell-O. "Why? Was there a robbery?"

The officer crossed his arms and stared. "You're kind of a big fellow aren't you?"

"That's what they say." An uncomfortable silence followed. Clement's chest tightened.

"Uh-huh," the officer finally said. "Well, you better get the vehicle. The store manager is complaining about it."

"Sure," Clement said, "Sure. I'll get on it."

"And, Clem, stick around, we might need to talk you again." He slammed his notebook shut.

He watched the officer leave. *Phew. That was close.*

He hugged Izzy. "Good job. Good job," she said.

A watermelon smile covered his face. "I pulled it off," he shouted. Now, all he had to do was go and get the pickup, but first, he'd check his mail. *Who knows? Might be another disability check.* He could never remember when they were supposed to come, just that they did.

He looked for his number—195—in the row of black metal mailboxes hanging on the brick wall. There were no envelopes or advertisements in his box—only a note pinned to the magazine holder with a clothespin. Clement unfolded the note and read: *I saw what you did. Wait for further instructions,* printed with a blunt, lead pencil.

Clement's whole body shook. He needed water for his suddenly dry throat. *Jesus, a witness.* Back upstairs Izzy said, "Oh no. Oh no."

While walking to Big Mike's, Clement belched up stomach acid. Without warning, he heaved his breakfast onto the asphalt, took a deep breath, and wiped his mouth on his sleeve. When he reached the parking lot, he looked over his shoulder. Nothing. He drove back home and parked his vehicle in the spot under the oak tree. At least he didn't have to mess with that damn bike.

Up in his apartment, he fumbled with the computer keyboard. After several typos, he finally wrote: *Talk to me. Talk to me.* This time in sixteen-point bold. "I'm desperate, Izzy."

He clicked on file, print, and held his breath. The printer made its initial chugging sounds before spewing, "Check again. Check again. Watch it. Watch it."

Clement spent another sleepless night. He didn't bother to pull open the bed, just laid on the sagging couch with a blanket and a pillow. The next morning, his neck hurt and his back ached. He dragged himself up and splashed cold water on his face before sneaking out his door and down the stairs. Careful to look both ways, he crept along the brick apartment walls and lifted the landlord's newspaper.

Safe in his apartment again, he brewed himself a cup of instant coffee by boiling water in a saucepan. He no longer used the coffeemaker because the grounds looked like dirt, and its gurgling and popping sounded like a drowning man gasping for air. *What was it saying?* It scared the bejesus out of him.

He blew on his coffee and took a long drink before thumbing through the news. Nothing. What did that mean? Was he being set up? Was that note on his box some kind of sting operation? Did that cop write it? He'd seen shows like that on TV. Well, when he had one. He couldn't remember when that was. Did he ever own a TV? Or, was it someone else's? The fog. That goddamned fog.

*The blue pills.* He went into the bathroom and swallowed one. Afterward, he retreated to his recliner and thumbed through a comic book, waiting for the medicine to kick in. *Was there another note out there?* He didn't want to seem overly anxious, in case someone was watching his moves.

Ah, 10:00 a.m. The mail would be there. He lumbered down the stairs and over to the mailboxes—only one envelope, his electric bill. Sure enough there was a note fastened with a clothespin. It said, *I'll be in McVeety Park tomorrow at 1:00 p.m. Bring cash. Go to the garbage can by the men's john. Wait there.*

*Blackmail!* It didn't say how much money. It probably would be a lot, but it was better than prison. He couldn't have Izzy in the slammer. He'd be locked in there with all those dirt bags. Bad people. People that would glare at him and God knows what. What would he do without Izzy? Who would talk to him and tell him what to do? Izzy was all he had. He didn't have a family, did he? If he did, he couldn't remember them. But sometimes when he was sleeping, he thought he felt his mother's hand covering him, like that big oak tree in the parking lot reaching for him. Maybe Mom would come tonight. Dr. Morrison said his mother wasn't really there, that he was hallucinating, but Clement knew it was her. She smelled like lilacs.

He lay awake all night listening to the clock ticking and the traffic moving. *Was there someone on the stairs? Maybe I should hide Izzy.* He heard the roar of the big metal dinosaur that came every Wednesday morning. It lifted the garbage bin outside and swallowed its contents, its two eyes gleaming in the darkness. He pulled the blankets over his head whenever that monster came, growling.

Bleary eyed, Clement forced himself to get out of bed. "Get it. Get it," Izzy said. Mid-morning, he put on a fresh black T-shirt, drove to the bank, and withdrew $4,000 from his account, leaving a zero balance. It was better than jail.

"Are you sure?" asked Chelsea, the short, chubby teller. "Are you closing your account?" Her black, curly hair and one squinty eye reminded him of his mother. Each time Clement went to the bank, he searched out Chelsea because she was patient and helpful. Besides, you could trust a person who seemed like your mother.

"No," he said in a quiet voice.

Chelsea gave him a long look.

"Somethin's come up. I mean, you can't leave a printer all on its own," he said.

She cocked her head. "What's that? Are you okay? You want me to call someone?"

"No. No." He looked over his shoulder to see if anyone was watching.

"You seem nervous."

"Don't be hassling me. It's my money."

"Yes, it is," she said. "Just wanted to make sure you weren't being scammed or something. There are a lot of bad people out there."

"No. No scam."

She counted out the bills and put them in an envelope. "You take care," she said and gave him that sweet Chelsea smile. "Don't be flashing your money around. Hear me?"

Clement turned and left. He'd have to wait for his next disability check to live on. He drove his pickup back to the apartment planning to walk to McVeety Park. Before heading out, he put the money envelope in a plastic Big Mike's bag.

***

There was only one set of toilets at the park. Ah, there it is—the garbage can by the men's john. That must be the one. He checked his watch—12:55 p.m. He waited.

Nothing.

*What was that?* Ah, a flushing toilet. Soon, an older man, wearing a blue sweater and slacks, came out. Tall and thin with a serious Clint Eastwood face, he loomed over Clement as he approached.

Clement shivered, feeling his damp skin under his T-shirt. Maybe the guy was an undercover cop. Maybe he should all out confess. "I didn't mean to," he blurted. His ears were pulsing. "The kid was ruining the apricots."

The man paused and peered at him. "Mean to do what?" He gave Clement a "go ahead and make my day" look.

"The bins. I was at the bins," Clement said.

"I don't know what you're talking about," the man said. "You homeless?"

"No," Clement said. "I came to pay up."

The man's eyes narrowed, his frown deepened. "Damn druggies," he muttered as he hurried away. "They're all over. Can't even stop to take a piss."

*False alarm.* Clement wanted to cry. He needed Izzy. *What to do? What to do?* He sat down on the ground and held his head. Minutes passed, but they seemed like hours. He opened his eyes and two feet planted themselves in front of him. He followed the feet up the pants legs, the chest, and finally the face.

Emery.

"It was you that broke my bike," Emery blurted. "You pay up or else, I'm reporting you. You can't trash someone's property and get away with it." He took a breath. "And I saw you steal the landlord's newspaper. For sure, he'll put you out."

*The little sniveling pissant.* Clement wanted to pinch his head. "Idiot. You don't leave a bike in a parking space."

Emery didn't budge. He balled his fists, his skinny body standing firm. "People say you're a real nut job, but you don't scare me. Pay up or else I'm telling."

"A nut job? Why you little pock-faced bastard." Clement leapt to his feet. He wanted to jerk those smart-ass glasses off Emery's face and stomp them into pieces—well, after he strangled him.

Emery hopped around in his tight jeans like a boxer shadowboxing the air. "Go ahead," he shouted. "They'll lock you up."

The word *lock* hit Clement like a wave. He stopped, fumbled with his plastic Big Mike's bag, until he found the envelope, and pulled open the flap. He held out two $100 bills. "That enough?"

"That's more like it." Emery grabbed for the money and stuffed the bills in the pocket of his hoodie. "See ya around." His mouth made a smirk before he scuffled off.

Drained, Clement watched him leave. He couldn't help it. He burst out laughing. He wasn't going to jail. No, he'd be able to see his Izzy again. Feed her. Listen to her. God, he needed Izzy. And now he knew. You don't harm kids. Izzy had been clear about that, "Bad thing. Bad thing. Never touch. Never touch."

"That little earwig didn't even say thank you," Clement said, talking to himself as he trundled homeward with $3,800 in his pocket. "The bike. It was all over that goddamned bike. Ha." People on the street stared at the orange-haired hulk walking along, babbling to himself.

*Home*. Such a precious word. Such a special, safe place. When he reached the parking lot, he threw his arms around the big oak trunk and rubbed his cheek against the rough bark. "Thank you, Mother." He chugged up the apartment stairs, unlocked the door, and hung his hat on the coat rack. "Izzy, sweetheart." He gently caressed and kissed a stack of twenty-four pound bright-white paper and lovingly fed her. Once he typed in his message and hit file, print, Izzy hummed and slipped into her tender rhythm. "Sleep now. Sleep now. Sleep now."

# Addie of the Strawberry Fields

A h, the strawberry fields—Mavis and me hoped to land rows next to Jakey Heiner, the coolest guy in sixth grade; one of the few boys who really knew how to dance. Instead, we drew spots next to Addie. She was a large woman in her middle years, with short blond hair and wide blue eyes. Normally, that combination could be pretty, but Addie, with her broad face and heavy body, looked like a clumsy tank with hair.

A light overnight rain made everything muddy. As we knelt on the damp earth at 5:30 a.m., searching the wet bushes for berries, I recalled the knowing looks my mother's sewing circle friends gave whenever talk turned to Addie. It never failed; some sweet-faced church lady bit off a string of thread, set down her thimble, and wound her finger in a loop by the side of her head meaning Addie was "not all there."

So naturally, we were leery picking next to her. I mean we'd never seen crazy up close.

"She lives with her sister in town." I said, whispering.

"The one with the hair lip?" Mavis asked her gray eyes wide, her voice equally soft.

"Yeah. Their house is over by the water tower."

"Scary stuff." Mavis's eyes didn't blink.

"Dad said it's a good thing they have each other." I'd seen the sister, Freda, at our church. Tall, thin, older than Addie, wore glasses, had gray hair pulled straight back into a knot at her neck and a jagged scar on her upper lip. Definitely homely. She worked in the next town at the hospital doing something, I wasn't sure what.

Addie worked in the fields. I guessed it was something folks thought she could do. I couldn't picture her checking in patients at Doc Hill's office or standing behind the soda fountain at the Rexall drug store.

She seemed to be a hard worker, humming "Rock of Ages" and other hymns to herself, snapping the red fruit off the vines with her thick, mannish hands, carefully filling the six hallocks in her wooden carrier. A fast picker, she was always a few feet ahead of us, much to my relief. I tried to sneak careful peeks whenever she hauled her filled boxes to the check-in table, to see if she had a crazed look or maybe was on the verge of exploding. My glimpses never got that high. The only thing I saw was a muddied green pad covering her bulky knee. When she returned to her row, it was back to humming.

Once that stopped, she blurted scripture to imaginary heathens. "Repent," she said, "And your sins will be wiped out." She glanced up, looked back at us, and smiled.

Our eyes widened and locked. Then, Mavis abruptly shifted from squatting to bending over, her long blond hair blocking her face. She spoke in hushed tones. "Don't ever look crazy people in the eye."

"Why not?" I asked.

"It can set 'em off," she said.

I tugged at the brim of my white bucket-style hat pulling it low over my brown curls to shield my face. I cast my eyes at the ground, glad they'd never gotten higher than her knee pad.

I heard Addie mumbling something else, but I couldn't make it out, and I wasn't about to look.

"Maybe she's going to attack us," Mavis said, her hand covering her mouth.

I couldn't tell. I was just grateful for the other pickers around us.

By mid-morning, the clouds disappeared and the sun was back; by noon, we were sweating. The crew, mostly kids and a few moms, stopped to eat lunch, gathering in our little groups, under a big Douglas fir tree at the edge of the field, chatting as we ate. I blew off Jakey Heiner. He was leaning against the thick trunk all ga-ga over Veronica Miller, the one girl in my class that wore a cup bra. Compared to hers, the cotton Maidenform Mom got for me at Sears, seemed like training wheels on a kid's bike.

Addie sat clear off to one side taking bites from a chunky sandwich of homemade bread that seemed to match who she was, smiling and talking to herself.

I wondered about that. I mean her over there all by herself. I couldn't help feeling sorry for her, but couldn't figure what to do. Our lives stretched ahead of us fresh as a new field of clover. Addie's had pretty much arrived.

"When you have plenty to say to yourself, you don't need to sit with anybody in particular," Mavis said, knowingly.

I opened my lunch sack. Discussion about Addie done, I said, "I'm gonna buy a pair of white saddle shoes. After today, I should have enough money."

That didn't impress Mavis. "I got shoes. I'm going to send away for another Elvis record."

"Fat chance." I laughed. You couldn't buy forty-fives in Rivers, the town where we lived. You had to go into Portland, and Mavis' mother would never hear of that. I doubted that she'd even let her order another one by mail, but Mavis claimed she'd already scissored the order form for the record store from the *Oregonian* newspaper.

"Hmmm, hmmm, yay, yay" Mavis slapped her thighs to the beat as she sang, her upper body gyrating, her small breasts bouncing. "I can't get enough of that man," she blurted, her voice loud.

That drew a look from Addie.

"Shhh," I said and nudged Mavis. "She might think we're heathens."

"Cripes" Mavis pulled a Hostess cupcake from her lunch sack. "Let's cash in some of our tickets, so we can go see *Old Yeller*. It's still playing at the show."

"Mom says berry money is for school clothes." Done with my sandwich, I tore the wax paper off my oatmeal cookie, but I eyed her chocolate cupcake with the white squiggly line of frosting across the top. Mom never got us store-bought cupcakes. She made everything from scratch.

"You don't have to tell your mom every *single* thing," Mavis said, taking a healthy bite.

"The field boss won't allow it, anyway," I said. Mavis was now down to the surprise-inside crème filling. My mouth watered. "You're supposed to cash in your tickets at the end of the season." I was glad when the rest of the cupcake disappeared into her mouth.

Lunch over, we stopped at the rickety wooden outhouse before heading back to work. It was out of sight a ways from the field behind a cluster of smaller trees, near where they parked the flatbed truck. I always hated using it because of the dead skunk smell in there, but we didn't have any choice. Mavis held her nose as she entered. I waited outside.

I felt a tap on my shoulder and turned around. Addie loomed over me like a giant walrus. My heart thumped, remembering what Mavis had said about making eye contact with crazy people. If she strangled me, who would know? There was no one else around, and Mavis was inside taking her time, probably drenching baby oil over her arms so they'd tan up.

"This yours?" Addie asked, holding out my white hat. I knew it was because of the red cherry image and the words, *Life is just a bowl of cherries* embroidered in black on the front.

How could she have my hat? I must have left it under the tree during lunch. It was precious to me, keeping the sun off my head and making me look cool.

"Yeah," I said, reaching for it.

She stood there for a moment, looking directly at me, her blues locked on my browns. It seemed as if she wanted to say more, but didn't; just stared with a kind of yearning expression.

I clutched the hat to my chest. She turned away.

I didn't even thank her. My feet glued to the ground, my legs still shaking, I watched her big body lumber back toward the field.

Who was she, really? Did she have friends? Ever? What made her crazy? A broken heart? Maybe she was born that way? How did you get to be "off"? Could that happen to anybody, to us?

I told Mavis about it as soon as she came out of the john, smelling like a new baby's butt. "Eeeew," she said. She held her nose, the same way she did when she went into the outhouse. "Have your mom wash the hat."

I didn't answer, because I couldn't stop thinking about Addie. She seemed stuck in a body that allowed no one in. Maybe she wasn't crazy, so much as misunderstood. I mean she knew the hat was mine and thought to return it. I didn't know, but that moment, that look, haunted me long afterwards.

***

Home from college years later, I learned Addie wandered through town, inviting folks over while her sister was at work, so she could give away "her" belongings—a cardboard box full of mason jars, a steam iron, some skeins of red yarn, her father's mantel clock, a crystal relish dish, and their upright piano. No one seemed to know where she was planning to go, just that the minister thought people who took the stuff ought to give it back to the sister.

I think most people did, except for the ones that took the piano. Mom never got over that. "The piano belonged to their mother. It had a lot of sentimental value. They ought to be ashamed, taking advantage of someone touched in the head like that," she said, as we peeled potatoes together.

"And they call themselves good Christians," she continued over dinner.

"Poor Freda," Dad said, cutting his meat into small pieces. "You have to feel sorry for the sister."

It wasn't long after, Mom said *they* took Addie away. I guessed that meant to some institution. I pictured Addie sitting on the edge of a metal bed in a narrow, windowless room at the asylum, rocking back and forth, talking to herself.

I remembered the strawberry field, earthy summer air, sticky hands stained red, and the day she returned my hat. I'll never forget the look she gave me that came somewhere from the depth of her soul. Maybe if someone had broken through and reached out to her back then, things would've turned out differently. Maybe in that little inch of time, that someone could've been me.

# The Promise

Killing your ex-husband isn't what most people think about during the holiday season, but that's exactly what Michelle wanted to do. She hopped from one foot to another trying to stay warm as she stood in line in front of Save-Mart at 5 a.m. on the Friday after Thanksgiving. There wasn't a drop of moisture in the air, just frost on the roof tops and a chilling wind that invaded her jacket and red wool hat. It was so cold she could see her breath. No wonder they call it Black Friday.

"Damn that Jerry," she muttered. She pictured herself dropping him into an icy green sea from a helicopter. He had promised their two small boys that Santa would bring them the very popular Rambo Danbo game if they were good. It was his way of keeping them quiet, so he could watch professional football. Now they, like every other kid, had their hearts set on this hot, new electronic novelty.

The Save-Mart line quickly spread like fast growing cancer cells until it snaked around the corner of the store and into the dimly lit parking lot, even at this hour, crammed with cars. Michelle had never expected anything like this. Several people had camped for hours in the darkness in front of the store entrance. They brought blankets and folding chairs and ate breakfast from Styrofoam containers. A chubby, middle-aged man stood directly behind her. His big stomach pressed against her as he craned his neck to see if the door was about to open. Michelle spun around and glared at him. He wore a black wool hat, gray jacket and had a large turned-up nose that seemed out of place on his face. His dull gray eyes avoided her stare. He sipped coffee from a paper Starbucks cup and munched on pastries from a white paper bag. Michelle had skipped breakfast. The coffee sent a twirl of steam into the dark air. The aroma of rich, good coffee coupled with the sweet smell of sugar and fat made her mouth water. She couldn't remember the last time she'd had a really good cup of coffee.

Her thoughts drifted back to Jerry, still in his warm bed, and then to the last conversation she'd had with him—if that's what you could call it. Talking to Jerry was like trying to teach music to a tone-deaf student.

"What were you thinking?" Michelle had demanded her hands on her hips. "All the boys talk about is this silly game." Jerry hung his head the way he always did. "I can't afford to buy them one," Michelle shouted. "Can you?"

Jerry hooked his thumbs in the waist of his jeans. He needed a shave and his unkempt brown hair hung over his bloodshot eyes. He was in between jobs—again. His gambling habit and allergy to steady work had destroyed their marriage. Despite his dark, once handsome looks, Jerry was about as solid as ice cream on a hot day.

"They'll get over it," he muttered.

"You just don't get it, do you?"

"Get off my back."

"They're children!" She tugged on the thin silver chain around her neck.

"Something will come up," he insisted.

"They believed you." The slim chain snapped.

"Maybe I'll get lucky." They left it there. It was always where they left it.

After Jerry stormed out the door, Michelle pulled her shoulder-length, light-brown hair into a ponytail and proceeded to paint her toenails bright red. The vivid color and slow, meticulous brush strokes had a soothing, meditative effect. By the time she reached the tenth toe with a second coat, the queasy feeling in her stomach had lessened.

The boys, six-year-old Jared and four-year-old Brandon, broke her heart. Both tried hard to hold their side of the bargain. When Brandon spilled his cereal, Jared ran for a sponge and wiped up the milk; something he had never done before the promise of the Rambo Danbo.

"I help," little Brandon said, not wanting Jared to win more favor with Santa.

Jared carried his dinner plate to the sink and picked up all his toys before he went to bed. Brandon did his own awkward imitation but couldn't quite reach the kitchen counter. He cried all the way home from the babysitter's house because he'd lost his mittens and thought Santa would hold it against him.

***

Since the divorce, Michelle worked as a waitress at a nearby sandwich shop. She barely made enough to pay the rent and buy food. Jerry seldom came through with child support.

Everyone at the restaurant liked Michelle. Despite the challenges in her life, she had a friendly disposition and was on a first-name basis with her regular customers. In between tuna melts, hamburgers and keeping coffee cups full, she listened to their chatter and happily exchanged stories about children. She was twenty-six years old, pretty, wholesome looking and it paid off in tips. No one would have guessed that behind the natural smile and warm, brown attentive eyes was a life teetering close to the edge.

The unusually cold winter had caused heating costs to skyrocket. On some days, she and the boys wore jackets in their small basement apartment in an older, drafty house. However, when little Brandon came down with a cold and then bronchitis, Michelle turned up the thermostat. At night, she tucked him into her bed to keep him warm.

She had hoped to complete a secretarial course so she could get a better job, but dropped out to pay the doctor and heating bills; then the brakes went out on her second-hand blue Chevy. She helped Alma, an older woman who lived above her, make slipcovers for her thread-bare love seat. Her sewing project and the more generous holiday tips enabled her to scrape together an extra fifty-five dollars.

When Michelle heard the Save-Mart was having a "door-busting" sale on Rambo Danbos for forty-eight dollars instead of the normal eighty-nine, she dragged herself out of bed at 4:00 a.m. All the trips to Goodwill for clothes, saying no to movies, candy, toys, and just about everything else that cost money made her determined to make her children's wish come true. Sure, it was just a game; but a promise was a promise—and granting it was within her reach.

"They're opening the doors!" she heard someone shout near the front of the line. "Go, go, go!"

The crowd began to surge forward; strange elbows shoved Michelle aside. She tried to push back, but her small stature was no match for the out-of-control wave of people that moved backward and forward until it finally pushed her through the door.

A throng of shoppers swarmed around the large table holding boxes of Rambo Danbo games. Michelle managed to squeeze in, but couldn't get to the front until a group behind her thrust her forward. She leaned against a heavy-set woman in a bright blue wool coat to keep from falling. Her awkward tilt created a gap through which she managed to stick her arm and grab one of the games. She was trying to pull it past the woman when she felt another hand suddenly lock onto the box.

"It's mine!" Michelle yelled into the blue coat. She tightened her grasp only to hear the cardboard tear as someone jerked the game away.

"That was mine," she wailed to the small piece of packaging she held in her hand.

The woman in the blue coat gave her a dirty look. "Quit leaning on me," she growled.

The public address system crackled, and a male voice announced that the Rambo Danbo game had sold out. The crowd groaned. Then the microphone hissed and popped and strains of "Frosty the Snow-man" floated over the din.

"Hurry!" someone shouted. "They've got some screamin' deals on aisle three."

Michelle's heart jumped in her throat, her head ached, and she felt dizzy from skipping breakfast. She needed to get outside in the fresh air. She hurried past the displays of ornaments, artificial trees, and banks of candy canes. A mechanical Santa waved his arm. "Ho, Ho, Ho, Merry Christmas everybody," said his battery powered voice.

A tall woman, owl-eyed behind thick eyeglasses, hit Michelle with her shopping cart. "Mildred needs a new Crock-Pot," she said to her companion. She didn't even apologize.

In the distance, Michelle saw two young women playing tug-of-war over a red jacket. A store employee wearing reindeer antlers tried to intercede, but ended up on the floor. Michelle ran toward the checkout counters. This was all so crazy.

Suddenly, she stopped.

The middle-aged man who had the coffee in line stood there with an armload of Rambo Danbo games resting on his big stomach that made him look about six months pregnant. He announced to people around him that he bought one game for his grandkid and planned to sell the rest on eBay.

"Say, don't leave empty-handed," he said to Michelle. "I'll sell you one right now for just sixty-five smackers." His pink, fleshy face beamed.

Michelle smirked. One of the games he held had a tear in the packaging. The anonymous hands now belonged to a face and its body to the sleazy underbelly of the secondary market. She felt like she just turned over a rock and was staring at a swarm of creepy dark things moving toward her. "I'd rather pay full price than line your pocket," she sneered.

He shook his head and laughed. "I'm giving you a bargain."

"It's Christmas," she said.

"That's the point." He snickered. His nostrils widened.

"I was ahead of you in line," she shot back. He just turned away leaving her to look at the fat folds at the base of his head.

Outside in the parking lot, Michelle welcomed the blast of cold air against her face. At least she could breathe. Her hands shook as she turned the key in the ignition. The engine made a groaning sound and then kicked in. "Phew," she sighed. Her tires squealed as she drove away and waited for a red light to change.

*It's hell to be poor. Children don't understand poverty. Maybe this is a blessing in disguise. What if I lose my job? What if we end up homeless and have to live in this poor excuse of a car? Christmas isn't just about things and presents, but it is hard to make children understand that—especially when their friends get piles of toys and that idiot, Jerry, made a promise he didn't plan to keep. For crying out loud, aren't children entitled to some magic in life.*

The light turned green and Michelle made her left turn onto the street that was busy even at this early hour. She longed to paint her toenails.

Out of nowhere, a police officer wearing a white helmet stepped from the curb and with sharp jabs of his arm motioned for her to turn right. At first, Michelle thought he was redirecting traffic, but then she saw the red and orange BBQ—ALL YOU CAN EAT sign and realized she was in an empty restaurant parking lot. She could see the cop's motorcycle conveniently hidden behind a large bush.

Michelle rolled down the window. She took a long swallow.

"Ma'am, I need to see your license, registration, and proof of insurance."

"What's the trouble, officer?"

"Your license, registration, and proof of insurance, please."

Michelle fished the license and insurance card from her purse and pulled the registration from the glove compartment.

"What's the problem?" she asked again.

"The reason I pulled you over," the young officer said, "is because you made an improper left turn."

"I don't understand."

"When you made your left turn, you pulled into the right lane. You should always pull into the left lane at an intersection. Did you know that?"

"This intersection is controlled by traffic lights, and I have to make a right turn up there." She pointed to the next corner. "I...I wanted to get over while I could."

"You'd have plenty of time to change lanes, once you made your turn, ma'am." He seemed to be smirking like a hunter that just snared a rabbit. "You know if an oncoming car was making a right turn—"

"Nothing was coming," Michelle interrupted. "If there was, I would not have turned."

"Sometimes there are pedestrians."

"There was nothing...nothing there." Michelle said firmly.

"It's still dark out, ma'am."

"There was nothing there." Her hand slapped the steering wheel. "Absolutely nothing."

"Some people, you know, don't heed stop signs when there's no traffic around, but the law requires that they do so." He sounded like he was talking to some backward child.

"I would never do that."

"I'm not saying that you would." He went off to his motorcycle to check her record.

Michelle waited. *That little snip. His slight build makes him look about twelve, and in that white helmet, he looks like a Martian.* She fought off an urge to drive away.

The officer returned, stood in front of her open window and scribbled something on his pad.

"Are you writing me a ticket?" She leaned her head toward the window, trying to see.

"Yes ma'am." He tore it from the pad and thrust it at her.

"Two hundred and forty-two dollars! For a minor offense, are you kidding me?"

"You have the right to appeal." There was that smirk again.

"You think this is funny?"

"Ma'am—let's not make things worse." He sounded irritated.

Michelle didn't care "Worse! How could things get any worse? You just took my Christmas...my savings...the kids won't have anything now."

"You can explain all that to the judge." He seemed pleased with himself.

"By then, Christmas will be over."

"You need to move on ma'am." He jutted his chin.

"Children don't understand that they're poor!" she blurted.

"Our conversation is over ma'am. You have the right to appeal." He sounded like a recording.

"But..."

"Drive safely, ma'am." He turned and walked away.

Michelle started the ignition. Her foot trembled as she pressed the gas pedal. Her head throbbed and she felt cold. Really cold.

After turning right, she pulled into the empty parking lot of a bank. The dizzy feeling returned, and she was afraid to drive farther. She stared at the idyllic snow scene painted on the bank's windows. A string of jolly snowmen in red and green wool hats, peppermint striped scarves, and mittens danced and skied against a background of falling snowflakes. There was no joy in her heart.

She dumped the contents of her purse on the passenger seat. Like an addict seeking a fix, she grabbed the Tylenol bottle, popped off the lid, and washed down three tablets with the plastic water bottle she kept in the car. She rubbed her sore neck waiting for the painkillers to take effect. If Jerry hadn't made that reckless promise, she would not have gone to the store and none of this would have happened.

She should not have married Jerry, but in the heat of one passionate moment, just that one moment, she got pregnant. She was only nineteen when Jared was born, and it changed everything. Everything. Two years later, she had Brandon. Why did it always take two kids and a few years before a couple realized their life together was a mistake?

The snowmen's smiles seemed to mock her. In their frosty faces, carrot noses, and coal black eyes she saw images of that big man at Save-Mart laughing because he had a pile of those games; Jerry standing there with that idiotic, ever-present blank look; the woman who bumped her in search of a Crock-Pot, and that stupid, smirking cop, a real life Grinch.

"People are no damn good," she cried. She crumpled over the steering wheel glad that she was alone. At first, the tears slid silently down her face and then gave way to body shaking sobs. "They're just no damn good."

Michelle rose early on Christmas Day. At seven in the morning, it was quiet in the apartment and very cold. There was hardly any traffic on the street. Occasionally, the older gas furnace would kick on and rumble in the background. Every time it did, she hung her feet over the register in the floor and waited for warm air to dry the cherry red polish on her toenails. When her toes were smudge proof, she hid them in a pair of heavy, warm socks. Then she scooped coffee from a can into her coffee maker. While it gargled and sputtered, she placed three bowls on the table. Even the bowls were cold. She pulled the big yellow Cheerios box from the cupboard and set it next to the jar of peanut butter. The boys would come bounding out any moment anxious to get at their gifts. She would make the toast after they settled down.

Not able to afford a Christmas tree, she had covered a small end-table with a green towel and decorated her potted philodendron with tiny ornaments. She taped the awkward glitter-covered star Brandon had made from yellow construction paper to a drinking straw and stuck it in the middle of the pot. She set a small red candle between the plant's flowing vines.

The boys pinned their stockings to the arm of a living room chair, and Michelle filled them with some candy she got at the mission. She picked up a small, red plastic fire engine for Jared from the mission's donation center and a blue plastic airplane for Brandon. The mission also gave her socks and underwear. She placed the gifts on the floor next to the end table and decorated plant.

She sipped her bland coffee, lit the candle, stood back, and sized up the plant and gifts. At least it looked festive. It wasn't exactly what she planned, but it was enough. The boys had gifts, they were all in good health, they had a roof over their heads, and they had each other.

She set a box of mac and cheese next to the stove. They would have that, hot dogs, and leftover apple pie from the restaurant for lunch. She also took home the split pea soup that wasn't selling well. The soup and some crackers and cheese would be their Christmas dinner.

Suddenly Jared darted passed her in the direction of the philodendron. Brandon was close behind. Michelle made them put on sweaters before they emptied the stockings and tore the paper from the gifts. Then in an act of defiance, she turned up the thermostat. They could at least be warm for one hour on Christmas morning.

"He didn't bring it." Jared shouted when he discovered the red truck. "We asked for a Rambo Danbo, and he didn't bring it." His lower lip trembled.

"Honey, we need to be grateful for what we have." Michelle set down her coffee cup. "Let's take a look at that nice truck."

"I was good and he didn't bring it." He glared at Brandon as if he had done something to cause this misfortune.

"I good too," Brandon said.

"Maybe he missed our house." Jared ran to the window. "Maybe, if we had a *real* tree." He ran back to the decorated plant and slapped a leaf causing a tiny ornament to fly across the room. "Maybe he didn't know we were here." He clenched his small fists.

Brandon set down his airplane. His brown eyes were big and sad. The Tootsie Roll he chewed dribbled down his chin.

"Maybe Santa ran out," Michelle said. "That could happen. Maybe next year..."

"But I told all the kids we were getting one." Jared stamped his little foot. His lower lip jutted into a pout.

"Just look at this fine truck." Michelle tried to distract him. "It even has a ladder that goes up and down."

Jared threw the truck down. "I don't want it! I'm telling Dad!" he wailed. Then he ran off to his bedroom and slammed the door.

Brandon climbed into Michelle's lap and buried his head in her chest. He got upset when his big brother did. Michelle held him tight and kissed his head. She wanted to scream. *Go ahead and tell your Dad. That'll do a lot of good. That bastard caused this problem. He ruined our Christmas, not to mention that piggish man at the store and that damn sniveling little cop.*

"Mommy, is Santa mad?" Brandon asked.

"No honey. It's not your fault." She squeezed his shoulder.

"Are you going to paint your toenails now?" he wondered. Michelle flinched—not because he asked, but because her little boy had noticed. That was the final straw.

"Mommy, why are you crying?" Brandon asked.

"Oh, honey...I..." Before she could finish, the doorbell rang—four rapid rings in succession. That had to be Jerry. That was the way he always announced his arrival. Impatient. Self-centered. Annoyed because he had to wait. He hardly gave a person a chance to respond before the sequence of four rings began again.

What was he doing here now? He usually didn't get up until noon. This time she was absolutely going to kill him. Maybe tell him to get the hell out. No, she had a better fate for him. She would make him go and explain to Jared why Santa didn't bring the game. That way he could see close up what a broken promise looks like. She set Brandon down, wiped her eyes on her sleeve, and flung open the door ready to do battle.

"Santa!" Brandon screamed. "Jared! Jared! Hurry! Santa is here! He found us!" He jumped up and down.

Michelle stared. Sure enough, Santa stood there with a young woman wearing a green fir trimmed elf hat that set off her short reddish hair and blue eyes. Michelle didn't recognize the woman, but the man in the padded red suit and white beard seemed familiar. There was something about his gray eyes. They definitely didn't belong to Jerry. Jerry's eyes were dark brown. Maybe this couple had come into the restaurant.

In a flash, Jared came running from his room. He grabbed the gaily-wrapped package from Santa's hands, and he and Brandon ripped the paper away.

"It's a Rambo Danbo!" Jared screamed. "He came. He came. I told you he would!" he said to Brandon, redeeming himself as the big brother. "Thank you! Thank you, Santa!"

Little Brandon ran to Santa. He hugged his knee and darted back to his big brother, leaving a sticky chocolate smear on Santa's leg.

Michelle was speechless, but glad the kids remembered their manners. "How did you know...I mean what they wanted?"

"I'm Santa. I keep lists." She'd heard that voice before.

"I know I should know you, but..."

"Something for you too," the elf interrupted. She handed Michelle a tiny, thin package wrapped in a red bow.

"Thank you." Michelle pressed it against her breast. "Are you folks from the mission?"

"Let's just say we're on one." Santa winked. "This is my big day, you know."

Michelle couldn't resist. She stepped forward and tugged at the white beard, pulling it away from his face.

Her eyes got big. Her mouth opened so wide, her jaw almost hit the floor.

"You're that cop," she blurted. "The one who wrote me that ticket."

Santa smiled sheepishly. He looked down at the floor.

"This is my wife, Jill," he said, introducing the elf. The young woman grinned.

"I hated you," Michelle said.

"I know," he said laughing. He put his beard back in place. "The kids think I'm real."

"But how did you find me?"

"I already had your address. I asked around, did some checking, talked to a lot of folks. You know, cop stuff. Do you really think I look like a Martian?"

Michelle's face flushed. She had told the traffic ticket story to just about everyone and always at the police officer's expense.

"I couldn't fix the ticket," he said. "So Jill and I—we decided the next best thing was to fix your Christmas."

"Merry Christmas," Jill said. She reached out and hugged Michelle.

"Mom, Mom," called Jared. "Come and see how this works!" Brandon clapped his little hands.

"That must have cost you a fortune," Michelle said. "I know those games are scarce, and they are not cheap."

"We found the game for sale on eBay," Jill said.

"Oh." Michelle's dark eyes were tearing. "I don't know how to thank you."

"Mommy! Mommy!" Brandon called.

"You have a nice day, ma'am," Santa said in his police-officer voice. Then they were gone.

Michelle stood for a moment looking at the closed door, until she realized she was still holding the small package. She pulled away the bow and opened it. Inside was a gift card for Safeway and a note with a telephone number scrawled at the top:

*Please call me after the holidays. In my real life, I am a social worker. I can help you get the services you need—Jill (the elf.)*

"I didn't even get his name," Michelle said aloud.

"Whose name?" asked Jared who suddenly stood in front of her. "I'm going to call Dad and tell him Santa came and brought the Rambo Danbo, just like he said."

"You better wait, Jared." Michelle felt a pang of anger that Jerry was somehow the hero of this magical moment. She would have loved to jolt Jerry out of bed, but she feared a woman might answer, and Jared would not understand.

"Your dad is probably still asleep. Let's eat breakfast. You can call him later."

She put slices of bread in the toaster and poured the milk over their Cheerios. Jared brought the Rambo Danbo to the table, and Brandon twirled the propeller of his blue airplane. Soon little boy chatter and the smell of toast and peanut butter filled their apartment.

Michelle poured herself a second cup of coffee and pulled open the blind over the kitchen sink. Outside the weather was changing. The sun, like a glaring light bulb, was winning the struggle to break through a gray, overcast sky. It streamed through the glass making the little ornaments on the philodendron sparkle.

# One Kind Thing

The towering, big leaf maple that grew in Albert Crowley's front yard dropped a never-ending pile of golden-brown leaves, so thick it looked like someone had spilled a giant box of corn flakes. Crowley worked for days raking the leaves and stuffing them into black plastic garbage sacks that now surrounded his front porch like a crouching swat team. He refused to rake any of the leaves that lay on the sidewalk or drifted into the street. "Let the damn city take care of 'em," he muttered.

Every time Crowley thought he'd cleared his lawn for the last time, he'd find another fresh layer of leaves. That afternoon, as he filled another garbage sack, he was grateful to see some bare branches. Most of the leaves had fallen except for a few clumps here and there. A big, impatient man, Crowley reached his rake up and swatted a branch causing more leaves to tumble and scatter.

"Come on, damn it," he nagged the tree and smacked another limb. Just then, a piece of folded notebook paper drifted to the ground. Its blue lines had started to bleed, but he could make out the message printed in a child's large scrawl:

*Dear Papa,*

*I miss you every day. Penny misses you, too. I know because she hides under the bed and won't eat. Momma says you are in heaven, and it is a nice place. But Papa, it's so hard without you. Momma says when people go to heaven they sit up on the clouds and watch over us. I have looked at all the clouds, but I can't see you. Please Papa, send me a sign, so I know you are watching me. I miss you so very much.*

*Love, Patsy.*

Crowley leaned on his rake and read the note a second time. Patsy lived in the white house on the other side of Crowley's big laurel hedge. He remembered Patsy's father had just died. It was a fluke, a heart attack or something. He was still a young man—maybe just forty or somewhere around there. He never trusted the guy. He worked with computers, had long hair, and a gold earring.

"Real men don't go around looking like women, unless there's something wrong with 'em," Crowley complained "No wonder he died." And computers—well, they were ruining the whole country in Crowley's opinion.

What was that note doing in *his* tree? Then he remembered. He'd left his ladder standing out after he painted the trim on a window. Little brat probably climbed on it. Now what would have happened if she'd fallen off? Damn people would have sued him, that's what. Damn those people anyway.

Crowley stuffed the note in his pocket. He didn't want trash blowing around his yard. Once again, he attacked the leaves with his rake. He always wanted to cut that tree down, so there wouldn't be any leaves; but Edna had liked it so much he'd let the idea go. Still, it gave him great pleasure to imagine himself attacking the tree with a power saw.

People pretty much stayed away from Crowley. He was a testy grump of a man with a shock of white hair that he combed straight back, a large bulbous nose with visible pores, and a stomach that hung over his belt. He always wore a white shirt tucked into dark trousers, even when he worked in the yard.

Whenever a ball or Frisbee came over the thick hedge that bordered three sides of his property, Crowley added it to his collection. "That'll teach those little snots. If they're gonna throw things around, they should find a park." If ever a kid snuck into his yard looking for what was lost, he'd squirt him with his hose. "Get out of here!" he'd yell. He wanted to put a fence across his front yard, but the big maple's thick trunk had grown so close to the edge of his property that any fence would have ended up in the sidewalk and violated a city ordinance.

Some scruffy older boys waited until dusk, about the time Crowley fell asleep in front of his TV. Then they'd sneak up his porch, ring the doorbell, and hide in the bushes waiting for him to come out. "Crowley Fowley!" they'd yell and run.

Sometimes bleary-eyed Crowley would chase them down the sidewalk lumbering like an old arthritic hippopotamus, until his lungs made wheezing sounds. "You damned gravel," he'd bellow in between gasps. After his heart started to weaken, he gave up the running. Crowley now kept a bucket of water by the door. He was still quick enough to douse one or two of them as they tore down his steps.

Crowley had been a grumpy fixture in town as long as anyone could remember. When he worked for that life insurance company over on third street, he'd crowd in the lunch line and mutter nasty things if people took too long deciding what they wanted. He'd pace in front of the copier if someone was ahead of him. Sometimes co-workers copied their stuff twice just to get Crowley's goat. Finally, his boss set him up at a desk in a windowless corner behind a row of gray file cabinets, where he reviewed thick actuarial reports that nobody much cared about until the day he retired.

Crowley's life had turned to vinegar after his first wife left him and took most of what he had. For a long time, he lived alone until Edna came along. She must have seen something good in old Crowley because she had the courage to marry him. People said she did it out of sheer loneliness; others just shook their heads. Her grown son, Eddie, never liked Albert Crowley, and he only came to the house when Crowley was gone.

Then there was the way Edna died.

During a late winter snowstorm, Crowley struggled to back his old, black Plymouth out of the driveway, but it hit a clump of snow causing the back tires to spin. Edna, a little bird of a woman with stooped shoulders, said he should get the shovel, but stubborn Crowley just pressed his foot down on the accelerator with Edna trying to push. Edna apparently walked behind the car to check the back wheels when Crowley's method of stomping on the accelerator kicked in. The car backed over Edna with such force, it killed her. People said it was just a matter of time before his impatience would come home to bite him.

Eddie was so distraught, he filed a police report; but after hours of investigation, they determined Edna's death was just a tragic accident. It left Crowley a bitter, bitter man. He only left his house to get groceries or to pick up something at the hardware store, and then he usually went during the dinner hour. "You run into fewer assholes that way," he grumbled.

Crowley sat in front of the TV set, in his dark house, eating his dinner off a tray when his nose started to tickle. "ACHOOOO!" he sneezed so loud it rattled the windows. He reached into his pocket for a tissue when Patsy's note fell out. He read it again. *Please send me a sign.* He remembered seeing the little girl stop in front of his house. She stared up at the stately maple and gazed at the sky.

*Please send me a sign.* Idiot kid, he thought. She thinks her father is in heaven, sitting on some damn cloud. She probably put this note in the tree because it was high up, and she figured her father could reach it. He shook his head. Kids these days were downright stupid.

At first, he thought he would wait for her to walk home from school. He'd give back her note and tell her there wasn't any heaven, so she should just forget about it and quit loitering on his property. If she ever put anything in his tree again, well, he'd fix her good. That oughta scare her. He turned to blow his nose and happened to look at the picture of Edna that still sat on end table cluttered with pencils, the phone book, an unwashed coffee cup, a screwdriver and an ashtray filled with nails. He remembered the small bunch of flowers he'd gotten after Edna died. He'd heard the doorbell ring and thought it was those pesky kids again. He got his bucket of water ready, but when he opened the door, little Patsy stood there trembling with an awkward bouquet of early daffodils and some blue, beady flowers wrapped in tinfoil.

"What do you want?" he asked. She handed him the flowers and ran for her life. But, she was the only person who ever came. She was just a little shaver then. He looked at the note again: *Please send me a sign.*

Well, there wasn't anything he could do about it. Her father died. Edna died. That's the way it was. Life wasn't fun. He glanced at Edna's picture again. He remembered how she used to talk to the little girl when she played hopscotch on the sidewalk. She and that awful orange cat, the one they called Penny. Crowley hated cats. They climbed through his hedge and pooped in his flowerbed. He should have had a big dog to chase them, but he hated dogs, too.

"Quit talking to that brat," he'd told Edna. "Pretty soon she'll wanna come in."

"Before you leave this earth Albert Crowley, I hope you do just one kind thing." Edna gritted her teeth.

"If I had a gun, I'd shoot that damn cat!" Crowley blurted not wanting Edna to have the last word.

"Just one!" Edna called out as Crowley slammed the door and went out to the garage. Edna had never spoken up to him, and it was only time she did. It wasn't long afterwards, that the accident happened.

Crowley looked over at Edna again, and his dark, squinty eyes actually got moist. He missed her. Edna had been the only person in the world that cared for him.

Ever.

Crowley fumbled through the cardboard box he kept in his basement searching for the baseball, among the other things that had come over his hedge. He especially remembered the ball because Patsy's father had come to his door asking about it. He explained that Red Bailey, a famous baseball player, had autographed that ball. Patsy's father said the kids had gotten hold of it when he wasn't home. They didn't know it was a special ball, and they lost it over the hedge. He wondered if Mr. Crowley had found it. If he did, he sure would like to have it back. Crowley claimed he never saw such a ball. Pasty's father just stood there looking Crowley in the eye, as if he knew he was lying. Crowley stared at his earring.

"If you should come across it please, out of the kindness of your heart, return it. It means a lot to me." Crowley shut the door in his face and left him standing on the porch.

"That'll teach 'em," he said after Patsy's father had left. "People should watch their kids. They shouldn't let 'em carry on like a bunch of wild Indians—especially people with long hair. Damn hippies shouldn't even have kids."

Hmmm, Crowley thought. Patsy gave him the flowers when Edna died, so he would return the ball. Surely that would work. Then they'd be even. It was just taking up space anyway. Maybe then that darn kid would quit staring at his tree.

How would he do it? He could speak to Patsy, except she'd be so scared she'd run away. Maybe he'd sneak over to her house after dark and leave the ball on the front porch. No, that would be too obvious. She always came down the sidewalk after school and stopped by the tree.

The next day, Crowley placed the ball and Patsy's note in the crook of one of the tree's big roots. He went back into the house and waited until school was dismissed. Then he peaked through the blind. Sure enough, the little girl came to the tree, stood for a moment, and gazed at the clouds.

"Aw, she's gonna miss it," Crowley muttered behind his blind. "Come on kid."

He'd just about given up when Patsy spied the ball sitting on top of her note. She scooped it up and held the ball close to her chest. She stared at the sky with a wide smile. "Momma, Momma!" she called as she ran home.

Old Crowley went back to what he usually did in the evenings eating his dinner alone off a tray, his dark house lit only by the flickering TV screen.

***

Patsy's mother got up early the next morning to bake her special coffee cake. She rang Crowley's doorbell with her cake in hand. She wanted to thank him for the nice thing he'd done. She figured it was him, because she and her husband always knew he had that ball. She braced herself for Crowley's cantankerous face and his lies, but she didn't care. She needed him to know how much his kind act helped Patsy. For the first time in weeks, her little girl slept clear through the night. When no one answered the door, she didn't give up. She walked gingerly to the rear of the house, ready for a bucket of water, a squirt from the hose, or whatever.

She found Crowley, alone on the back porch. He was sitting there slumped over a bit. "Mr. Crowley," she called, approaching with caution. "I wanted—" Then she gasped almost dropping her precious confection. He was stiff and cold with a trowel still in his lifeless hand and a strange smile on his blue lips.

# No Exit

Wayne had just come in from watering the geranium pots on his patio for the third time. The thermometer was already approaching 107 degrees, and it wasn't even noon. This heat wave had plagued them for seven days with no end in sight. Still, he felt lucky. Floods and violent wind storms wracked other parts of the country, half of Europe was on fire, and there was famine in India and Africa. He wiped perspiration from his forehead, grateful for the air conditioning, but with the extreme heat outside, he could hardly feel it.

What was that? A loud knock on the front door. Now what?

A tall man dressed in a black T-shirt and khaki pants with his dark hair undercut on the sides and a sloppy man bun on top stood there with a clipboard, his penetrating blue eyes sizing up all six feet of Wayne, including his sloping shoulders, thinning white hair, and his New Balance dad shoes.

"Wayne Daniels?" he asked.

"Yeah."

He gave Wayne a one-sided smile because his mouth drooped on the right side, said he was from the government, and handed him his ID. Sure enough, it had the man's picture and identified him as Felix Cunefuegos from the Federal Bureau of Transformation (FBT).

Wayne shuddered. He kinda heard about these visits on "Straight News," a multinational cable news television channel based in New York City, but the anchors were laughing. He thought it was a joke, but you could never tell these days because big corporations owned most of the media and objective reporting had gone the way of phonograph records.

Cunefuegos handed Wayne a white number ten envelope. "You'd best read it now. So I can be sure you understand what's required and can answer any questions you might have before I leave."

Wayne pulled his reading glasses from his shirt pocket and ripped open the envelope. The letter, in so many words, pointed out that Wayne was seventy-five. Once you reach that age, it said, there's no point in you continuing. The earth's resources were scarce due to climate change, global warming, wars, pestilence, and overpopulation. Too many people on the planet were causing the earth to struggle. It was a hard decision, but for the sake of everyone else, Congress, whose members grandfathered themselves in, decided the older generation needed to go.

"You only have about five years of life left anyway," Cunefuegos said. He checked his well-manicured fingernails. "Your wife is deceased and you have no children. So what's the point? You might as well get it over with." He fiddled with the diamond stud on his left earlobe. "I mean you're taking up space, consuming goods and services, and you're a drain on our health care system."

Wayne sucked in stale air. "I've lived in my modest house for fifty years," he said, his hand waving across his small living room, like an actress showing what one could win on a quiz show. "It's paid for. I have a pension from my years working as an accountant. I don't need much, and I hardly go out anymore. Sure, I had the shoulder operation, struggle with arthritis, and have a sensitive stomach, but the only medication I'm on is a statin, so how could I be—"

"Sorry," Cunefuegos interrupted, "It's the *law*. You might have heard the Supreme Court recently reaffirmed it. There's no point to your life anymore and with all your aches and pains, you're like a parasite gobbling what others could use."

"Wait," Wayne blurted. "I'm not ready to go. I still have things that need taking care of," all the time thinking what was happening to his country? Congress banned abortion and contraceptives to foster a younger generation. Shelves in grocery stores were often empty, gas prices were sky high, and there was a demand for young workers.

A sneer crossed Cunefuegos's face. "Things to do? Oh, the old bucket list. We get that a lot. So what's on yours? Grandchildren?" He looked at his clipboard. "You don't have any. Can't be a trip. Trips just contribute to your carbon footprint. And under the law, people your age, are not allowed to fly anywhere anymore. You must know that."

Wayne bit his lip. "I just want to outlive my dog."

Cunefuegos's droopy mouth produced that weird slanted smile. "You can't be serious."

Just then a little black-and-white terrier with perky ears and a wet nose came into the room and jumped up on Wayne's leg. Wayne reached down and scooped him up, to shield him from Cunefuegos's malevolent blue glance.

"See," Cunefuegos said, pointing at the dog. "It's just like with pets. I mean that's the way Congress saw it. When your dog or cat gets old, you don't let it linger or rack up enormous medical bills. You take it to the vet, give it a peaceful death, and leave with its collar. That's what we're offering you."

"The government is putting me down?"

"So, how old is your dog?"

"Seven. Henry is seven."

"Tsk.Tsk. That won't do. That dog could live another eight years. That means you'd be eighty-three." He checked his clipboard. "It also means you'd be exceeding your life span."

"What? The government has determined how long I live? Giving me an expiration date like a carton of eggs?"

"Wayne. Wayne. Wayne. Get real. Lots of organizations have life expectancy tables. And, if you've been paying attention, you'd know they've been declining in our country." Cunefuegos brushed off Wayne's concern like he was a fly who settled on his sleeve. "You get to choose how you want to leave. You can have a party with your family and friends." He paused. "That is, if any of 'em are still around. Medicare will pay for a nice sheet cake and the balloons. It all comes with a packet of Instant Release. As they say, a bit of sweetness makes the medicine go down."

Wayne's jaw dropped. "Say what?"

Henry's ears perked.

"Instant Release, or IR as we call it. Heh, heh. It's like instant coffee. You mix it in hot water and take a healthy swig. Well, along with your cake. Voila." His hand rose. "You fall into a deep sleep and never wake up." His lips formed that lopsided grin again. "Best to consume it while you're sitting down. It even tastes like instant coffee." He checked his clipboard. "Oh, and you get your choice of three delicious cakes—chocolate, spice, or carrot. They all come with swirls of frosting. And, of course, there's the balloons and confetti."

Wayne was speechless. He couldn't believe what was happening, and he didn't know what to say or do. He cleared his throat. "Well, I have to think about it. I mean, what will become of Henry? Who will sell my house? What about all my things?" He thought about the special coffee mug his wife, Claudia, had given him for his birthday that time, the one that said, "You're my favorite brew." He used it every morning. Then there was his gray cardigan sweater, a long ago anniversary gift. And what about his favorite recliner, his ten-year-old Subaru wagon, the sweet little dog bed he'd bought for Henry, and his brand new kink-free garden hose? Most of all, he thought of Henry—all alone in a cruel world. "Now, if you'll excuse me," he managed to say and tried to shut the door.

Cunefuegos blocked it with his foot. "Wayne, Wayne, Wayne. You don't understand. See, you don't get to think about it. You get to *plan* it. We usually give you ninety days." He gave another shrewd grin. "You know, like if you were living in a rental and the landlord decided to evict you. Ninety days, get it?" His hand cut through the air. "Whoosh, you're gone." He reached into his pocket and handed Wayne his card. "When you decide on a date, let me know. But don't be too long. Or, you know, we'll have to move in."

"What? Move in here?" Wayne clutched his arms and squirmed.

"That means we'll arrest you. Take you downtown. Fix you a soothing cup of IR which you can drink in your cell with two chocolate chip cookies and be on your way. No charge to you. Medicare covers the cookies and the drink." He thrust his clipboard with an attached pen toward Wayne. "And, I need you to sign here. Just to indicate you were informed and understand what we require of you."

Wayne gasped.

Henry wiggled out of Wayne's arms, jumped to the floor, and bit the man on the leg.

"Ouch!" Cunefuegos yelled. "For Christ's sake!"

"I'm so sorry," Wayne said, secretly pleased. "Henry has never done that before. Bad dog," he scolded in a feckless voice.

Henry sat alert. His ears perked.

The man wasn't listening. He lifted his pant leg and rubbed the sore spot, which looked pretty superficial. His face turned beet red with anger.

Henry continued to growl.

Wayne scooped him up for fear Cunefuegos might hurt him.

"Dammit." Cunefuegos jerked up his clipboard and wrote something down. "That does it," he shrieked. "I'm cutting your notice time to sixty days. Now get with it and do something with that incorrigible mutt. Sign here on line sixteen, indicating our little adjustment."

Wayne's shaking hand reached for the pen.

With that, Cunefuegos left muttering to himself about needing a tetanus shot but fretting about there being a vaccine shortage.

Wayne hugged all thirteen pounds of Henry in his arms and retreated to the couch, stunned. Henry had bitten no one in his whole, little life, but, on the other hand, he was an excellent judge of character.

After stroking Henry's ears, Wayne looked into his two dark eyes. "There's only one thing to do, pal."

Henry whimpered and rested his head on Wayne's thigh.

"Run!"

***

Wayne packed up his things. He didn't need much—a loaf of bread, a hunk of cheese, packages of Chex Mix, sleeping bag, small tent, a change of clothes, his toiletry bag, Henry's kibble, treats, leash, dog bed, favorite ball, and Lamb Chop squeak toy. After that, he and Henry jumped into his Subaru, crossed two state lines for a grueling eighteen-hour trip to the Oregon coast. They overnighted under the stars near a campground outside of Pocatello.

How could this be? Wayne thought the next day as he drove on and Henry dozed on the passenger seat. How could a group of elected officials who were supposed to represent you vote you off the planet?

The coast probably wasn't far enough, he knew, but whenever he was troubled, he headed there. Listening to the roaring sea, its beckoning, its vastness, had always calmed him. He remembered going there after Claudia passed and spreading her ashes in the sea as she had wished. It was there he found Henry. After saying farewell to Claudia, he'd gone into a coffee shop, feeling empty and alone. While there, he spotted a notice tacked on the bulletin board from a family that had to move and needed to rehome their puppy. He remembered the sad parents and  tearful children. He couldn't put Henry through that again.

Besides, didn't all life come from the sea? Maybe that was why Claudia wanted to rest there, and why he found the coast so comforting.

He and Henry spent the day walking along the beach getting lost in the ebb and flow of the tides, welcoming the brisk breeze, snagging an occasional shell or a smooth rock polished by the waves, listening to the call of the seagulls, and being in awe of the thousands of tiny creatures living in the wet sand and tidal pools. There was joy, too, simply watching Henry running back and forth, his mouth open as if he were smiling.

Even at the coast, it was hotter than usual and windy. Just before dusk, he tootled down an old logging road until they retreated to a wilderness area where Wayne pitched his small tent and spent the night on a sleeping bag cuddled with Henry, listening to the sound of crickets. The light from his battery-powered lantern lit the tent, making it glow like a small green globe against the dark towering trees. There was no one else around.

What to do next? he thought as he laid there, his mind like fingers leafing through his Rolodex.

He remembered Myra, the kind widow up the street in his neighborhood, had disappeared. She'd always greeted him on his walks with Henry and kept a stash of Henry's favorite biscuits. Folks said she went to live near her daughter in another state. Did she? Or, or did Cunefuegos come knocking? Then there was Phil McElroy from his coffee group. He no longer showed. It was shortly after Phil turned seventy-five. Someone said they thought he moved to a retirement village, but no one knew which one it was, only that homes and villages for older folks seemed to be shutting down. Hmmm. Neither one of them invited him to a going away party with cake, balloons and, oh yeah, confetti. Did that IR drink come with a cover story? Were there others out there like him, hiding in the shadows, waiting for the Cavalry? It was as far as he got before his exhausted body fell into a deep sleep.

Each day Wayne and Henry made do with their routine—going into town, picking up a few groceries or pet supplies; later taking long walks on the beach and returning to their camp at night. It was strange, though, because in town he didn't see many senior citizens.

Finally, the miserable heat wave broke. Wayne was beginning to feel a little better. Maybe sweating through the summer had caused him to imagine Cunefuegos's visit. Maybe he would try to return home, talk to the guys in his coffee group; see if they knew more about this termination project thing. Besides, he missed sleeping in his own bed, the comfy pillows and the pleasant scent of freshly laundered sheets.

He gave up on that idea the next day.

He'd gone into the grocery store to buy a case of bottled water, which was expensive and scarce. When he returned to his car, Henry was all agitated. That's when he noticed a note on his windshield. *You can run, but you can't hide. It's day thirty-seven—your clock is ticking. Never forget that.* It was signed Felix Cunefuegos with a crude smiley face sketched under his signature.

Wayne began to sweat as if the temperature suddenly skyrocketed. What to do? What to do? He hugged Henry. He couldn't imagine life without him, and what would happen to Henry? Maybe they should go out together. No, that would be so wrong.

Wayne knew he couldn't live forever, but he always thought the Angel of Death would be some old skeleton, clothed in a dark robe carrying a scythe, not a smirking Cunefuegos with his foo-foo hair style, evil blue glint, and a clipboard, offering sheet cake.

He couldn't go on like this, where someone was counting his days and now stalking him. No, he needed to be realistic and provide for Henry's future as painful as that would be. And who knows, maybe the right person would let him keep Henry until day sixty. Then again, maybe that wasn't fair. A gigantic clock embedded itself in his mind's eye, its black hands ticking, each tick getting louder and louder until he thought his head might explode.

Wayne and Henry escaped to Brentwood State Wayside, a small inviting park nestled beneath large trees with a picnic area, restroom, and short trail leading to the beach. Here he could toss the dog's ball and get exercise before heading back to his camp and deciding his next move. He also wanted to sit and watch the waves. This spot had been one of Claudia's favorite places. She liked it because it had a good view of the ocean, was shady, had clean public bathrooms, and a drinking fountain. It was where she wanted to go in her final days as cancer consumed her body. He had been so lucky to find someone in life who truly loved him. He remembered the calmness her touch could bring, the sound of her laughter, her love of small things like jam-filled doughnuts and of himself gently wiping the inevitable small, jammy splotch from her face. Coming to the place she loved was the right thing to do. It made him feel whole again.

He gave Henry's ball a healthy throw. The dog dashed off while Wayne sat on the picnic table bench, snacking on pepperoni and breathing in the ocean air. Now where was Henry? The dog always returned with the ball, waiting for him to throw it again. He could feel his heart beating in his throat. Did something happen?

He leaped up. "Henry!" he called. "Henry, come."

Then he saw them. Henry running toward him with a giggling, small boy who said his name was Eddie. He had sandy hair, a smattering of freckles over his nose, and a few teeth missing from his smile.

"Mister, can I toss the ball?"

"Sure," Wayne said. He watched as the boy raised his small arm, his tongue perched on his lower lip, and threw with all his might. Not bad, Wayne thought, even though it didn't go that far. Nevertheless, Henry took off like lightning to retrieve it, and then they both ran toward Wayne, Eddie all smiles, Henry clutching the ball in his mouth.

A young woman wearing jeans, her brown hair pulled into a ponytail, approached. She had the same sprinkling of freckles as Eddie. She said her name was Delia and that she was Eddie's mother. Eddie, she said, had just lost his father. The doctor said getting a pet might help the boy cope. "Thanks for sharing your dog. He hasn't smiled like that in a long time. Now, I know what I need to do."

Wayne returned to the wayside numerous times, each time running into Eddie and Delia. Henry loved romping with Eddie, who could move a lot faster than Wayne.

"I'm trying to find him his own dog," Delia said, sitting on the picnic bench next to Wayne, sharing a bag of Fritos, "But I'm not having any luck. There seems to be a dog shortage. I guess that doesn't surprise me. There are shortages everywhere these days. I don't know what the world is coming to."

The minute she said that, Wayne thought of Cunefuegos. "I need to ask you something."

"Shoot," said Delia.

"I'm not well," he lied. "I've only got a few days to live." Well, that was the truth. His hand touched his chest.

Delia's face fell. "I'm so sorry to hear that. Is it cancer? I lost my husband to cancer."

"Uh, no. It's my heart." It was sort of the truth. This whole mess was heartbreaking. "I, I need to find a home for Henry."

"Are you sure?" Delia asked. "I mean your dog is so comforting to you and—"

"I would feel so much better if I knew Henry was loved and safe."

"Sure," said Delia. Her brown eyes brightened. "We'd love to have Henry." She reached over and patted his hand.

So Wayne told her all about Henry. His likes, his quirks, his loving stubbornness about some things. How his mouth made little noises at night when he slept. How to tell when he needed to go out.

"He's not fond of cats. He hogs most of the bed, and he's a picky eater."

"You can visit him," Delia said. "Come to our house?"

Wayne just shook his head because he was approaching day fifty-eight. "That would confuse Henry, and there's not much time left. I'll need to go back to my camp and get his things."

"Take your time," Delia said. "I'll have to tell Eddie, and we better make a place for Henry. Of course, he'll sleep with Eddie, but he'll need his own space, too." She reached over and hugged Wayne. There were tears in her eyes. "It's okay to think it over."

Was he doing the right thing? When he and Henry reached their camp, he found a note pinned to his tent.

*We know where you are, and we're counting. If you don't turn yourself in, our armed agents will call on you. IR is also injectable, you know. Tsk-tsk. We'll take care of the mutt,too. Oh, and Wayne, nobody wears golf sweaters anymore.*
*Xoxo Felix.*

Inject him? Wayne shuddered, staring at his precious, now crumpled sweater lying on his sleeping bag. Cunefuegos had been to his camp site. Touched his things. Eeew. It couldn't get any worse.

That pretty much cinched it. Wayne spent one last night with Henry. He stroked his ears. "What's coming down is the best I can do for both of us." He thanked Henry for coming. "The years I had with you were great, buddy. I wish Claudia could have met you." He couldn't help it. Tears rolled down his face, followed by body shaking sobs. When hope dissipated, you needed your dog more than ever.

Henry sensed his emotions. He grabbed his Lamb Chop toy and invited Wayne to play. It was something he always did when he knew, in the way only dogs can, that Wayne was sad. Wayne looked into his two dark eyes and welcomed the sloppy kisses for the last time.

The next day at the wayside, he handed Henry over to Eddie, who was delighted. He brought Henry's ball, his bed, the little Nylabone he loved to chew on, his favorite blanket, all of his toys, and, of course, his treats and dog food packed in a paper shopping bag.

"I'll take good care of him," Eddie promised. He threw his arms around Wayne who patted his back.

"Thank you very much," Delia added. She handed him a piece of paper. "Look, if you ever need something...if there's a change in your diagnosis...or if you just want to talk, see the dog, whatever, give me a call."

Wayne stuffed the paper in his pocket, shrugged his shoulders, and managed a grin. "Sure. Thanks. I don't have many options."

"Well, okay then."

Wayne bent down to give Henry a final hug and kissed his furry cheek. Finally, he took out the leash and fastened it to Henry's collar so Delia could lead him away. Henry didn't understand. He pulled on the leash, trying to get back to Wayne.

"I better carry him," Delia said, her voice choking. "I know this is hard." She picked him up. Over Delia's shoulder, the dog's face turned toward Wayne.

Henry's last confused look etched itself in Wayne's memory. How Henry wiggled to get free, wanting to get to him, so they could romp together. Wayne watched until they got to the car and Delia put Henry and Eddie in the back seat. She waved and honked as they drove away.

His chest ached, his soul wounded, like the time he leaned over the narrow hospital bed and kissed Claudia's cold lips for the last time. But, in his heart he knew it was best. Henry was safe now and loved.

Wayne drove back to his camp, his tent a blemish on the pristine wilderness. He looked at the business card Cunefuegos had given him—a call, the party, that drink. "Bosh," he said out loud. He tore the card to bits and tossed it to the wind.

At midnight, the beginning of day fifty nine, Wayne donned his gray golf sweater and drove to the seashore. He removed his sensible shoes and socks and waded into the cold water. The wet sand squished between his toes, as darkness enveloped him only revealing pins of light from a nearby town. He paused and took a deep breath wishing he could stop time, but it was not to be. His hand lovingly stroked his cherished sweater and settled it close around his body. The roaring waves lured him on and on, until swirling water reached his neck. If he had to leave the earth, he would go out, in his own way, and that would be in Claudia's arms.

# Stalked

The homeless man was hard to miss. He looked like a ragged mushroom sprouting out of the asphalt—shaggy hair, beard, rumpled brown clothes. He'd plopped himself down in front of the chain link fence that surrounded the cruddy lower parking lot behind the gym.

Rita had no choice. She was late for her evening yoga class, and no other spaces were available.

*Was that guy planning to spend the night or break into cars?* She sat for a moment giving the trespasser a wary look, before hopping out and jerking her rolled yoga mat from the back seat. She continued her long stare. A few items from his tattered backpack—crumpled jacket, water bottle, white plastic spoon, Ritz cracker box, a knife stuck in a red apple—lay scattered before him.

"Hi," he said as she passed, a quizzical look on his face. He nibbled crackers.

"Hello." Her dark, suspicious eyes met his. A musty odor came from his direction.

He swallowed water. "You want me to leave?" Crumbs lingered in his beard.

She forced a smile. "Up to you. I don't own the gym."

He nodded. "Okay."

Hurrying to class, she debated about mentioning his presence to management, but checked her watch and decided there wasn't time.

Still, she worried. Now that fall had begun, it would be pitch-black when yoga class was over. *What if he's still out there?* He was a big man with a good-sized knife.

Unable to concentrate, her down dogs caved and her side planks crumpled. Finally, Sue, the instructor, dimmed the lights for *Shavasana*, the final relaxation pose. Ambient yoga music played in the background. "Breathe," Sue said. "Relax all the muscles of your body. Let everything go."

Rita couldn't. Visions of a shadowy figure flitted through her mind. After class, she lingered, hoping to walk out with others, but they either headed toward the front lot or hung around to visit with each other or with Brad, the club's personal trainer.

*Walk with purpose. Have the car keys ready.*

Rita took quick steps to the back lot, lit by two weak floodlights on each side of the building. Why hadn't she asked Brad to go with her? She knew the answer. She didn't want to give ol' flirty, stuck-on-himself Brad any encouragement.

*Too late for that now.*

If that homeless guy tried anything, she'd unleash a glass-shattering scream. Her eyes searched the dim lot. He wasn't there. Or, was he? He could be behind the sprawling bushes that lined part of the fence.

*What was that? Footsteps?*

Her shaking hands clicked her key fob and tossed her yoga mat on the front seat. Once inside, she immediately locked her doors, flicked on her headlights, and readied her cell phone on the console. Driving out, she scanned the area. No homeless guy, only shadows and a flattened Ritz box. If he tucked himself behind those bushes for the night, she didn't want to know.

Rita pulled into her driveway, pressed the button on her garage door opener, and drove in. How silly all that was—just some poor bloke needing a break in life, stopping for a while in a parking lot. Sheesh. She'd jumped to all the wrong conclusions.

In the bathroom, Rita splashed cold water on her face and ran a comb through her curly dark hair. After brushing her teeth, she wrapped dental floss around the middle fingers of both hands and began sliding it between her teeth, fretting about the novel she was writing and the place where she was stuck. *Hmmm. I could punch up the setting or...dammit the phone.*

"Hello," she said, floss hanging from her mouth.

"Hi," said a male voice.

"Who is this?"

No answer, but she could hear breathing.

"Listen," he finally said, in low, but gruff tones. "I wanted to thank you for what you did at the gym. I mean not askin' me to leave...not turnin' me in."

"What?" She pulled the floss from her mouth. "What are you talking about?"

A pause, measured breathing. "I didn't mean to make you mad."

Her voice rose and tightened. "How did you get this number?"

"Listen, Rita..."

"How do you know me?" Her brown eyes widened with alarm.

More breathing. He cleared his throat. "Are you alone?"

Rita slammed the phone down, her heart banging her chest. Could this be the homeless man she saw earlier? He mentioned the parking lot, but she'd told no one about it. How did he get her phone number and name? She flicked on the hall light before climbing into bed and kept the lamp on her nightstand burning for several hours, reaching to turn it off when she became drowsy. After a few hours of sleep, she lay awake, listening to the creaking noises houses make at night.

Two days passed. Nothing. Probably some nut wanting a thrill, she assured herself. Gradually, her calm returned. She went to her yoga class but made a point of arriving early enough to park in the well-lit front lot.

"Hi, Rita." Brad stood behind the front desk, looking like a Greek god with his blond hair sleeked back and his muscles rippling in his gym stringer tank top. "Enjoy your workout." He winked, his eyes roaming her body.

Rita swiped her membership card. "Thank you. I will." She turned away.

Inside the yoga room, Rita rolled out her mat and sat down. Poppy, a red-haired cutie in green paisley tights and clinging pink top, warned the group about a car break-in that happened down in the back lot.

"I saw a scruffy homeless guy hanging there last week," Rita said.

"This happened to Brad during the *day*." Poppy's gray eyes expanded to the size of golf balls. "I mean broad daylight. He discovered it at noon when he went out to run errands. Brad said the thief stole all his DVDs." She flipped back her long hair and began doing warmup stretches, showing off her shapely yoga butt.

"The guy I saw looked pretty desperate."

"Brad's going to check Craigslist to see if any of his DVDs end up for sale there."

Brad this. Brad that. Poppy seemed to know a lot about Brad, but then Rita had seen them smooching in the hot tub. Nothing more was said, and no one asked Rita for details.

Tired after a long day of writing and editing, and slightly relaxed by yoga, Rita flopped into bed and fell asleep while reading a John Grisham thriller. Eventually, she woke up, killed the light, pulled the covers up to her chin, and drifted off. Her ringing bedside phone jolted her bliss.

"Rita?" said the familiar low, gravelly voice.

She yawned. "Uh-huh." She ran her fingers through her hair.

"I was passin' by and—"

"What's that?" she asked, slowly coming to. She glanced at the clock—3:00 a.m.

"Saw your light on. Thought I'd give you a call."

"You have the wrong number," she said, now fully alert, tense, and shaking.

Pause. Breathing into the receiver. "Why'd you turn off the light? Need some company, huh, Rita?"

*My God. He's outside somewhere, watching me.* She dropped the receiver like it might explode and rushed through her darkened living room where she carefully shifted the drape, sneaking a peek from the side. Nothing moving. The street appeared empty, except for cars parked in driveways, a couple of huddling garbage cans, and a porch-light two doors down splashing yellow light on the pavement.

Back in bed, she stared at the ceiling, until she finally fell into a restless sleep. The next morning, after downing two cups of strong black coffee, she called the police.

A nice, young policeman, who introduced himself as Officer Kendrick, came to her house that afternoon and took her report. She told him about her experience outside the gym, described the homeless man and the telephone calls. He listened politely while writing in his pad.

"Did this man threaten you?"

"No. He was sitting there eating."

"Did he threaten you on the phone?"

"Not exactly. He seems to be watching me, wanting to make contact."

He scribbled her response in his notepad.

"He had a knife."

The officer looked up from his pad. "What kind of knife?"

"I'm not sure. A knife. It was sticking in an apple."

"Hunting knife, kitchen knife, sword? What?"

"I can't say. I...I wanted to get past him. Uh, it wasn't a paring knife."

"Okay." He continued writing. "Did you leave your car unlocked at the gym? He could've read your registration."

"No, I locked it."

The officer raised an eyebrow. "Are you sure? You said you were in a hurry." He tapped his notebook with his pen and waited.

"I always lock my car."

"Sometimes when we're distracted, we forget." He gave her a smug grin.

"When I saw him sitting there, I was leery, but I locked it." *I did, didn't I? Is he blaming me?*

He asked about friends, former boyfriends, neighbors, and anyone with whom she might have quarreled.

"Nothing like that," Rita said to all those questions.

"We can patrol the neighborhood," the officer explained, "but unless something more happens, there isn't much we can do. Keep your doors and windows locked. Give us a call if he continues to harass you." He slapped his notepad shut and left.

***

Over plates of spaghetti carbonara at Dino's, her writing partner, Maryanne, a small woman with black-rimmed square glasses and dark hair scraped into a hasty bun, suggested she change her phone number.

"What good would that do?" Rita poked at her pasta. "He knows where I live."

Maryanne twirled spaghetti strands around her fork, accidentally splashing creamy sauce on the stylish purple scarf that hung around her neck. "Then unplug the darn phone at night so you can at least sleep. I mean, you have a cell phone."

"If he can't reach me by phone, then what? Would he come to the door? Follow me someplace, break in? Like I told the cops, this creep wants to make contact."

"Oh my." Maryanne reached for her water glass. "A lot of those street people have mental issues or are drugged out."

Rita gripped her fork. "I'm aware of that. I just want my life back, to feel safe again, to take walks in my neighborhood without looking over my shoulder, to be able to read my writing in public without fear..."

Maryanne tipped the glass, moistened the end of her napkin, and rubbed the spot on her scarf. "You might have to move."

"Move? I can't. I'm paying down a mortgage." Her hand massaged her temple. "That's not even an option."

"What about Luke? Maybe he could move in with you."

Rita set her fork down and held her head in her hands. "We're not an item."

Maryanne's voice softened. "Maybe he'd like it to be more. Maybe—"

"We're just friends. He's in my meditation group. Luke's left brain. I'm right brain. No. It wouldn't work." Rita pushed aside the manuscript she'd critiqued for Maryanne. "Sorry, I can't seem to get into this."

"We can do it later," Maryanne said.

"I've been reading a Grisham novel. Now I feel like I'm in one."

Maryanne gave her a sympathetic look. "I hear you." She reached into her jute sling bag and handed Rita a small canister of pepper spray. "I always carry this with me when I'm out. Especially at night."

****

After hearing about Rita's phone calls, Luke volunteered to spend a few nights on her couch. He arrived in a blue Seattle Seahawks T-shirt, his brown hair askew, juggling a duffel bag, a stack of IT journals, and a six-pack.

Having her geeky, sports-crazed guy friend around wasn't such a hot idea. His constant cleats-and-pads chatter made writing difficult. When his eyes weren't glued to ESPN, they hungrily explored Rita's fridge.

"I can't find the mustard," he called from the kitchen.

Rita found him standing by the counter looking like a helpless child. She eyed his three-slice bread tower filled with alternating layers of Swiss cheese, tomato slices, lettuce, olives, and left over potato salad. "That's because there isn't any."

"Aw man. What am I supposed to put on this thing?"

"Try sticking it together with hummus," Rita said amused, handing him a small round carton.

He screwed up his face and returned it to the fridge. "That stuff sucks."

Rita watched him pad off to the living room, balancing his sandwich on a plate. "Your next best option is Gorilla Glue," she called after him, "it's in the middle drawer." He didn't respond. She could hear cheering coming from the tube and the sportscaster yelling, "The Seahawks just downed a punt inside the ten-yard line."

While she appreciated Luke's ham-fisted efforts to protect her, his departure brought sweet release. Unfortunately, it was short-lived.

***

October arrived with clear azure skies and a riot of autumn color, but Rita was too distraught to appreciate the fiery splendor. Her life had become cautious. She only went to her curbside mailbox when the traffic on her street was busy, locking the door behind her. Before pulling out of her garage, she clicked the car locks.

*I can't concentrate. I can't write. This is crazy, and it's no way to live. How long can I do this?*

After grocery shopping, she noticed a basket of yellow and orange roses studded with maroon carnations left by her front door. She picked it up and drank in the spicy fragrance. *How lovely. Probably from Luke, thanking me for the free room and board and apologizing for being such a butt.*

She read the typewritten note: *I didn't mean to upset you*. The name following the message said simply, *Your Admirer*. Was Luke trying to be funny? He always did have a weird sense of humor. Once she shelved the groceries, she gave him a call.

"They're not from me," he said. "Why would *I* send flowers?"

She slapped her forehead with her hand. Good question. Luke never said thank you for anything. What was she thinking?

Hmmm. She'd participated in a panel discussion on critique groups last week. Could that explain it? But she didn't leave upset, and no one gave out her address. But these days, if you did a savvy Internet search, you could find out a lot about people.

At the end of the week, she found another arrangement by the front door—a bouquet of stunning white lilies, accompanied by a typed message: *Your Secret Admirer. I'd like to be less secret.*

She'd been home. No one rang the bell to indicate a delivery. There was nothing on the note or bouquet to identify a florist or a courier service. The flowers must have been personally delivered.  Homeless guys couldn't afford flowers. Maybe he wasn't homeless, maybe he was a thief, somebody on the lam…a serial killer.

***

The Indian summer dissolved into gusty winds and drenching storms. Rita found no more flowers on her doorstep. Still, always on the alert, she double-checked the deadbolts and all the window locks before heading to bed.

That night another freaking call. Up on her elbows, she swiveled toward her bedside clock. The red dials said 2:00 a.m.

"Rita?"

She clutched the receiver but didn't respond. It was the *same* voice.

"Rita. Hi. Thought I'd check in." Heavy breathing "How are you?"

"To whom am I speaking?" Rita barked. *Hopefully, I can trick him into giving a name.*

"Your secret admirer."

"So where are you, admirer?"

"Can I come over?"

"Yeah, if you want me to shoot you."

A pause. More heavy breathing.

She said, "I think you're a coward, hiding behind phone calls and flowers. A damn sniveling, bastard, coward."

"Oh Reet-tuh, you turn me on when you get like that." He laughed and hung up.

***

"I can't take it anymore," she told Luke the next morning over coffee at the Cake Walk, a local bakery. "I contacted the cops again. Told them about the continuing phone calls and the anonymous flowers."

"And?"

"Same ol,' same ol.' Not much they can do, unless he tries something." She took a deep breath filling her nostrils with the scent of cinnamon and fresh-brewed coffee. "I'm going to lure the creep over and shoot him." She thumped the table.

Luke rolled his eyes. "You can't be serious. You don't own a gun." He took a bite of his gooey chocolate butter cake.

"Well, I'm going to get one and learn how to use it."

"Not a good idea." He wiped his mouth with a napkin. "Guns are dangerous."

She set down her coffee cup. Her hand formed a finger gun. "Kapow. Dead."

His shoulders shook when he laughed.

She gave him a hard look. "What's so funny?"

He patted her hand. "S-o-o-o not you. As I recall, you wrote a pretty strident letter to the editor on gun control."

"I'm desperate. My insides are in knots. I can't write. I can't focus. Especially since Halloween is this Friday. I'm *scared*. That creep might come to my door dressed as God-knows-what?"

Luke agreed to sleep on her couch again for three nights. He answered the ringing doorbell and handed out candy to all the little goblins, while Rita peeked through the blinds to see if any adult ghosts were lurking out there. At 9:00 p.m., Luke switched off the porch light. He and Rita munched popcorn, read, and did a brief but calming meditation before turning in early.

For the rest of the long weekend, Luke watched football on TV. He whooped and yelled at little helmeted men running across the screen, guzzled beer, ate most of the pizza she ordered, and all of the leftover Halloween candy, leaving a pile of tinfoil wrappers on her coffee table.

Nothing happened.

"Listen," Luke said, when preparing to leave, "if you still feel uneasy, I could always go to yoga with you."

"Thanks, Luke." She gave him a platonic peck on his cheek. "I feel better. Don't worry, I'll be okay. You're a great friend."

He smiled, put his arm around her shoulder, and gave her a hug. "Hang in there. Call me if you need me. You can bet I'll come running." He cleared his throat. "Don't expect flowers."

***

That night the stranger called again. *He's watching me. Calling when Luke's car is no longer in my driveway.*

The police had warned her not to engage her stalker, but sleep-deprived Rita wanted to reach through the phone and strangle him.

"Let's meet, but not here," she said. "Somewhere in public...Starbucks?"

Heavy breathing. "No," said the gravelly voice. "How about the Blue Roof Motel out on NE Reynolds?"

"You're on. Name your time."

"Nine, tomorrow night?"

"How will I recognize you?" she asked, fishing.

"You've seen me before...in the parking lot, remember?" He made a guttural snort. "Go into the lobby. Wait. Wear somethin' sexy." A sleazy dark laugh, more breathing. Finally, the haunting dial tone.

The Reynolds neighborhood, Rita knew, was a seedy area. She immediately called the police who agreed to set up a sting.

"You go inside and wait," said Detective Winslow, a tall, thin man with an authoritative voice. "We've made contact with the manager out there. We'll be in plain clothes in the lobby. When he comes in and approaches you, we'll toss a flash grenade to distract him. Once that happens, our guys will move in. Don't, under any circumstances, leave the premises with him. We'll see that you get home safe."

Rita sat in the lobby of the Blue Roof for three hours, along with one police officer dressed in jeans and a sweatshirt and another who stayed out of sight. The lobby's moldy air irritated her sinuses. *Why did cheap motels smell like old bedding?* She dabbed her nose with a tissue, read the entire newspaper twice, and thumbed through three rumpled copies of *Entertainment Weekly*.

He didn't show.

***

Wired from her experience at the motel, she lay awake most of the night. At exactly 3:18 a.m., the shrill ring of the phone jangled her already overwrought nerves.

She lifted the receiver, but didn't speak.

"You should not have brought the police, Rita," said the croaky voice followed by more heavy breathing. "How stupid do you think I am?" *Click.*

*Now what?* She cradled her knees and rocked back and forth. *My life is going to hell, all because I was nice to some homeless guy in a parking lot. I should have reported him then.*

She could disconnect her landline, but her home phone number was on her business cards, and she didn't want her cell number to become public. Instead, she contacted the phone company and installed Caller ID. Sure enough, another middle-of-the-night call. She flipped on the light. Caller ID said *anonymous.*

She let the call go to voice mail. "Hey Rita. How are you? I know you're in there." Rita spent most of the night sitting up clutching her pillow.

At 4:00 a.m., she got up to write, hoping to engage her mind. Sipping black coffee at her desk, she revised the ending of a short story. *Was that cigarette smoke?* She stopped and sniffed the air. It could be coming from someone walking past the house on the sidewalk. *Wait, that smell is so intense, like he's right by the window.* She fought off the urge to peek through the mini-blind, terrified he'd be looking back. Instead, she switched off her desk lamp, hurried into her dark bedroom, sat on the bed, cell phone ready. No use calling the police about tobacco smoke. After the motel "no show," would they even respond? Maybe her mind was playing tricks. Maybe she was losing it.

***

"Dammit," Rita muttered. She'd forgotten the gym's popular pre-holiday nutrition class, "Eat Fit," began that night. Parking spots were scarce. To make matters worse, a light November fog hindered visibility. Rita circled the upper lot several times hoping someone would pull out. Maybe she should forget it and head home, but yoga helped quell her anxiety.

Other cars arrived and headed for the lower back lot. *Safety in numbers.* At least she wouldn't be back there alone. She parked, grabbed her yoga mat, and ran toward the building.

The nutrition class was still in session when yoga finished. That possibility hadn't crossed her mind. She tried calling Luke, but her call went to voice mail, so she left a message explaining her predicament. "Please come if you can."

She paced, used the restroom to kill time, and constantly checked her cell phone. There was no message from Luke. She'd been waiting thirty minutes. According to the wall poster, "Eat Fit" would go on for another whole hour.

*I can't hang here much longer. Don't be stupid. Don't go to the back lot alone. Ask for help.*

She hurried to the reception desk. "Hey Brad," she said. "I realize you're busy, but do you mind walking me to my car. It's in the back lot. I...uh...have been having a little problem with a stalker. Maybe you heard?"

Brad set down his pen. "Sure Rita." A smile crossed his chiseled face. "Yeah, we're aware of your situation, an' believe me, we're taking it very seriously."

Phew. Brad, with weight lifting trophies, was six feet two and built like a young Arnold Schwarzenegger. She fished in her purse and pulled out her car keys.

"Absolutely, no problem," he said as they walked, "I'm off the clock." Outside, the wisps of fog had thickened into a dense soup making her very relieved Brad agreed to accompany her.

"The boss is gonna put some cameras out here, but it takes time, ordering them an' all. We're also gonna upgrade the lighting. Guess you heard, someone broke into my Camaro."

"Yeah, I did. Sorry you lost your DVDs." Rita pointed. "I'm over there. The blue Toyota." She pressed her key fob. The lights on her car blinked in the damp mist.

Brad stood by her car. "Okay, I'll wait till you get in."

Rita opened her door and turned to thank him. "Be careful going back."

"Oh I will." He smiled. Suddenly his body crashed against hers, slamming her up against the car, causing the door to close. He seized her keys. Her yoga mat hit the ground.

"What are you doing?" She gasped.

"You stuck up little tight-ass," he said, his voice low and throaty, his laugh familiar and sleazy.

"You!"

"Nose-in-the-air Rita. Now, I've *got* you." His hazel eyes turned hard and unfeeling.

Every muscle in her body tightened. "You better plug in your brain. You'll lose your job. Get twenty-five years in the slammer."

"Oh but, Rita. You walked right into my little web. Told the cops about a stalker, a homeless guy." He snickered. "In great detail."

"How did you…?"

"Know? I was in the parking lot that night, too—emptying the trash into the dumpster. Thought I'd have a little fun. You fucking dumb bitch. What a perfect alibi for me." His arms gripped tighter.

"Let go of me!" She tried to pull free; her purse went flying. Now, there was no way to reach the canister of pepper spray.

"We're going for a little ride...in *your* car. How convenient."

*Don't get in the car.* "Help!" she screamed. But, with the first shriek, Brad pressed his hand over her mouth and banged her head against the car. Everything got hazy. He dragged her across the asphalt toward the passenger side. She bit and kicked, missing his groin, but succumbed to a fierce blow to her gut. She couldn't breathe.

Brad pulled the car door open. The dome light came on, exposing his eyes narrowed to slits, his lips curled in a determined snarl.

That treacherous look, like an animal before the kill, would be the last image she'd ever see. *It's over.*

An arm came out of the foggy darkness. It encircled Brad's neck in a chokehold. Gagging, Brad loosened his hold on Rita. The anonymous hand tightened something around his neck, pulling hard, until Brad crumpled to the ground. Feet kicked Brad's head and chest until he lay flattened on the asphalt, a broken Hercules, unconscious, blood oozing from his nose and mouth.

On her knees, Rita looked up into the face of the bearded homeless man she'd seen in the parking lot. She stared at the bungee cord dangling from his hand. He picked up her car keys and came toward her. Like a defenseless child, she raised her arms in front of her face, too weak to fight.

He grabbed her arm, pulling her to her feet. "Are you okay?"

"I...I thought..." She coughed to clear her throat. Her lips quivered, her face covered with tears. "My head... I feel wobbly." Her hand touched her swollen eye.

"These belong to you." He pressed the car keys into her hand. His arm wrapped around her shoulders to steady her. His musty smell like a pile of old, raked leaves filled her nostrils. They walked to the other side of the car. He bent down, picked up her purse, and handed it to her.

She clutched it to her chest. "Thanks," she murmured. *Does he want something? Should I offer him cash? Probably not wise to open my purse.* Her caution gave way to body racking chills and nausea. She wanted to lie down, to rest, to clear her mind. Now wasn't the time.

He pointed toward the building. "You need to go inside. Report this. Get you some help."

She glanced toward Brad. "Is he...Is he..."

"Dead? Naw. He just got a little taste of street justice. Can you walk?"

"I'll try." She started to move, but stumbled.

"Hang onto me."

He put his arm around her. She clung to his jacket, taking careful steps in the dim light.

"Name's Berkette," he said. "Folks on the street call me Bucket." He gave her shoulder a slight pat. "Always did mean to thank you for your kindness."

# A Safe Place

Needles of pelting rain fell from the endless gray sky for three straight days causing every body of water in Oregon's Willamette Valley to swell near flood stage. I stood watching thick drops hammer the ledge of my Red Lion Hotel window. *Head home now. If the Willamette River goes over its bank, I'll be stuck in Portland for days.*

On the southbound freeway visibility was treacherous. Traffic crawled. Muddy water pooled on both sides of the pavement. I cringed every time a big eighteen-wheeler passed, throwing a spray of water, causing me to drive blind. At times, I felt my Taurus hydroplaning. The car was twelve-years-old, running on tires I'd been meaning to replace. It might easily skid off the road. If it overturned, I feared drowning in that deep, standing water. My arms and neck ached from gripping the wheel, and I had twenty-five more miles to go. *Oh, dear God.*

Through the rain-swept windshield, I could barely see the green exit sign, but I was sure it was the one leading to Maxine's, a small diner off the old highway. I sometimes stopped there on my way back from writing workshops in the city to relax, people watch, and gather my thoughts in the notebook that I always carried with me. Once I made it to the diner, I could wait out the storm.

*Whew.* The big red neon sign announcing Maxine's glowed in my windshield like a candle in a dark window. I pulled into the gravel lot, jerked up the hood on my coat, and dashed for the door, shielding myself from wind and bombarding rain.

Inside, I inhaled warmth and the welcoming smell of coffee and grill.

"Hey," said Maxine from behind the counter. "Haven't seen you in a while."

"I'm s-o-o-o glad you're open." I removed my wet coat and collapsed onto a chair of a table close to the entry. I fluffed my dark curls while hungrily eyeing her pastry display case that featured batches of heart-shaped cookies and cupcakes with red sprinkles on white frosting in anticipation of Valentine's Day.

At mid-afternoon, the diner was almost empty. I recognized Ted, a regular, who sat hunched at the counter working on a burger and a mound of fries. He nodded as he lifted a steaming mug of coffee to his lips.

An older couple sitting across from Ted appeared to be involved in a tense conversation. "When you're eighty-eight anything can happen," I heard the woman tell the man.

Ted, I knew, was a long-haul truck driver, and Maxine's was a noted truck stop. She considered the guys to be her extended family. Framed pictures of various truckers holding a prize fish or standing behind birthday cakes with goofy balloons covered almost every inch of the oak-paneled walls. A realistic painting of Mt. Hood hung behind the counter. Above it was a grinning Kit-Kat Klock with plastic eyes that swiveled in time with its pendulum tail.

Maxine was proud to have those big rigs parked in her gravel lot. "The best advertisement a diner can have," she'd claim. She once told me that her third, now ex-husband, drove truck. "I have as many miles on me as most of them big wheelers out there," she'd say and flash that big, dazzling Maxine smile.

Ted never said much. Maybe it was because he spent so many years alone in his big B&L Transport. When he did talk, it was mostly with Maxine who I guessed was about the same age—probably pushing fifty. Sometimes, as I sat writing in my journal, I'd overhear them chatting about the weather or trips to Spirit Mountain, a casino on the way to the coast. Maxine carried most of the conversation while Ted, in work boots, jeans, and a black windbreaker, always perched on the third stool from the left, usually said, "Yep, Yep," or "I get what ya mean."

As a writer, whenever I struggled to describe characters, I'd imagine a huge box of crayons and ask myself what colors I'd select if I were coloring that person. For Ted, I decided I'd pick tans and grays. Mostly grays.

"I'm hoping to wait this out," I said to Maxine when she approached for my order. "I've never seen anything like this."

"Tell me about it. We're getting hit with a Pineapple Express." Maxine's reddish hair was pulled back in a ponytail. She wore a thick black sweater with tweed slacks and sensible Sketchers. She drew an order pad from the pocket of the white apron neatly tied over her slim figure. "A lot of homes north of here are underwater and evacuation warnings are increasing. Now, we've got wind. There's talk of closing the south end of the highway because of water pooling in fields. I guess it's startin' to flood the road. Sent my cook home at noon." She raised a well-penciled eyebrow. "I'da gone home, too, but folks depend on me. You know how that is."

Drifting water would mean I couldn't use the old highway, but would have to get back on the freeway. I wished with every ache in my shoulders that I was home watching the rain from my couch with my dog, Abby. I worried about home. I didn't live in a flood plain, but the grated storm drains on my street were easily overwhelmed during downpours.

And what about Abby? She was a Golden Retriever with even temperament, but kennels made her antsy, and she'd already been at Dog Haven for three days. She'd whimpered when I left her and gave me her you're-not-leaving-me-here look, but at least she was safe. *Wasn't she?*

While Maxine filled my coffee and grilled cheese sandwich order, a young couple rushed in, shaking the rain from their jackets.

"Can't see anything out there," the young man gasped.

"Last I heard, the Willamette has crested about ten feet above flood stage and is within inches of going over its seawall," I responded. "I had no idea what it was like to drive in something like this."

"Yeah, visibility is like nil with that wind kicking up." He shepherded his female companion toward a table.

The warm cup of Maxine's brew soothed my frazzled nerves. I sipped and nibbled my sandwich while watching the rain make rivulets on the window and the already somber sky turn gloomier. The Kit-Kat said 4:00. I hadn't driven very well during daylight; having to do it in darkness terrified me. I tried to remember if any of the little towns along the highway had motels when Maxine announced, "Sheriff's office just called. They closed the bridge down the highway on a count of some downed trees, and we got a slide up north. They'll notify us when the coast is clear, but it looks like no one is going anywhere for a while." She pursed her lips.

"Oh no, Nick," said the young woman. She set down the cupcake he'd purchased for her and shook long brown hair out of her anxious face. "What if we're trapped here and get washed away?"

"Now, Nancy..." Nick began. He cleaned his wire-rimmed glasses with a napkin. His thick, sandy curls needed a comb. They both wore green and yellow sweatshirts that said *University of Oregon*, and she had a diamond stud peeking out of the side of her left nostril.

Maxine delivered the bowls of chili they'd ordered. "This diner's no ark, but we're on a bit of a hill here, so the water would have to get mighty high. The problem is you can't go anywhere now."

I was actually relieved. Not that I wanted to spend the night in a diner, but it sure beat drifting off of the road somewhere and drowning in the darkness alone. Maybe I should've stayed in Portland, but it was too late, now.

The diner didn't have a TV, so Maxine brought out her small, transistor radio, placed it on the counter tuned to KJR, a Portland station. Local rivers and streams remained at flood stage, the weather forecaster said, and they were still concerned about the Willamette. North of Maxine's, flooding was especially severe with the Clackamas River over its banks. We listened silently. I shuddered at the report that two Hispanic farm workers traveling southbound had ignored barriers blocking access to a portion of the highway underwater. Authorities said their pickup had apparently drifted into a flooded field. They were presumed drowned.

The windows facing the parking lot grew black. Wind whistled and rain pelted the glass in sheets. *What if those tall firs bordering Maxine's gravel lot toppled and crushed our cars?*

The older woman stood. "Since we're all stuck here, we might as well introduce ourselves." She was thick-bodied with bright red lips and a head of beautifully coiffed white hair. She adjusted her beige fisherman's sweater over ample hips and thighs which filled her gray slacks.

"I'm Caroline. This is my husband, Walt."

He turned and nodded.

"We drove up from Eureka to see my elderly mother, but didn't count on flooding. They've moved her to the hospital in Portland. I have to get there and…" she twisted her napkin. "You know…in case…to say…to say goodbye. I'm just so…conflicted." She tossed the rumpled napkin on the table.

Walt, a slight bald man in a brown golf sweater, frowned and looked over his bifocals. "It'll be okay, honey." His wife's unbridled emotions seemed to embarrass him.

Maxine collected the dishes from their table. "Sorry about your mother."

"I'm Nancy," said the young woman speaking in rising intonations. "Funny, Nick and I were trying to get to my parents' house in Vancouver? Funny, we've been living together and were worried Nick would have to sleep in the guest room? Now, I guess we'll be together after all. Funny, who'da thought?" She giggled, tossed her head to shake the hair out of her face.

Nick grinned. Caroline and Walt gave them a cold gaze. It must have been the "living together" comment.

Ted said his name and that he "drove truck." He quickly turned back to the counter. We all knew who Maxine was.

"I'm Rita," I said. "I'm on my way home from a writing workshop—"

"I just feel so bad..." Caroline, still standing, cut my introduction short. "I hope she doesn't go before I get there," she wailed. "She's eighty-eight, you know. I should've spent more time... you know, she'd call and I was too...well engaged. Now I feel so conflicted."

Walt's face reddened. Maxine insisted that Caroline use her cell phone to call the hospital.

*Good idea.* I pulled my cell phone from my purse and dialed Myrnie, my elderly, nosey next-door neighbor, to find out how things were on my street. If a pin dropped in our neighborhood, Myrnie could tell you all about it before it hit the ground. My call went to her answering machine. Odd. I hoped she was okay. There was no point calling Luke, my guy friend. He was attending an IT conference in San Francisco. No one answered at the kennel, so I left a message saying I'd been delayed and asking them to call me. *Poor, poor Abby. I'd make it up to her with treats when I got home.*

We passed the time listening to weather updates on the radio and eating Maxine's complimentary Valentine cookies. Nick and Walt talked sports for a while. Nancy wished there were magazines and a big screen TV. Nick said it was too bad nobody had a deck of cards. I tried writing in my journal, but found it hard to focus, so I doodled. Ted continued to give us his back. Maxine ran her cloth across the already clean counter and busied herself in the kitchen. Every so often, Caroline called the hospital. Then she'd tell us about the times her mother needed her, but how her life was so "engaged." Off she'd go on her guilt trip, calm down, and then start all over.

"They said her blood pressure was low. I thought low was better than high. How low is low, Walt?"

Walt's shoulders slumped. He looked weary.

"I just feel so conflicted." She held her head.

I couldn't help it. I quit drawing weird shapes and wrote: *If that woman says "conflicted" one more time, my head will explode.*

"This god-awful storm is not your fault." Nick finally said, trying to make Caroline feel better. "Everybody is guilty about something, that's for sure."

Nancy helped herself to another valentine cookie. "Really? Everyone is guilty? Funny, that must be because you were raised Catholic."

Nick chortled. "That's a load of guilt all by itself." He sipped his Pepsi. "I spent most of my life worrying about everything I did. When I went to confession, I made stuff up so the priest wouldn't think I was lying. Then I felt guilty about that because I was. Lying, I mean."

Nancy licked the chocolate frosting on her cookie. "You made up stuff? Like what?"

"He wanted to hear my sins, but I didn't have any really good ones. It was dark in the confessional, and I was scared. I stuck my hands in my pants pockets and felt my pack of Juicy Fruit gum. I told him I went into Mom's purse and stole her gum. Actually, she gave it to me, so I'd sit still in church."

"And he believed you?"

"All he said was say three Hail Marys and four Our Fathers. I was so shook up over my lie, that I stuffed three sticks in my mouth right before mass. Afterward, I snuck out the side door. Ran right into *that* blasted priest and stood there with a big wad of lying gum in my mouth. I didn't know what to do, so I swallowed it. I was scared shitless because all I knew about gum wads was that hard stuff you find under theater seats. I thought I was gonna die."

"Good God!" Nancy laughed and slapped her hands on the table, knocking a spoon to the floor.

Ted turned on his stool and stared at her as she bent down to fetch it. His hand fiddled with his thinning hair.

"I thought it might stick to my heart or lungs or something. Hell, I was a little kid," Nick protested. "Sure glad to be done with that crap." He gave Nancy a serious look. "Get real. There must be something that you—like maybe us living together and not telling your Mom."

Nancy giggled. "Funny, I'd worry more about Daddy." She broke a piece from her cookie and put it in her mouth.

Caroline's face flushed and Walt's left eyebrow twitched. I could see they didn't want to hear about Nick and Nancy's living arrangements. Maxine was back to wiping her counter, while Ted looked amused. The Kit-Kat said 10:30.

"I don't feel guilty about that. You sorta do because of your Catholic upbringing. But okay, okay, well, there was this one time. I was a freshman and skipped a lot of those boring American history classes?"

Nick snickered. "Ha! Cut me a break. Everybody does that."

"No, no, it wasn't the skipping. There was this guy, Chester? He wasn't very attractive, wore glasses and all that stuff? Very shy, a little heavy, not fat, though."

"You left out the pocket protector." Nick grinned.

"Seriously, Chester was nerdy, but a real nice guy. He had this crush on me."

Nick rolled his eyes. "Sounds like a dork."

Wind-whipped rain strafed the roof. The lights flickered.

"Oh my." Caroline's hands cradled her cheeks.

"Anyway," Nancy continued. "He never dared ask me out...and well, I never read any of those assigned paperback books. So, I asked him to tell me what they were about. Chester came over to my dorm and patiently told me all the main points while I took notes."

"So, *that's* your guilt trip?" Nick laughed.

Their banter brought a smile to Ted's thin lips.

"Let me finish. The mid-term came, and I went in there and put down all the stuff that Chester said, and well, I got an A on the exam. Just like that." She snapped her fingers in Nick's face.

He didn't flinch. "Yeah? So?"

"Chester only got a B, and it was a weak B at that."

"Hah!"

"After that, I sort of dissed Chester. I know I wounded him. I saw it in his eyes."

"Oh, jeez Nance, you're breaking my heart." Nick played an imaginary violin with his thumb and forefinger, until Nancy smacked his hands. "He probably found some other chick and forgot all about you."

"Listen. Every time I ran into him, I saw the hurt. One day, he disappeared from the campus. Never said goodbye. Like poof!"

Caroline sniffed. "Well, I guess we all do stupid things when we're young."

Walt stiffened, bracing himself, I guessed, for her guilt travail, but she didn't say anymore.

The room got quiet. Everyone was looking at me. Not all of my guilt pangs were suitable for public discussion. Hmmm. I could talk about leaving Abby, but the topic seemed to be youthful indiscretion. Ah, there was one thing, and it genuinely did bother me even to this day.

"I was in the eighth grade in my small school," I began. "We were all excited about going to high school. Girls, who weren't popular, not neat dressers, and on the slutty side, were dubbed *scrags*. I learned this from my older brother who told me if I didn't change my slobby ways and wear this or that, I was destined for *scragdom.* He said scrags were dippy girls who stood at the end of the hall and opened the doors for the cool guys hoping to get dates. I stuck my tongue out at him. I wasn't holding doors for anybody."

Nancy burst out laughing. Walt and Caroline looked bored, while Ted sat quietly, his eyes fixed on Nancy watching her finish her cookie. Since we'd already devoured Maxine's valentine cookies and most of the cupcakes, she gave us another complimentary round of coffee, a basket of chips, and a plate of onion rings.

"A group of us girls were standing by the drinking fountain worrying about how popular we'd be in high school. 'You sure don't want to end up being a scrag,' I said knowingly.

"A scrag? They leaned in wanting to know what that meant. Since, I couldn't really explain it, I opted for an example: 'Mary Dicksen would be one.'

"Suddenly they gasped. I thought it was because of my insider information, but no, it was because Mary was standing next to our circle and had heard what I'd said. I didn't have a clue in my young head how hard those words must've hit. Mary didn't say anything; she stepped back into the shadows. The thing is Mary wasn't a dippy girl. She was poor."

Caroline dismissed my story with a wave of her hand. "Children can be *mean*. Walt, it's cold in here. Are you cold, Walt?" She rubbed her upper arms.

Walt didn't answer, probably relieved that Caroline wasn't talking about her mother.

"I never told Mary how sorry I was," I continued, miffed that Caroline interrupted me. "I was young and too stupid to know I should apologize. In her sophomore year, she dropped out of school."

"A dropout, like Chester!" Nancy chimed in.

"Hey, maybe Chester and Mary found each other." Nick's hands drum rolled on the table. Nancy playfully kicked him.

"To this day, I wonder if those words…I really hope she had a happy life."

No one said anything more, so I kept talking. "There's a small cemetery outside of the town where I grew up. My family has a plot there. One Memorial Day, after I placed the flowers on my grandparents' graves, I walked around reading the headstones. I noticed Mary's brother's name on one. He apparently was killed in Iraq. There weren't any flowers there, so I went back and got a few of mine. Now, when I bring bouquets for my family, I stop and leave at least one bloom for him…because there never are any there."

"Well," said Walt, "I'm surprised you remembered *that* after all these years. But you know, she could have forgotten all about that incident and dismissed you as an insensitive little fluff brain."

His words stung. "I know, but I wonder if she did."

"Did what?" asked Nancy

"Made it…you know…had a happy life. I hope she did." My throat tightened. I took a swig of coffee.

A gust of wind slammed the rain hard against the windows, the lights flickered again, and the door rattled, reminding us that the angry storm was still out there.

Surprisingly, Ted began to talk. He hadn't said more than a few words all evening. "I, I, uh, my little girl…" His voice was raspy.

Here we go again. Another youthful *faux pas*.

"I killed my daughter," he said. The words came out like a wail.

"Killed your daughter!" Caroline gave Walt a baffled look. "Whatever are you saying?"

Even Maxine's eyes widened, but she calmly refilled Ted's mug. "I didn't know you had a girl, Ted."

Ted swallowed hard, hesitated, and licked his lips. "Ayla," he said. He stopped and coughed. "It was my turn to have her. I rushed around gettin' things ready. I was late."

He paused and reached for his coffee again. "So, after I picked her up from my ex's house, I pulled the pickup into the gas station. While they was fillin' up, I went inside the food mart to get Ayla some candy. I couldn't remember which ones she like best...the gummies or those little chocolate balls." The mug started to shake in his hands. He set it down.

"When I got back to the pickup, Ayla was playing with my gun." Ted's voice trembled.  "I...I thought I'd locked the glove compartment."

Caroline's mouth dropped open. "A gun!"

"I ditched the candy." Ted wheezed. "And grabbed for the gun. It...it went off." He gasped for air. His voice broke into a shrill hoarse howl, like an animal in distress.

My mind shot back to the time I was fourteen and our dog got hit by a car. He made a wailing sound like that before he died in my arms. I cradled him tight, but it was no use. Powerless, I hung on, his blood staining my jeans and T-shirt.

The wind howled, driving hard rain against the diner like a bunker being shelled.

Caroline exhaled loudly. "You had a gun in your vehicle...with a child?"

"Worked in construction back then. Took a gun with me to the remote sites. I didn't think..."  His lips moved, but made no sound. Finally, he said, "I thought it was locked."

The lights blinked off, then came back on.

*Jesus. I hope we don't end up in the dark.*

"Boy, oh boy," said Walt, "We almost lost power that time." He stared at the ceiling light.

I was grateful somebody said something else.

Maxine turned the conversation back to Ted. "What happened? I mean how—" She had a pained looked on her face.

"My new insurance cards come in the mail. I put one in the glove compartment. I must've forgot to… " He made that sound again, shrill and piercing and then low and mournful.

"Oh, Ted," Maxine said. Her red-tipped fingers patted his arm. "I'm so, so sorry."

"There was blood all…the medics showed up, but it was too late. She just turned seven." He gulped more coffee. Some dribbled down his chin. He wiped it on his sleeve.

Every time he wailed like a distressed animal, Walt winced. Caroline's hands held her face. Nancy nervously twisted the ends of her hair. Nick's eyes found the table. I could feel my nails digging into my palms.

"It's okay, Ted, it's okay," Maxine's hand stroked his arm.

*Was he crying? With Ted, I couldn't be sure.*

"I held her, you know. Ayla always felt safe when I held her. It didn't help." He shook his head and mumbled. "Got a job driving truck, been driving, just driving…all these years."

"For God's sake, it was an accident," Nick said.

I couldn't help it. I nodded and smiled at him. *Nick's a good kid.*

Ted wiped spittle from his chin using his sleeve again. He gave Nick a pleading look. "They couldn't save her. I shouldn't have grabbed for the gun. I shouldn't have gone in there for candy."

Maxine pulled several napkins from the holder on the counter and handed them to Ted. They bunched in his hand.

Caroline rose to her feet. "Are you churched?" She straightened her sweater. "You should pray about this."

Walt shifted uncomfortably.

Perspiration dripped from Ted's forehead. "It was too late. Just drive truck." He wiped his face with the napkins. They dropped to the floor.

"I can still see...but I wasn't able to do nothin', you know, to save her." He gave Nancy a pleading look. "She was gone. I don't—she'd be all growed up now."

"God is very forgiving," Caroline said, her voice priggish. "You need to talk to a clergyman."

Ted didn't respond. The silence was unnerving.

"Maybe you just need to forgive yourself," I heard myself say. "You can't take back what happened. You can only fix the future. You—"

"She looked so peaceful." Ted turned away from us. "So peaceful. Her face, I mean, her sweet little face, her head of brown curls. I don't know...I don't know if she pulled the trigger or if I did." He placed his elbows on the counter, his hands cupping his face, his head shaking back and forth. "I shouldn't have gone for the candy, I shouldn't have gone..."

I couldn't think of what else to say. Like a turtle, Ted retreated to his shell taking his anguish with him. Nick's face went blank. Nancy had tears in her eyes. Caroline had offered Ted a spiritual road, but he was more comfortable driving round and round on the real one.

Caroline wasn't about to let it go. "Well, I think we should *all* pray for Ted." she said. "Walt—"

"Nance and I are not...we're, uh, we're not mainstream believers," Nick blurted.

"What?" Caroline pulled on the wattle under her chin.

"We...we...we're sort of New Age." Nancy patted Nick's hand. "Kinda."

"That's not to say we don't respect what others believe," Nick added.

"Yeah," said Nancy, "as long as they don't try and make us believe it."

"Or hurt anybody over it." Nick smiled. "So please, you folks go ahead. Pray if you want."

Caroline looked like she'd swallowed a sour pickle. She gave Walt a *not only are they sleeping together, but they're heathens* look. "Walt," she said, "do something. Why don't you do—"

A limb battered a small window on the side of the diner shattering glass. Cold wind gushed in and rain puddled on the shards. Nick and Walt jumped up, seemingly glad to have something to do. Ted, his face drained, stayed put. Maxine directed them to a couple pieces of odd-sized plywood and some nails in a back storage room, which they pounded over the window. Walt tacked down several green plastic garbage bags over the awkward wooden bandage. They helped Maxine sweep up the glass. She got her mop out to soak up the water.

Maxine glanced at the Kit-Kat. "It's almost midnight. We better get some sleep. Find a comfortable spot, lay your head on the table, or push some chairs together." She looked tired and sounded irritated. It had been a long day, and she was stuck with us.

Maxine turned the heat up and the lights out before disappearing to her office behind the kitchen. Nick and Nancy huddled together in a corner on the floor. Walt and Caroline pulled chairs to accommodate their legs with Caroline muttering about what this would do to her back and Walt saying, "It's our only option. Pretend you're camping." I wrapped my coat around me and stretched out on three chairs the best I could—at least they were padded. *What if we have to spend days here?*

Ted still sat at the counter—a lonely figure in the night with the ghost of a young girl, huddling in his mind. He'd made one mistake, and it gnawed away at him like a cancer until it had consumed his life.

Would he forever roam the freeways running from himself? And, what made him suddenly uncork his past? Did he see flickers of little Ayla in grown up Nancy? Did it feel safer to unload his grief without any other burly truck drivers in the diner? I couldn't picture him bearing his soul to some counselor or sitting cross-legged in meditation, doing deep breathing, but at least he'd gotten his pain out. A first step? Maybe being trapped in this place together was meant to be. Maybe there was something to that old adage: *Nothing happens without cause, even the chance brushing of one's sleeve against that of a stranger's.*

My stomach, filled with black coffee, cookies, and onion rings, churned. The Kit-Kat Klock ticked softly keeping time while its glowing eyes kept watch. Walt was snoring. No answers came.

The wind wailed outside like a banshee and heavy rain gurgled down the drainpipe. The bright, red sign that said *Maxine's,* gleamed through the droplets on the window, a neon beacon in the cold, bitter night. The last thing I remembered before drifting off to an uneasy sleep was seeing Ted still sitting there hunched and alone.

***

I awoke to the smell of fresh brewed coffee. The Kit-Kat said 7:30. Ted, it appeared, hadn't moved.

I sat up and checked my cell phone. There was a text message from Mandy, the kennel manager, that had come in overnight:

*Abby is fine. We weren't impacted by flooding. Other places, especially those near the creek, had to evacuate. We'll keep Abby until you get here. Stay safe.—Mandy*

If the kennel wasn't affected, that would mean my house was okay and Myrnie probably was, too.

"Got a phone call from the police. The bridge is still closed, but the slide's been cleared," Maxine called through the order window. "So you can drive the highway north and with some detouring hit the freeway. KJR News says traffic's moving okay."

Outside, the wind and rain had stopped. *Silence. Sweet silence.*

"I'm fixin' us some muffins and coffee, and it's on the house," Maxine said. She flashed her bright smile.

After trips to Maxine's small bathroom to relieve ourselves and freshen up the best we could using paper towels, we assembled at the counter.

Ted, looking pale and drawn, kept to himself, third stool from the left, drinking coffee, staring straight ahead, locked into his own world, a plate of buttered toast in front of him.

I slid off my stool and moved toward him wanting to pat his shoulder or at least say something consoling, but Maxine waved me off, shaking her head, mouthing *no*. I assumed she worried he might have a further meltdown. So, I let Ted be.

My back and neck ached from sleeping in an awkward position, but that didn't stifle my appetite. I inhaled Maxine's coffee. The warm muffin topped with butter and apple jelly slid down my throat and tasted like manna. We ate quietly, used the restroom again, and gathered our things, anxious to be on our way.

Walt reached for his billfold offering to pay Maxine for what we'd consumed during our stay, and we all echoed his suggestion.

"No. No. You folks get along, now. Get home safe. That's reward enough." We thanked her, gave her hugs, and wished each other luck.

It was time to go.

We left Ted where we found him, sitting there with Maxine who was talking softly and plying him with coffee warmups and orange marmalade. That's probably best, I thought. If God couldn't break through to him, I had a hunch Maxine eventually would.

Outside, a bright, but cold day awaited us. The parking lot was a battlefield of scattered pieces of fir branches and pinecones. Off in the distance, a chain saw groaned, most likely working its way through the trunk of a toppled tree. I stretched my body and twisted my neck getting ready for the drive, my thoughts turning toward home, my precious Abby, and a hot shower.

Nick and Nancy pulled out of the lot first, waving from a cute, yellow Volkswagen with a U of O bumper sticker. Walt and Caroline lingered in their maroon Buick talking. Ted's silver semi with the bright blue B&L logo on the door sat off to one side, a fir branch precariously teetering on the cab.

# One Last Shout

$\mathbf{M}$ost people get a mother-in-law when they marry. Mine came with the house.

When I first moved next door, she seemed harmless enough—a little old lady living by herself in a ranch-style house with a lovely yard. But I soon learned Myrnie, somewhere in her mid-80's, had one of those touchy personalities that began at the point where water hit electricity. Everything was her business and it all bothered her. Unfortunately for me, her windows put me in her constant line of sight.

Myrnie was a short, stocky woman with sparse cinnamon hair flecked with gray and enough vanity to spread on toast. I first drew her ire because my friend, Luke, regularly parked his old, dented Honda Civic on the street directly in front of her house. "That car's gotta go," she said standing on my front porch, feet hip distance apart, wearing a pink and navy blue flowered shirt and boxy white pedal pushers. She shook her crooked finger at me and then at the faded car. "When it's parked there, folks don't stop in. They think I already have company."

She stopped to glare at my dog, Abby, a golden retriever. "He's not a barker is he?"

"No," I said, "*she's* a good dog." Abby gleefully wagged her tail at the compliment. "As for your potential guests, maybe they could call ahead."

Her jaw jutted out revealing two long chin hairs. "Have your friend park on *your* driveway," she ordered. "You got plenty of room."

Speechless, I stared at the bright, red plastic nails that tipped her short, gnarled fingers and enhanced the age spots clustered below her knuckles.

"Not much of a car to begin with," she muttered and stomped off.

Whenever my guests did park on *my* driveway, I could always count on a probing telephone call, along with feigned concern. "Is everything all right over there, Rita?"

I assured her it was.

"Lots of cars always means a funeral or something," she said, fishing. "Somebody die?"

I consulted the neighbor across the street. "Aw, Myrnie's always been that way," he chuckled. "Lived here for years. You just have to let her blow."

And blow she did.

Myrnie got into it with just about everybody over barking dogs. "You gotta nip that in the bud."

"Maybe you could talk to the people; work it out," I said, making a plea for compassion. "I'm sure the dog is part of their family."

"Been there, done that. A dog is an animal."

"That's all we are," I said. "Animals."

"A dog," she paused, her eyes narrowing, "can only bark for fifteen minutes." She checked her watch. "He's got five more." Then she marched into her house to make the inevitable call to animal control.

"Shad up," I heard her say one afternoon to Abby who was barking at a squirrel in *her* tree. After that, I kept Abby in the house whenever I was gone, and only let her in the yard if I was out there, too.

When Frank, a neighbor on her other side, let his homeless mother park her camper on his driveway, Myrnie had a conniption fit. Her arms flailed the air. "I turned them in," she said.

"It's not just *anybody*." I protested. "It's his mother."

"Can't have people living out there on the driveway."

"It sounds like he's trying to help her," I said. "Cut them a break."

Myrnie's jaw locked into that familiar, pugnacious angle. "You give those squatters an inch, and well, you know the rest. They don't have a pot to pee in or a winda to throw it out of. First thing you know, the garbage will be knee high, and we'll be overrun with rats."

God help the Ridgeways. Their yard spouted clumps of dandelions. Myrnie, face flushed, ready for battle, zeroed in. "Those things spread like the chicken pox. Looks like an epidemic over there. I'm calling the city."

She took down the license plates of "all the cars" visiting "the drug house," a duplex across the street and a few houses up, only to discover that their children, complete with friends, were home from college.

She was upset when I put a blind over my garage window, because she couldn't see in. "How will I know when you're gone?" And, she didn't like the fact that I locked my backyard gate. "What if there's a fire?" She also thought I needed to notify her every time I went out of town to avoid disruption to her life. "I always head for bed, when I see you put the dog out."

***

To celebrate the March equinox, I invited my meditation group over. We were sitting in the living room, cross-legged, eyes closed, deep into Samadhi, I on the verge of nirvana (well, hopefully) when, after five silence-puncturing rings, my answering machine took Myrnie's desperate call. "Did something happen?" she squawked. "I seen all those cars over there. People walkin' in with food. You sick or something?"

"God knows what she'd do," I complained afterward, over potluck, to my amused visitors, "if she knew we were burning incense and had a Buddha on the coffee table. I swear that woman can see through cement."

All six feet of Luke hooted. "Call her back, Rita. Invite her over. Tell her we're having the blood sacrifice right after dessert. By the way, what *is* for dessert? Ah, cookies."

"She'd probably storm the place and bat a few heads with her garden shovel."

"We could always sacrifice my car. That would make her happy."

I couldn't resist. "That would make *a lot* of people happy."

"Come on, Rita. You're a writer," Luke said, his dark eyes amused. "Think of all the good material living right next door. She's one hell of a character study. And, this is one hell of a good cookie. Chocolate chip." He brushed crumbs off his shirt onto my floor.

I had to smile. He was right. Pieces of Myrnie already floated through many of my characters, but so did pieces of him.

One windy evening, I hosted a birthday dinner. We were about to cut the cake when a loud noise stopped our chatter. Six seconds later, the telephone rang. "Someone's shooting in the neighborhood," Myrnie declared, out of breath.

"It's pretty blustery out there," I said, trying to calm her, "but we'll check it out."

"*We?* You're not alone?

"No, I've got company."

"There's no one over there that's got a gun?"

"Of course not," I said, irritated.

"What about that Luke fella? The one with the crummy car?"

"He's unarmed."

"I had to turn the TV off when I heard that shot," she insisted. "A person can't even sit in their living room and feel safe these days."

The next morning, I directed her to a large tree branch that had fallen on the metal shed in her backyard.

A month later, Myrnie hired a handyman to repair the shed's dented roof and its decaying floor. I happened to be standing there as the befuddled man walked toward her garbage can with a clinking box full of empty liquor bottles.

"I see you're quite fond of Jack Daniels," I said to Myrnie.

She blanched. "The guy that fixed the leak in my roof that time was an alco-hawlick. Dang fool hid all his bottles under my shed."

"Gee," I said. "I don't remember seeing a roofer at your place."

"I'm just glad the idiot didn't fall off, break his neck, and sue me or something. Gotta go." She hurried inside. I heard the door slam.

After Myrnie discovered the neighborhood association, she became a regular. "You know me, I just bite my tongue," she said, but insisted that I go there and help her complain. "I can't do it alone. You gotta have *people* behind you. They just think I'm an old crank."

*If the shoe fits*, I thought, but feigned other commitments.

Myrnie was not to be put off. She tacked a plastic zip-lock bag containing copies of the association newsletter to the fence between her yard and mine with a big plastic clip. *Keep one for yourself and hand the rest out to the neighbors*, her handwritten note ordered. I dropped them into the trash. Sometimes I just ignored the parcel. Sure enough, the phone would ring. "What I put out on the fence, hasn't moved.

You been gone? I can't see in your garage since you put that curtain there."

Like a person breaking in a pair of new shoes, I thought I was starting to get comfortable with Myrnie's cantankerous ways until she started in on my climbing rose, Joseph's Coat. The ten-foot climber burst into a gorgeous kaleidoscope of orange, yellow, red and pink blooms each June. I had lovingly planted it in an obelisk wrought iron trellis by our shared backyard fence directly in front of Myrnie's patio.

I did have a motive. I wanted to block her view into my life.

As the rose grew and the trellis aged, its metal legs loosened in the soil. Periodically, the wind caught the rose's leafy top, causing the trellis to bend slightly on an angle, but not enough to harm the vigorous rose.

Needless to say, Myrnie was on it like a fire in dry underbrush. "Why don't you fasten that thing to *my* fence?" she squawked. "Its leaning there like that makes me crazy."

I simply straightened the trellis, but I wasn't strong enough to push its legs into the earth.

Not to be put off, Myrnie ordered the yard service crew we shared to straighten it. "They just stood there like fence posts, until I told them I think of you as my daughter," she said smugly.

*Daughter?* I thought of *her* as a thorn in my side. Of course, the two intimidated Hispanic workers did her bidding and pushed the legs into the ground. Still, the next strong wind gave the trellis a slight tilt.

I let it go. It wasn't harming the rose and secretly, I was glad it irritated her. "Don't worry about it," I told her. "The canes are firmly entwined. It'll be okay."

"No." Myrnie bristled. "A trellis should be straight. That's why you have one in the first place." She insisted that the yard crew fasten it to the fence. She even provided the wire, but alas, a windy night caused the trellis to lean sideways again.

Myrnie pointed it out several times. "It gives me fits," she said in that shrill, scratchy voice which rivaled fingernails against a chalkboard.

I took my time straightening it, much to her chagrin. Maybe, that's when she started really hating that rose bush.

***

"So how are you?" Myrnie asked. I had just come home after a long day to a ringing telephone.

"Fine," I said fidgeting and checking my watch. "How are you doing?" I knew her cancer had returned and spread to her kidneys. Her doctors did not recommend treating the reoccurrence with radiation or chemotherapy and because of her age, they'd ruled out surgery. For that, I was genuinely sorry.

"I just wanted to tell you," she continued, "I had the guys trim your rose."

"Oh?"

"I had them cut mine back, so I thought they might as well trim yours. There's no need for you to be climbing on the ladder, cutting those buds. I mean you could fall or something." she said, layering on her concern for me.

"You might want to give it a shot of fertilizer. You know, to perk it up."

"Oh, uh-huh," I said half listening. I sorted through my mail. The rose did need to be deadheaded.

"You there?" she asked.

"Yeah."

"And, I had the guys wind your clematis on it, too. Not that I minded it climbing on *my* fence."

"That's nice," I said, my mind miles away.

"Now it looks good," she insisted. "And the trellis is straight. There's no reason you need to be on a ladder."

Who did she think climbed on the ladder to clean the drains or to paint the house trim? "How thoughtful. Thank you," I managed. Abby anxiously pawed the door wanting to go out.

"I've been busy getting all my things settled. I can't talk too long because home health care is coming."

I'd seen the ambulance parked outside her house in the wee hours of the morning a couple of weeks ago, but I didn't realize things had become that serious.

"And, my sister's got a tumor."

"I'm so sorry," I said.

"It's in her liver."

"Is there anything I can do for you?" I asked and meant it.

"When you get some time, come over. I'd like to see you. Maybe in a couple a weeks. You know, when you got the time...for tea."

This was such a different Myrnie. Tea? Did she want to say good-bye? I didn't know. Of course, I needed to visit her. Maybe I'd bring her a bouquet of roses from my yard.

"I have a twenty-year-old mind in an old body." Her voice cracked.

I had heard her say that many times. In fact, I enjoyed entertaining my friends with "young" Myrnie stories. Like the time, she'd strained to squeeze her full bottom into low slung jeans "that gals these days wear." And the toe ring she tried, but had to give up because of her diabetes. Instead, she sported an ankle bracelet and painted toe-nails. One day, she even came home with new eyebrows tattooed on her crinkled forehead. When she lost some weight, she went around with her shirt tied up around her waist to show off her bumpy, cellulite-studded butt.

Now, all of that belonged in the past. I felt a strange ache. What did it feel like to be her? To wake up in the morning, look outside your window and know all of what you saw and sensed was now beyond your control.

*Losing control.* That especially would be hard for Myrnie.

"Feeling young is okay," I said. "It can help. It really can." Actually, life in the neighborhood without her would seem bland. She knew everything that went on and then some. I'd miss the stories, her corny observations, and the fun I had doing imitations of her for my friends. Who said you had to like every aspect of a person anyway? I'd miss her, I guessed, the way I missed that tacky chalkware bird figurine I used for a paperweight. Funny, how I didn't realize its value to me until it tumbled to the floor and shattered. "You take care," I said. "Abby is about to break down the door, so I need to let her out."

That's when I saw my rose.

It wasn't trimmed. It was stripped of blooms, buds, and all of its leaves. Now it was just a stalk—gray, barky and naked in the middle of a "straight-as-a-pin" trellis. My purple blooming clematis vine that grew nearby and had previously made its way up *her* fence now curled around the trellis.

Myrnie had done it again.

I wanted to wring her wrinkled neck. The yard guys would not have demolished my beautiful rose, unless someone specifically ordered them to do so. Why for God's sake did this woman, at the end of her life, do this nasty thing?

Enough was enough. Period.

In a huff, I marched inside and grabbed the phone. I intended to spew fire. Don't you *ever* make decisions about *anything* in my yard. I'd call the yard service, too, and raise hell.

I stopped.

Myrnie was dying; her life now grains of sand slipping through the narrow channel of an hour glass. My throat tightened. Her cancer hadn't quenched her flame. No, that irascible, fiery woman was still in her failing body. I took a deep breath and dropped the receiver in its cradle.

Maybe in the end, clinging to who we are is the last shout we get at life. I wanted Myrnie to have her unique roar.

# On Edge

"**M**adge says I'm boring," Chuck confided to Max. "I think she's going to leave me." The old dog looked up with his one good eye. The other was swollen and sightless, destroyed by a cataract and glaucoma. His furry body drooped, still submissive after Madge had scolded him.

Madge had spent most of the morning mopping the kitchen floor and vacuuming like a soldier on a mission, until she discovered the wet spot on the living room rug. "I told you to put the dog outside," she roared at Chuck from the kitchen. "Is that too much to ask? I still have to make the potato salad...and take a shower."

She'd invited the Hackleys over for a Fourth of July potluck out on the deck. Chuck wasn't looking forward to the Hackleys. Oh, Pete was okay, but Ruth and Madge constantly tried to one-up each other. That always put Madge on edge, and she was already out there teetering. Their besting used to be about the kids, clothes, or cars, but after they retired, it was *travel*.

Chuck bent down and scratched Max's ears. The Hackleys were travel whores—always off to some place. All you had to say was pass the salt, and they'd tell you every detail of their trip to Ireland where Pete got hooked on potato pancakes, or the time Ruth got stuck in a sauna in Finland. After they discovered cruising, it got worse.

Once the Hackleys visited, they'd reciprocate with a dinner invitation. Chuck shuddered at the thought because he'd have to sit through a boring slide show of their endless travel photos. Now that Pete had learned how to hook his iPhone up to the TV, there'd be zillions of shots of him with his big, hairy stomach hanging over a pair of ugly, flowered shorts and more of Ruth standing next to him smiling, totally unaware of her cottage cheese thighs sticking out of a bulging swimsuit.

"Shit," Chuck muttered. "Why do people have to define themselves by where they go?" Max didn't look up.

"You asked 'em how they are, they tell you where they went."

Max whimpered.

"Harrumph. Those Hackleys travel thousands of miles just to eat and shop." He patted Max's head. "There are two things in life anyone can do, ol' boy. One is travel and the other is get married."

Chuck was perfectly content with his routine—playing golf, having coffee downtown with the guys, puttering in the garage, browsing at the hardware store, or whiling away the afternoon lounging with Max, reading sports magazines and murder mystery paperbacks.

He surveyed the wet spot on the rug. Max hung his head.

"I'll clean it up," he called from the living room. "Do we have some Nature's Miracle?"

He barely finished his question when a red and white container flew through the air and bounced off the wall landing next to Max with a thump. A few seconds later, the raging Madge tossed a roll of paper towels.

"This house smells like a monkey's cage!" she bellowed. "And, there's dog hair everywhere."

Chuck said nothing. Max just cowered and shook.

The weather wasn't helping either. It rained in the morning, and the still chilly day coupled with a threatening gray sky meant the potluck would move to their small dining room. Several miniature American flags, originally intended for the deck, found a home in the chipped philodendron pot. A festive streamer of tiny red, white, and blue stars wound its way around the large dining room window.

Chuck led Max outside to the backyard and put him in his kennel. Max flopped down waiting, while Chuck grabbed the garden hose and filled his water dish. "There you go, ol' boy." It seemed like yesterday when he brought the squirming, golden lab puppy home to fill their empty nest. Now suffering from arthritis, Max's old body just wanted to sleep.

"At least out here, you won't be trapped around the table with those mind-numbing bores." Chuck's shoulders slumped. He'd hoped to busy himself barbecuing chicken breasts over the grill, but because of the weather, Madge decided to oven roast them instead. Now, with his plan foiled, there was no way to escape the Hackleys, not even for a few minutes.

Back inside, Chuck sopped up pee with a thick layer of paper towels and poured the cleaning fluid on the wet spot.

"I know it's hard," Madge yelled from the kitchen. "But you just have to face it. Max is up there, and...and I think it's time." She slammed a cupboard door.

Chuck, ignored Madge's comment about Max, covered the spot with a fresh layer of paper towels, and pressed down with his full weight. His thoughts shifted to his haunting discovery. He'd been checking the sent mail file on the computer to make sure he'd included Clyde in his e-mail message about their Thursday golf game. That's when he spotted *it*—a message from Madge to Robert, her old college boyfriend. It said she'd found his web page while surfing the Internet and got to thinking about old times. After two children and a long teaching career, she'd finally retired. She didn't mention Chuck. She said she was going to be in San Francisco, and she'd love to meet him for lunch...*to catch up*. Chuck read it several times slowly. He felt like he'd been hit in the stomach with the head of a 3-iron.

That next morning, during a nice breakfast of pancakes and strawberries, Madge abruptly announced, "I'm going to San Francisco to see Amy." That news caught Chuck with a big strawberry in his mouth. Before he could reply, she quickly added, "It's a mother and daughter thing." By the time he swallowed, she was already on her feet, taking militant strides toward the sink with her empty plate. For days afterward, Chuck mined the e-mail files looking for Robert's response, but found nothing.

2.

For Madge, it all started the night she fled to Amy's bedroom to avoid Chuck's guttural snoring, which sounded like a jackhammer on steroids. Maybe it was Amy's school pennants hanging on the wall or the full moon shining through the oak tree outside the window that spurred her on. At any rate, a vivid image of Robert popped into Madge's mind transporting her back to her youth. *What would her life have been like if it had worked out with Robert?*

She slipped out of bed and scuffled down to the den, where she plugged his name into Google. Her search produced several hits. He was a successful real estate lawyer in San Francisco and served on a prestigious city planning commission. Back at the Google site, she clicked on Images, which took her to a web page about some conference where Robert was a speaker. She pushed her red-framed reading glasses farther up on her nose and moved her face close to the computer screen to study his image. Unlike Chuck who had a belly and bald head, Robert was trim and handsome in his dark suit. His full head of dark hair grayed gracefully around the temples. Beneath her nightgown, her heart fluttered. She hastily composed an e-mail suggesting they meet. As soon as she hit the send button, she felt like a huge weight had dropped off and she was floating toward a new beginning.

3.

Chuck continued to blot the wet spot on the rug. He remembered seeing Robert around campus a few times. He couldn't picture him exactly, but he did remember Madge saying he'd broken her heart. Why, after all these years, would you want to see some jerk-face who did that? He pushed another paper towel down hard against the rug until no more liquid appeared.

The first time he'd met Madge back in college, he was instantly attracted to her dazzling smile and the way her brown pageboy bounced every time she turned her head. Slender and perky, she kept the conversation going no matter who they were with—something he wasn't good at. Over the years, Madge's waistline had gotten thicker, but she still wore her hair like that, although now it was much shorter and steel gray. After their first date, Madge seemed aloof; but he pursued her until they became a couple. *All marriages had their dry spells, didn't they?*

4.

In the kitchen, Madge, wielding a knife, swiftly removed the skins from the boiled potatoes, her thoughts shifting to Robert. To a small town girl, Robert, who sat next to her in an American lit class, was handsome with that dark curl in the center of his forehead and an easy smile. He was exciting, too, always talking about going to law school, having his own practice, and spending the summer in London. He took her to plays, to frat parties where they danced until midnight, and surprised her with a French kiss. She fell hard, like a giant redwood crashing in the forest, her heart pounding every time he came near. She was dreaming about the details of their wedding right down to the cake, when Robert ditched her for Connie somebody, that well-stacked sorority queen. Madge picked up a large skinned potato and viciously diced it, the knife clacking against her wooden cutting board.

After hunkering down in her dorm room, crying her heart out, she began stalking him, running for blocks, hoping to *accidentally* bump into him at the student union or the library. Nothing worked. So, when Chuck asked her to go to the game that weekend she said yes, secretly hoping to cross paths with Robert.

Madge pulled a bowl from the cupboard and whisked together mayonnaise with yellow mustard. She'd met steady, reliable Chuck at a dorm social featuring dessert and conversation. He was attentive and she felt comfortable with him, but Chuck never stoked her fire the way Robert had.

"Chuck's a good man," her dad had said after meeting him twice. "Sensible. Both feet planted on the ground."

"Have you decided on *your* colors?" her mom had asked as she hemmed the green taffeta bridesmaid dress Madge would wear for her younger sister's wedding. "You need to do that, you know."

"Mom, please." Madge clenched her hands and took a deep breath, wondering if another Robert might come along. "We're just dating."

Her mother bit off the end of the thread and shook out the skirt. "I'd love to make your dress."

*A dress? Was marriage about a dress? What about love? London? The world?*

"You know, Madge, your Aunt Ruby could've gotten married lots of times, but she was too particular." She wrinkled her nose when she said *particular.* "You don't want to be too darn picky or you'll get left."

Aunt Ruby. That shriveled husk of a woman they always had to invite on Thanksgiving and Christmas. She reminded Madge of those corn kernels you always found at the bottom of the popcorn bowl that failed to burst into a wonderful fluffy delight.

After her sister's wedding and after Madge's best friend eloped, the pressure increased. "You're not getting any younger," her mother insisted.

"That Chuck," her dad said, peering at her over the sports section. "You can set your clock by him. Don't know too many men like that."

One month after graduation, she and Chuck married. Everyone said it was the next logical step. *It was, wasn't it?*

Madge added salt and pepper to her mixture, whisking vigorously. Chuck, a history major, ended up working at an insurance company while she taught second grade. After a couple years of apartment life, they bought a tract house in the suburbs and had Amy, then John. When John started school, Madge went back to work. Chuck settled down in the underwriting department and stayed with the company for thirty-two years.

She banged the wire whisk against the bowl to shake the mayonnaise from the tines.

5.

Chuck grabbed Madge's hairdryer from their bathroom, so he could dry the wet spot. He glanced at the tiny heart-shaped clock on the windowsill—the one he'd given her as an anniversary present. Why did she put it there, instead of on her nightstand?

*Time.* It fixes everything. At least that's what Clyde had said when the two shared cheeseburgers at the club after a round of golf. Chuck's angst poured out slowly like the thick ketchup in the Heinz bottle he held over his fries. "Madge is on my case all the time," he'd confided, watching the red sauce puddle on his plate. "Do this. Do that. When I do, it's never right. If I say something, she loses it." He didn't mention the e-mail affair. That still made his stomach lurch.

"Give it *time*," Clyde had said. "When I retired, me and the wife had to adjust to each other all over again. I used to go to work while she did her thing with the kids, the house, whatever. We did that our whole lives. All of a sudden, I was in her space. Let me tell you, we drove each other crazy. Now things have settled down...somewhat. I go off and play golf. She joined a book group. Trust me, it gets better."

Chuck aimed the hairdryer at the spot on the rug. Maybe he should insist on going to San Francisco with her. Maybe he should fly down there later and surprise them. He grabbed a can of Lysol and gave an imaginary Robert a quick spray. "Real men don't have web pages," he said to the rug.

6.

Madge jerked the shells off the hard-boiled eggs. She decided to toss in a little chopped celery to jazz up the salad. Pete always bragged about Ruth's cooking. Chuck just sat there like a bump on a log.

She hacked away at the celery, muttering to herself about Robert's response to her e-mail. Wagging her head, she mimicked his voice. "How nice to hear from you. Unfortunately, I can't meet for lunch because I have to be in Toronto for a seminar. Have a nice day. Blah, blah, blah." The tone of his message was matter of fact...not even a maybe-I'll-see-you-around sometime and absolutely no details about his personal life. She closed both eyes—such hope, such anticipation. Then pow!

She'd been in the den with Max when she read Robert's reply. Max was always at her feet whenever she used the computer. "He did it again," she'd blurted. "That bastard dumped me." She slid down, threw her arms around the old dog, and cried into his neck—not only about Robert, but about everything else bottled up inside. After a few moments, she got up and hit the delete key. "Take that!" she muttered as Robert's e-mail disappeared from the screen. She clicked on the trash file and annihilated him again. Zap!

7.

The dinner with the Hackleys went as expected. Pete and Ruth were so tan from their latest vacation to Bora Bora they looked like two roasted turkeys. Ruth talked endlessly about the massage she'd gotten on the cruise ship, the delicious *Poisson Cru* salad with coconut milk, the midnight buffet complete with ice sculptures, the entertainment, the waiters with cute butts. Next, they were going to try trekking, she said, or perhaps an African safari.

"So, where have you *been*?" Ruth asked. She gave Madge am innocent smile.

"We're going to travel one of these days," Madge replied. "But it's hard to find someone to care for Max. He's an old dog. We could board him, but Chuck doesn't want to do that."

"Actually, Madge is planning a trip to San Francisco to...uh...see Amy, aren't you dear?" Chuck studied her face, but Madge took the conversation in a different direction.

"We've been working on the kitchen," she said. "Did you notice we painted the cupboards and updated the knobs?"

Chuck shifted in his chair.

Ruth's eyes blinked; then blinked again. "That's why we sold our house and moved into a condo. Houses, like dogs, just *tie* you down."

"We took a trip to Victoria a few months ago," Madge said. "We took the dog."

"We've been there...several times," Ruth countered, "*before* we retired. I'm talking about excitement—the lure of distant lands."

"Beans?" Madge handed the bowl of baked beans to Pete.

Chuck could see Ruth was getting to Madge, so he jumped right in. "I take trips every day to Home Depot, Walmart, SavOn Foods." He grinned. "You don't have to hide your money in your underwear, and the people are happy to see you."

Pete gave him a condescending smile.

"Travel is so *broadening*—" Ruth began

"Some of us are broad enough," Chuck laughed and patted his belly. "Right, Pete?"

Madge kicked him under the table.

"Is there celery in the potato salad?" Ruth suddenly dropped her fork as if she'd been poisoned. "I never touch the stuff!" She grasped her throat. "I got sick on it when we were in France, just as we were going to that alpine village, the one with magnificent flowers and cobbled streets. Even the sight of it makes me—"

"I—I thought celery would perk it up a bit," Madge stammered.

Ruth quarantined the mound of potatoes to the far side of her plate.

"Ruth makes a hell of a potato salad," Pete said, "But she *never* puts celery in it."

Chuck was glad when they got to dessert because that meant dinner was over and the Hackleys would be leaving soon. Ruth had brought a luscious lemon soufflé cheesecake topped with blueberries. He gobbled his portion, all the while picturing himself at the door waving goodbye.

Pete took it as a sign that he liked it. "Would you look at that, Ruth. The man just inhaled your cheesecake. Ruth makes a hell of a cheesecake."

Ruth beamed.

Madge looked mortified.

Chuck sat there like a bump on a log.

8.

After they left, Madge sought refuge in the kitchen. While loading the dishwasher, she thought again about Robert, the jerk...and then about her children. They were great kids. Did Robert have children and was he a good father? She rolled her eyes. He probably was too busy, distant, and always jetting off somewhere. At least Chuck loved his children. Cared. Spent time with them. She'd give him that.

She saved a piece of chicken breast for Max, planning to surprise him with it in the morning. She felt bad about yelling at him and guilty for wanting to end his life. Max, her once loyal guardian. His scruffy, eager ways had filled the empty spots in her life. She couldn't count the times she'd taken him for a walk, just to get out of the house. She needed to walk right now, but Max was old and had hip problems.

*Maybe I should have an affair? Would Chuck even notice if I did? He gave me a silly clock for our anniversary. What ever happened to a dozen roses, dinner out, dancing, romantic sex?* She threw open the kitchen window and took several deep breaths.

"You better go get Max before the fireworks start," Madge said when Chuck brought in the last dishes from the table.

"He doesn't hear like he used to," he mumbled.

"Bring him in, but make damn sure he's does his business beforehand." Madge banged a pot. She would go to San Francisco by herself anyway...to clear her head...to get away...to decide her future.

9.

Chuck, happy to duck out, scuttled to the backyard. "Okay, big fella, the coast is clear." Max lay still. He probably didn't hear me, Chuck thought, so he gave him a gentle nudge. Max's old body felt stiff and cold.

"Oh no, Max..." his voice broke. Get Madge, he thought. He turned, took two steps, threw his hands up, and stopped. All she cares about is her trip to San Francisco and seeing that wimpy Robert. He made a farting noise with his mouth.

Instead, he grabbed a blanket from the station wagon and carefully wrapped it around Max. He carried the lifeless dog across the lawn, and gently lifted him into the back. Tomorrow he'd take him to the vet and have him cremated.

Chuck sat on the tailgate next to Max for a long time, just watching a clump of ominous, gloomy clouds move above him, his throat choked with emotion. As it got darker, the clouds disappeared into the inky sky. He could see Madge's silhouette against the upstairs window. His heart sank. She was sleeping in Amy's room *again*.

He heard a popping noise and saw the sky light up as a colorful red flare burst into millions of tiny lights. Except for shouts and children laughing in the distance, the backyard seemed like a battlefield with whistling sounds and bright explosions. He remembered when they used to picnic in the park with the kids waiting for the fireworks to start...how little Amy squealed and ran to his protective arms; how he carried a sleepy John from the car to tuck him into bed. Now they called him Pops. They were a family. He and Madge had a history together...over forty years. Surely, she wasn't going to toss that away. Maybe Clyde was right—you just had to give it some time.

The bedroom window was black, and except for an occasional bang, the night was still. Chuck slid off the tailgate and stared at the bundle in the back. Max seemed so all alone lying there. For just a second, something stirred deep in Chuck's gut that made him want to linger; as if he just finished the final chapter in a good book but didn't want the story to end. In the darkness tears came. He patted the blanket one last time and slammed the door shut. "Good night, fella," he said. "Thanks for everything."

# The Invitation

Arlene hid the binoculars behind some cookbooks in the kitchen when she heard Liz tapping on the back door.

"Come on in," Arlene called. She wiped her hands on a faded kitchen towel and carried the basket of freshly baked muffins to the table. The scent of apples and cinnamon wafted through the air.

"Oh gosh, but those look good," Liz said, "And it smells like heaven in here." Liz was a plain, thick woman who favored jeans with elastic waistbands. Her short, straight white hair hadn't seen a beauty shop in years.

Petite, chunky Arlene, on the other hand, loved her weekly visits to the Cut 'n Curl where she chatted it up with the regulars and got her thinning brown and gray hair shampooed and sprayed into place.

Arlene and Liz had tea together on Tuesdays for as long as they had been next-door neighbors.

Liz's heavy behind made the cushions on the kitchen chair squish as she plopped herself down. She reached for a muffin.

"It's a new cranberry, apple, walnut thing," Arlene said. "I found it in the lifestyle section of the paper." Arlene enjoyed baking muffins. She knew the basic recipe by heart, so she didn't even have to think. She liked measuring flour, pouring in milk, breaking the egg, and stirring the ingredients in the pale rose-tinged bowl she'd used for years. Seeing her colored measuring cups lined up on the counter, feeling the copper measuring spoons between her fingers, and hearing the jingling noise they made comforted her. On restless nights, alone in her bed, she'd trundle down to the kitchen after midnight and bake muffins. The sweet-scented air made her world feel like someone had switched on the sun to bright, if just for a moment.

Liz's square fingers searched the red apple-shaped ceramic canister for her favorite Earl Grey tea bag. She ripped open the wrapper and bobbed the bag in her cup as Arlene poured the hot water.

Arlene's small, dark eyes searched Liz's face. "What's been happening?" Surely, Liz would tell her if she'd gotten an invitation.

"Not much. Edith is having her gall bladder out today. I guess these days they just suck those things right out of you. Whoosh! Used to be they cut you open, and you spent weeks recovering."

Normally, Arlene would ask what Edith wore to the hospital, if she got her hair done before going, and did they make her remove that loud nail polish she always wore. But today, Arlene was on a mission. "You got some plans for this weekend?"

"I think I'll take some broth over there. Edith has to be on liquids for at least twenty-four hours." Liz spread a thick layer of orange marmalade on her muffin and helped herself to the slices of white cheddar cheese and apple wedges Arlene always placed on a bright blue tray.

"So you're planning to be home...I mean...all week?" Arlene probed. She cut her own muffin into tiny pieces.

"Uh-huh. I got Edith a card, if you want to sign it. You know, cards these days cost almost as much as a dozen eggs."

Arlene impatiently dabbed her tea bag up and down. She pursed her lips. She'd have to be more direct. "I heard the Archers, those new people who bought the big colonial across the street, are planning a housewarming." She popped a piece of muffin into her mouth, chewed, and waited.

"I suppose that's the next step. They've been in there a month."

Arlene continued to prod. "I saw a carpet cleaning truck pull up the other day. Then their yardman brought in some extra plants. But I haven't heard anything about a housewarming, have you?" She studied Liz's face.

"Well, no."

"Have you actually met them?"

"He came over and borrowed Milt's wrench. Said there was a plumbing problem in the basement. Seemed kinda nice. Hmm, I think he did say something about us coming over—"

"So you got an *invitation*?" Arlene leaned forward in her chair; both of her elbows were on the table, her fists propping up her chin.

"Just what he said, but I don't think he mentioned anything about a housewarming. I don't recall any specific time. Then again, I wasn't listening that close. If it was a housewarming, you'd think we'd get something more formal, like a note or something. Did you get anything?"

"No. Not a thing."

"I'll have to ask Milt just what it was he said." Liz's eyes got wide behind her thick bifocals. "If it's a housewarming, I supposed that means a gift."

Arlene could see the wheels churning in Liz's head. She knew how tight Liz's husband could be. Milt, she always thought, still had the first nickel he ever earned.

"Well, it's only Tuesday. I suppose there's still time. Seems odd he'd invite us, just like that." Liz snapped her fingers. "I mean it was just a wrench. Uh, I forgot exactly what his name was."

"Bill...Bill Archer. He's a partner in that big CPA firm here in town. Each morning, he jogs down the street with...with their black lab."

"Oh, so they're the ones with the dog that gave you all that trouble. The one you told me about a zillion times." Liz winced and quickly put her hand over her mouth. "Oh, I mean—"

It was too late. Arlene exploded. "That darn dog barked on and off all night that first week they moved in...right on the side where I sleep. I had to get up and shut the window, and then the room got so stuffy it irritated my sinuses. I can't believe I was the only one that heard it." Arlene could feel her heart pumping blood. She paused and gagged as if she'd just swallowed a pit. "I...I had a terrible headache all day," she finally said.

"We never heard it. Our bedroom is in the back of the house. Why didn't you just move to one of your other rooms?" Liz asked. "I mean you have the whole house to *yourself*."

Sometimes Arlene just wanted to slap Liz. One of these days, she was going to know how it feels to be a widow...to wake up alone, to make all those decisions about the house or the car without a sounding board, to watch Jeopardy with the cat. "I guess they have him under control...now," she muttered. She regretted the dog incident and wished she hadn't said anything to Liz. She didn't know they were *the* Archers the morning she stormed over there about the dog.

Bill Archer was just about to step into his Volvo station wagon when Arlene accosted him. "You gotta do something about that damn dog!" she blurted. "Barking all night like that."

Startled, Archer tossed his heavy briefcase into the front seat. "I'm very sorry about that," he said, and placed the large, green mug of coffee he carried on top of the roof. "He's a young dog and the surroundings are new—"

Arlene didn't know why that should make a difference. "I couldn't sleep all night!" she screeched.

"Give us some time with him. Ranger is part of our family, and we're—"

Arlene's voice jumped a whole pitch. "The law says a dog can't bark more than fifteen minutes." Her thin mouth puckered; her eyes shot daggers.

"Have you ever had a dog?" Archer's brows knitted into a frown over his dark-rimmed glasses. He folded his arms across his chest, standing in his three-piece suit like he was ready to give a lecture on debits and credits. His tall, lean figure towered over Arlene's round body, which looked even more bulky in the light blue sweats she wore.

"No, and if I did, I'd keep him quiet," she shot back. Then she stormed off in a huff. When she looked over her shoulder, she saw the maroon Volvo heading down the street with the coffee cup still on its roof sending little ringlets of steam into the cool morning air.

Two days later, she stepped outside to pick up the morning paper only to discover the paperboy had missed her front porch. Again. She didn't want anyone to see her in her quilted, pink polyester robe that had gone out of style years ago, and she hadn't combed her hair. Parts of it stood straight up exposing her scalp in the back where her frizzy hair was thinning. She tip-toed gingerly trying to hide behind the big camellia bush.

"Dang kid," she grumbled as she bent down to grab the paper. "Don't know what's wrong with this fool younger generation." That's when it echoed right in her ear—a great big "woof!" She almost peed her pants. That big, black dog was in her front yard! Arlene bolted up so fast she nearly threw out her back. The damn dog trampled her flowerbed. Arlene shook her fist at him as he took off across the street.

Later, when she was out pulling a few weeds, she found the stinking present that he'd left right next to her crushed Alexander Fleming peony—the one her husband had given her; the one that came back every year, making her heart smile. Now its deep, pink blooms were all catawampus. Furious, she marched into the house and armed herself with a plastic dustpan. After she scooped up the poop, she tramped across the street like a warrior on a mission. Once there, she pulled back her arm and flung it right on the Archer's front doorstep. "Take that!"

That was before she knew *who* they were. Now, she hoped no one had seen her, and wished she'd counted to ten, maybe to twenty, before confronting Bill Archer.

It was down at the beauty shop last week that she found out that Bill's wife, Meg, was *the* Meg, president and founder of the Wednesday Society. She heard it from that snooty Valerie Carter. Valerie, who used to teach third grade, until she married a dentist and her nose shot up as high as those geysers at Yellowstone Park. Arlene and Valerie both had their heads hanging over the shampoo bowls when Valerie said, "Have you met the Archers yet? Meg's your new neighbor." Arlene gasped. She felt her face flush purple.

The Wednesday Society wasn't just any book group. It was *the* book group in town. They met mid-week, once a month to discuss literature. Somebody led the book discussion, while another person gave a report on the author.

There were about eighteen women in the group. You couldn't just join The Wednesdays, as they called themselves. No, you had to apply. Arlene heard they had fantastic potlucks, sometimes car-pooled to hear authors speak at the auditorium, or went to movies together. Meg also belonged to the Forest Hills Country Club known for its interesting people, elegant dances, sumptuous brunches, a huge swimming pool, and a fancy restaurant that overlooked a lush green golf course.

Valerie, already a member of The Wednesdays, enjoyed baiting Arlene by dropping little tidbits about the group. She never failed to mention the waiting list. "How long have you been on *the* list? Of course, even if your number comes up, we have to vote you in." She'd puff up and get that little smirk on her long, horsey face. Actually, Arlene had applied about two years ago, but The Wednesdays restricted membership to keep things "cozy" as Valerie put it.

"Meg is having us Wednesdays over on Saturday for her house-warming," Valerie said, holding a towel to her drenched locks. "She said she was also inviting some of the neighbors. I suppose I'll see you there?"

A picture of the coffee mug on top of the Volvo and the dustpan caper flashed before Arlene's eyes. She was actually relieved when her hairdresser pushed her head back and turned on the cool water to rinse her soaped-up hair.

While they were both drying out under the hair dryers, Valerie shot a glance at the *People* magazine, Arlene was reading. "Of course, we only read literature." She waved the copy of *Mansfield Park* that she'd brought with her.

It gave Arlene some satisfaction to know Valerie's auburn hair came from a bottle.

Surely, the Archers would invite her. After all, she was on the waiting list, she used to substitute teach at the grade school in the language arts program, and she knew a thing or two about Jane Austen. That should count for something. Dogs weren't supposed to bark at night in neighborhoods. They must know that.

"Hate to cut things short, but Milt and me need to get down to the Mercantile this morning," Liz said. "They're having a big sale on marigold flats."

Arlene gave a relieved smile. It was almost an hour since she had a chance to point the binoculars at the Archer's house. Liz wouldn't understand how important this was. Membership in the Wednesdays could open up a whole world, a chance to meet people...and maybe a future husband. Liz only read those trashy romance novels and wouldn't know how to hold a fork at the country club. Arlene couldn't imagine Liz's chubby ankles in heels.

"I suppose there's still time." Liz carried her plate and cup to the counter near the dishwasher and dropped her tea bag into the garbage pail.

"What...to buy marigolds?"

"No, I mean for us to get formal invitations to the housewarming...if it really is this Saturday. I mean the week is still young."

Arlene sent some muffins home in a plastic bag for Milt. After Liz left, she took aim once again with her binoculars. Now with the big oak tree trimmed, she could get a good shot at the Archers' sparkling white front door. Aha! She spotted a worker in denim coveralls washing the living room windows. They were definitely getting that house ready for a party. Which neighbors would be there? Surely, they wouldn't leave her out, especially since she would see all the cars and the people.

The next morning Arlene's binoculars picked up the arrival of a leather couch and love seat. New furniture was a sure sign of a housewarming, in Arlene's opinion. She stepped away from the window when she saw the mail carrier approaching her house and eagerly watched the bills and advertising flyers dropping through the slot near her front door. She was about to return to the window when something caught her eye. There it was, among the flyers, a square buff-colored envelope with her name and address handwritten in black ink. Arlene turned it over in her hand and fingered the linen finish. There was no return address, but then why should there be if it just came from across the street. This was what she'd been waiting for—the invitation!

She held the envelope to her chest and did a little dance. "Hallelujah!" she called out to the emptiness. Maybe she should call Liz. No. No. Maybe Liz didn't get one. She couldn't picture Milt, with his thick brows and huge stomach bulging over his belt, holding a champagne glass, making small talk with Bill Archer about his bowling scores and the price of bananas.

What should she bring? A bottle of wine was always a safe gift. What was she going to wear? She carefully placed the invitation on the kitchen table before dashing to her bedroom where she slid open the closet doors and shifted the clothes back and forth on the rack. Nothing seemed quite right. Maybe she should buy a new pants suit. That's what she would do...right after lunch...go downtown and shop for a new outfit. It'd been a long time since she bought anything new. Maybe this was Meg's way of asking her to join the Wednesday Society, too. If she bought a new pants suit, she could wear it to the meetings. She just couldn't wait to see Valerie's face. That Valerie!

Back in the kitchen, Arlene fingered the invitation and gave it a loving pat. Then she filled the teakettle with water, heated some leftover split pea soup and grabbed a package of saltine crackers from the cupboard. Sometimes an invitation told you what to wear—like casual or semi-formal. Maybe she needed a dress or shoes with heels. Could she even walk in heels anymore? Her heart thumped in her chest and her neck got warm. A flood of panic coursed through her body. She got those feelings every time she had to go places *alone.* For her, that was the hard part. She took several deep breaths and sipped her tea.

At least they invited her; that was the important thing. Arlene nibbled on her crackers as she carefully slit the envelope. "It's show time!" she said out loud and flipped open the matching card. Then she dropped her soup spoon.

*Thank you for the opportunity to be of service. We look forward to helping you in the future, and we truly appreciate your business.*

It was from Larry's Landscaping, the folks who trimmed her tree last weekend.

# Walk to the Gym

I hurried out the backdoor on a brisk, dark morning to use the gym at the school. It was eerie being on the street alone so early and a little risky—especially since an elderly woman was murdered in our neighborhood. It was right after Labor Day, when people start thinking about picking apples, turning the soil in their gardens one last time, and storing their white shoes.

Someone broke into her house and stabbed her. They never did finger the guy who did it.

The nippy wind cut right through my sweats, so I wrapped my faded Indian blanket snuggly around my shoulders. The one I got a while back with green stamps. Why did I leave the warmth of my bed to do this? I needed to exercise that was why, and once I did, I would feel warm again. And calmer. My doctor said exercise would be good for me. I know he said that because I wrote it down.

A street light splashed a yellow glow across the wet pavement. Some of the houses already had big orange pumpkins displayed on porches smiling their crooked grins. A ghost made from a white sheet flapped high in a tree. I could feel the slick leaves that covered the sidewalk squish under my feet, so I slowed my pace to avoid slipping.

An ashy smell hung in the air. That, I knew, came from the smoke that constantly belched from the Beeler's chimney. Ray Beeler always got in a big stack of wood in the fall. "There's nothin' that warms a house like wood heat," he'd brag. As soon as the temperature dipped, he'd get up early and pack a hefty bundle of it over wadded newspaper into that old woodstove they had in the family room. Then, by golly, he'd take a match to it. Folks said one of these days, he was gonna burn the house down.

I turned my attention back to the leafy street. That's when I saw *him*.

The shadowy figure of a large man came toward me. He wore a dark overcoat and a black cap. A red, wool scarf peeked from his collar. No one else was around and no cars passed, so I crossed to the other side. The man kept coming, continually looking in my direction. I let the blanket slip from my shoulders, so I'd be free to run. I cut down an alley and through an empty lot. I could hear him running too, making heavy breathing sounds like a horse after a race. I didn't stop until I reached the corner and could see the school yard lights.

Out of breath, I pulled open the heavy door to the gym and made my way inside. I blended in with the children and began walking slowly around the perimeter until my breathing became normal. Actually, I was surprised to see so many kids there at such an early hour. They were running, jumping, yelling, and tossing balls. I ducked to avoid a wayward basketball that almost hit me in the head, but I kept walking until I heard a whistle.

The sound came from a portly man in a black-and-white striped shirt. He blew on his whistle again and started a class. There were so many kids, it was impossible to continue on my own, so I found myself in the midst of them trying to do the things the instructor man demanded. For some reason, he constantly corrected me. "Sit up straight. Shoulders back and down," he barked. I got exhausted doing the sit-ups, so I just laid down right there on the floor. I didn't care what he said. He stood over me, shook his head, and smirked. Why was I getting all this attention? Surely, he knew I wasn't a student. As far as I could tell, I was the only other adult there. Still, I tried the best I could to do the exercises correctly, but I was getting a little annoyed.

Once the bell rang, everyone scampered off. I was alone in the gym and glad of it. I decided I would not go back there again. It was never like this before. No, I'd ask the doctor to write me an excuse. I wasn't going to do jumping jacks again. Ever.

It was still dark and cold outside when I started back toward my house, so I searched the street for my blanket, but found only a tattered, yellow corduroy potholder that someone had tossed. In a strange way, it was comforting. It looked like the kind my mother made out of scrap material from the big bag she stored in the back of her closet. Those were the days. I missed Al, too. I needed him now more than ever.

I saw a woman tending potted plants on the porch of her rundown house. She had apparently found my blanket and used it to protect them from the frost. I stood for a moment, clutching my potholder. She flicked on the porch light, reached for a broom and began sweeping her front steps. With that hooked nose of hers, she looked like a real live witch. I stared at the blanket and up at her. She didn't speak but gave me an ugly, suspicious scowl, so it didn't feel right for me to grab my blanket. After all, I had thrown it down on the street. "Finders keepers," they used to say.

I hurried away when all of a sudden that eerie feeling came back. It's hard to describe. The area seemed familiar enough, but strange, too.

I could not find my house. I sniffed the air for smoke, but couldn't locate the Beeler place either. If I could just smell the smoke, I'd know I was close. I must have taken the wrong street. But how could that be when that was my blanket back there? Maybe I walked too far. How could I be lost in my own neighborhood? Al and I used to walk here all the time when the kids were little. Maybe someone moved the street sign. Maybe it was a Halloween prank. Well, it wasn't funny.

There he is again! *That man.* I know it's him because of his red scarf. He's staring at me. Oh my God, he's coming closer. I know he's after me.

I was almost to the corner, so I turned and ran. Several dogs barked in the distance. That was good. Maybe someone would look out a window. I crouched down behind a big rhododendron bush on the side of a white house and waited. I could hear his footsteps against the sidewalk. His shoes squeaked as he came closer. Through the bush, I could see his dark pant legs. I watched them as they went by. Then he turned, and I watched them go by again.

Soon, it would get lighter. Maybe I should hide here until then. I wished now that I'd never left my house. The cold gave me goose bumps, and I missed my cozy kitchen. When I get home, I'm going to make a big pot of coffee and sit in front of the fire. Coffee fixes everything. My knees ached from squatting, and the branches poked my chest. If Al were here, we'd snuggle and I'd get warm. I wouldn't have to crouch behind any dang bush either. God, I miss Al.

I checked my pocket, but couldn't feel my keys. There was nothing in there but a cough drop. A wave of panic surged through my stomach. In my haste, I must have left the keys on the counter or maybe I lost them at the gym or on the street. Oh God. How would I get in now? What if I forgot to lock the door? What if someone was in my house? What if it was that man! I leaped from the protection of the bush and started running back to the corner and down the street.

Then I stopped dead in my tracks.

That man stepped out from behind a tree and was right in front of me! I could feel my hands shaking as I backed away. He carried a big black bag. What was in there? A gun? Rope? Or maybe a knife?

"Who are you?" I tried to sound brave. "What do you want?"

"Edith." He smiled and reached his hand toward me.

*Edith?*

"Murderer!" I yelled. "I know who you are. You're that murderer!"

"Edith," he said again.

"You stay away from me! I'll scream if you come closer."

He reached into his bag.

"Stop right there." I doubled my fists to look menacing and bounced on my feet like a boxer ready to land a punch.

"Edith, please. Look, I brought Al."

He pulled a white stuffed rabbit out of the bag and thrust it to toward me. Its ears flopped over and one eye was missing. It was Al all right. I cried out in surprise.

"I'm here to help," the man said, patting my shoulder. "You wandered away from the state hospital again."

I hugged Al close and stroked his soft head. I could even smell smoke from the Beeler's chimney.

# Robby Goes Home

*H**ome.* At first a dim memory and then a yearning so vivid, it pulled him along like a lost dog sniffing the earth, sensing its way back. Across the bridge, past the park, twelve more blocks; then six. Turn left. Three more to go. There it is! The small tan bungalow with the steep red roof—the last happy place he'd lived.

That's how it was for fifteen-year-old Robby—tall, skinny, and pale-faced with dark, puppy-dog eyes—alone in the city on Thanksgiving. He no longer had a real family. He'd lived there with Roseanna, his mother, but after Gram passed, they'd lost the house. After that, they'd taken refuge in Gram's old maroon Buick until it sputtered and died. No money for repairs, Roseanna lost that too. It couldn't get any worse, except it did. "I can't take care of you anymore," she said, her eyes rheumy, her mind fogged by whatever drug she was on.

Care? That was care?

Roseanna hooked up with some guy—there always was a guy. The last Robby had heard heroin fried her brain which left her vegetating in the state mental hospital.

Robby made his way on the streets of Portland, hanging at a shelter or couch surfing until his friend's parents had had enough. Now Robby curled up at night on a slab of cardboard, wrapped in a tattered sleeping bag, shivering beneath an overpass with traffic thudding overhead. He huddled there with his street family—Alf, a thirty-something tweaker, and three other callow boys with vacant looks. The "family" offered protection from evil dudes roaming in dark places, but he still had to be careful because Alf had expectations.

He needed to get away from the squat, away from Alf who was leaning on him, away from the crazy yelling, the panhandling, the piles of rubbish, empty syringes, the stink of urine and sweat and having to do things he wanted to erase from his mind—forever. If he could be any place else, even for a while, he could clear his head and maybe find his soul again.

Hell, it was Thanksgiving. The day people drained out of the city to head home, except for those like himself who huddled in abandoned buildings, trash-strewn alleys, and other fetid crannies. Sure he was grateful. He was getting by eating at the rescue mission when convenient, but it was crowded there, and then there was that lingering body odor. The smell of despair. On his last visit, he nabbed a small bag of Fritos he carried in his backpack and new wool cap to protect his ears from the frigid air.

He just wanted to see the house again. Stand there and pretend he could still run in and crash on Gram's sagging floral couch. A stocky woman with a shock of straight, silver hair, she'd beckon him to the kitchen with a smile and hand him a saucer of freshly baked oatmeal cookies. Afterward, he'd play with that cat—the orange one that used to visit and meow on the porch.

He walked by, turned, walked by again. Paused. Why did the new people replace the front door with that red one? Weird.

Overcome by emotions he couldn't understand or describe, tears hung in his eyes. He wiped them away with the sleeve of his jacket.

"388 SE Walnut," Gram had said, handing him his lunch in a brown paper bag on his first day of school. "Remember that in case you get lost."

*388. 388.* How could a place be your home one minute and not the next?

Robby ambled up the sidewalk and climbed the concrete steps to the porch, not planning to stay, just to touch the tan shakes and feed that yearning bottled in his chest.

He glanced through the curtainless bay window. No lights, no movement inside, so he rang the doorbell. *What will I say if someone answers? I'll claim I'm lost.* He smirked. That actually was the truth.

He rang again. No one was home. Woot! He bounced on his heels before heading to the rear of the house to check out the yard. The gigantic oak he once climbed, pretending to be Captain America, was gone. In its place was a weathered stump with a happy garden gnome on top. They'd manicured the lawn into a kidney-shaped green mass banked by a lot of bark dust—not the kind of place a kid could play hide-and-seek or hit a baseball against the rickety wood fence replaced now with a shiny chain link.

Flat, gray stepping stones covered the little patch of ground where Gram used to grow tomatoes, onions, a few peppers, and short rows of beans and pumpkins. She'd kiss the packets before tucking the seeds into the warm dirt, laughing as if she were a child, a smudge of earth on her nose, claiming love was a better fertilizer than the chicken shit she couldn't afford.

He didn't mean to. Honest he didn't, but his hand tried the doorknob. The backdoor was unlocked! He'd sneak a peek. Look around.

God knows, he didn't want trouble. There was enough of that on the streets.

They'd painted the kitchen a cheerful yellow. Gram would have liked that. In his mind, he saw her leaning over the stove, her thick arm stirring a pot of porridge. "You don't have to say anything about your father," she said as she ladled the mush into a bowl. "If other kids ask, say he's away...on business." Another Gram rule: never say that awful word. The one Roseanna never hesitated to use, especially when she was looped, and he did something that set her off. That word he'd hidden in the ridges behind his heart once he'd learned what it meant: *Bastard. Bastard. Bastard.* Sometimes he looked in the mirror and thought he saw his ol' man in the features that weren't his mother's.

He sauntered into the living room. They'd replaced Gram's puke green carpet with a tan shag. That was okay, he'd never liked their green one all threadbare and stained. He looked up to see they'd fixed the crack in the plaster ceiling. The dark wood paneling was now stark white with an enormous picture of the ocean above a brown leather couch. A tall oak bookcase, with one shelf dedicated to happy family photos, filled a corner of the room. He leaned in. An older couple, sitting close, with their heads touching, smiled back. Smaller photos showed them gushing over a baby who, in other pictures, morphed into a squirming toddler and, finally, into a giggly yellow-haired girl.

*Family.* He swallowed hard and pinched the tip of his nose.

Next to the book case was a huge flat screen TV on a stand. Gram's television was a bulky old-style one that had "Dr. Phil" blaring so loud, it made the windows rattle. She had no framed art, and the only thing on their wall was the round clock she got at Target. That and two green plaster fishes swimming in opposite directions. He used to pelt their silly, grinning faces with spit wads. Fish shouldn't grin.

Robby took a deep breath. A faint familiar whiff made his nose stuffy—musty old house smell, tinged with something pleasant. Still, you couldn't really cover up that stale odor.

Enough, he thought. He should split before the new people came back and caught him there. He turned and headed for the kitchen.

Something made him stop.

Once he saw it, he immediately knew what else had teased his nostrils—a luscious pumpkin pie cooling on the Formica counter. His eyes teared again. It looked like the ones Gram baked. Roseanna never was any good at baking, or cooking, or cleaning, or much of anything. How could he have missed this when he first came in?

He bent over the rich cinnamon-colored pie with its golden halo-like crust and sniffed. His mouth watered and hunger pangs clutched his stomach. How long had it been since he'd eaten? He jerked open kitchen drawers searching for a knife. Bingo. He cut a small slice. Surely that wouldn't hurt, and he'd be long gone before anyone noticed. He chewed slowly, letting the sweet spice-filled taste linger on his tongue. A powerful sensation swept over him. He saw Gram, her wrinkled face beaming, motioning to him to sit at the head of the table and to preside over their simple meal—boiled potatoes, a piece of fried chicken, green beans, biscuits, and fruit cocktail. After they finished dinner, Gram would light her stub of a candle and bring in the grand finale—that splendid pie.

He couldn't help it. He carved a second, bigger piece, held it in his hand, and gulped it down. Better go before the people who live here return. He wiped his mouth on his sleeve. No, wait. There was one more thing he *needed* to do.

His room.

IIe had to see it—the only place that had truly been his. Ah, the staircase. There still was that chip in the handrail he made after he banged it with a toy truck when he was a toddler. Gram made him stand in the corner, but she couldn't stay angry for long. Soon, she had him sitting at the kitchen table with a glass of milk and a hunk of her butter cake. He fingered the gash, bent over, and kissed it. Love you Gram, he mouthed. These new folks couldn't erase him entirely.

He skipped stairs to the tiny room at the end of the hall. Jesus—pink walls! A white ruffled bedspread topped with matching pillowcases and a heart-shaped red throw pillow covered a single bed. A girl's room? Or, was this a guest room? It didn't have many personal items. The kind you'd have in there if you lived in it. The closet was bare except for a pair of bunny slippers and a few lonely wire hangers.

He flopped on the bed, laying his head in what had been his special place. The bedding smelled fresh and sweet, like lavender, but it made him feel dirty. He scratched at the insect bites on his leg, unable to remember the last time he had a bath. There were all kinds of creepy crawly things in the dirt under the overpass. His mind drifted to that kid they called Skeeter who spoke with a southern drawl and got bit by a nasty spider causing a red splotch on his thigh that was almost the size of a dinner plate. Skeeter almost died. What ever happened to that guy? He shuddered. Maybe he did die.

Lying in a clean bed brought back the longing—*388 Walnut Street.* He said those words several times as if doing so would conjure up strange magic that would keep him in this place. He stared up at the angled ceiling thinking. *I can't go back to Alf. I've got to escape, but how?* No one would hire him for much at fifteen but one more year and he'd qualify for full-time work. He had to survive until then. Wouldn't Alf come looking for him? Then what? There used to be a church around here. Would they help him? Could they? There'd be fewer people at a church shelter, and they wouldn't steal his shoes.

What a homecoming—all of it, the house, the pie, his room. *388. 388. 388.* Anything was possible.

Just a few more minutes and he'd go. The sugars from the pie made his lids droop. Before he realized it, the soft pillow lured him into a deep sleep. His lips curled into a grin as he dreamed of happy times, feeling Gram's hand pulling the blanket around him. "Sleep, sleep," she whispered, patting his shoulder.

"Harold!" screamed the distraught woman. "My God, he's in here. A tramp! Sleeping in our little Annie's room."

Robby bolted up like he'd dodged a bullet. He looked into the horrified face of an older woman with sparse graying hair and very red prune lips—the lady from the photo! Did she say tramp?

He felt that feral urge to run for his life, like he did when he picked a pocket or lifted a carton of chocolate milk from that 7-Eleven store. "I'm so sorry. Gosh, I'm sorry." He rolled off the bed, glad he'd left his shoes on.

She clutched her forehead. "Good God! Those shoes...on my bed. What filth!"

"I'm going, okay?" He raised his arms to shield himself.

"H-e-e-e-l-p. He's going to assault me! Har-r-r-rold."

Her loud screeching made his eardrums vibrate. He darted by her, down the stairs, passed a heavyset, older man, standing at the bottom of the staircase, with a cell phone in hand and a baffled look on his fleshy face. That must be Harold.

Run for God's sake! He grabbed for the door and bolted out, straight into the arms of a burly cop.

"I didn't take anything. Just a piece of pie." The words tumbled out. "I used to live here."

Hands grabbed him. "Get on the ground," the cop ordered.

"Not all of it. I didn't eat all of it." No one heard him. Why should they? No one really saw him, and God knows they never listened to him.

Now there were two cops. They cuffed his wrists, yanked him up, frisked him, and shoved him in the back of the patrol car. *The police.* The word on the street: Stay under the radar. *Alf will kill me when he finds out.*

Robby turned his head. An officer was talking to the older couple who stood on their porch, waving their arms, and pointing their fingers. A group of dismayed neighbors gathered around them. Harold waddled over carrying Robby's backpack, holding it out in front of him like a diseased rodent. He handed it to the cop standing by the car. "The wife's gonna hafta delouse that bedroom," he muttered, wiping his palm on his pants. "No one's gonna touch that pie."

The cop set the pack on the hood of the car and unzipped it. Satisfied there was nothing stolen or otherwise untoward inside, he opened the cruiser door and plopped it by Robby's feet. "Now you've done it," he said with a sardonic grin. "You ruined their pie."

The squad car pulled out. Robby took one last look at his house before his old neighborhood whizzed by the windows, all the time Roseanna's voice played in his head: *Bastard. Bastard. Bastard.*

# Lost Christmas

*I don't love you anymore.* Standing alone in the cemetery on a cold, gray December afternoon, those words kept echoing in my mind, each one striking like a hammer hitting concrete. I didn't think real love ever died.

Visiting the cemetery was the last thing Bill and I did each Christmas Eve. He always placed the swag on our baby's grave. Then we'd head home to sit by the fire and prop our feet up after days of shopping and the traditional round of parties. Bill mixed hot buttered rums, which we savored before opening our gifts. On Christmas Day, we'd drive across town for dinner with Bill's brother and family. After that, we'd take down the tree, carefully pack the ornaments and lights; then hurry off for a luxurious cruise to some sunny Caribbean spot.

Now, it was just me.

I laid the swag with a huge red bow on the grave of my parents and the one decorated with tiny toy soldiers and drums on that of our stillborn baby. The cemetery was deserted, but then it was Christmas

Eve. There would be no celebration at my dark house—no tree, no presents, no carols, no buttered rum toasts.

No Bill.

After fifteen years, he wanted a divorce. I was putting away the Thanksgiving groceries when he picked up a can of black olives and nervously tossed it in the air. "Listen," he said, his blue eyes cold, "I don't love you anymore. I...I'm leaving tonight."

Just like that.

"Are you kidding me?" I sputtered. "What am I supposed to tell our guests?" I pointed to the twenty-pound turkey defrosting on the kitchen counter.

"Tell them anything you like." He set the olives down on the counter with a thud. I just stood there with a carton of heavy whipping cream in my hand.

"You can't just leave. Not *now* for heaven's sake—it's the holidays." I was angry and tired, not to mention stunned. "We need to talk, but I still have a pie to make," I said to the back of his curly, dark head. He slammed the door. The car engine revving in the driveway sounded like a small jet taking off.

*Varoom.* He was gone.

I stared at the closed door until I heard a dripping sound and realized that I had squeezed the carton of cream so hard it burst. The thick cream dripped into my shoe and made a puddle on the floor.

Bill had been distant and moody for some time, but I thought that was because of the problems at his company—new management, followed by staff shifts, increased workloads, and lots of overtime. On top of that, I still grieved for my mother who died in September after a long illness. It so consumed me, I didn't see the breakup of my marriage coming.

"Why," I asked my mother's headstone, "did this happen to me?" I crouched down on the damp grass. "I tried to do everything right. Plan my life. I lost my child and now Bill." I clutched the headstone. "It wasn't supposed to turn out this way." Hot, bitter tears streaked my cheeks. I needed my mother more than ever, and I wanted to hug my baby boy who would have been ten this year. I only held him briefly when he was born, but I always thought I could see Bill in that little pinched face, dark lips, and curly damp hair peeking from the small cap covering his head.

I stood up, but my knees shook and I felt lightheaded. The tombstones seemed to swirl and mix with the dark, brooding sky. Like a trapped animal, I had an intense urge to flee. I darted past lines of headstones to a path, which led to the parking area where I sought refuge in my car. I rolled down the window and took several gasps of cool air before making my way down the steep, winding cemetery road. When I reached the city street, I drove and drove. Finally, I crossed a bridge and the lights of the city glittered in the rearview mirror. Now, I was on the highway heading toward the Oregon coast. I gripped the wheel and, like a robot, kept going until the traffic thinned and totally disappeared.

In the quiet countryside, I passed modest homes with awkward strings of blinking Christmas lights. Every time I saw a tree sparkling in a window, I fought back tears. I imagined wonderful smells coming from kitchens, families sitting down to dinner, and wide-eyed children anxious for morning to come. I thought again about the baby I had lost. My son. Bill wanted to keep trying, but I couldn't go through that again. I wished now we'd given our baby a name. The light from the warm, yellow windows beckoned, but I was a stranger—passing through to somewhere. I pressed my foot on the accelerator trying to speed away from my sad thoughts.

A large, inflated Santa with his hand raised stood in the front yard of the last farmhouse I passed as if he were waving goodbye. The happy homes disappeared, and I was somewhere in the coastal range, surrounded by tall trees and eerie fog. In the rearview mirror, I only saw darkness. The fog thickened, so I switched on my bright lights and even my windshield wipers. Neither helped much, but I didn't care. Alone on the road, I thought of the families in those cozy houses. I had a family once. In the silent darkness, tears came again, and I struggled to concentrate on my driving.

The low, hanging fog made the pavement wet and slick. It occurred to me that I should slow down and head back. Instead, I turned the heater up a notch, determined to keep going, to get away. When I reached a coastal town, any town, I would find a motel and rest there—maybe have some strong, hot tea to take the chill off and just listen to the comforting pounding of the sea.

I felt dizzy again; then realized the car was sliding. I hit the brakes, but the car jerked, skidded onto the shoulder, and bounced down the embankment. The door flew open; I tumbled out, my body slamming against the ground as the car rolled past me and crashed into a tree. For a moment, I lay still. Was I dead? My head hurt and blood dripped down my face. Sharp pains came from my right leg. I felt cold, very cold. Cracking sounds came from the overturned car, but in the darkness, I could not see the damage. I tried to raise myself on my elbows, but my arms shook. My one leg didn't work. The grassy bank was wet and I shivered.

I would die here—alone in the foggy night. The black emptiness engulfed me, except for what seemed like a small light in the distance. They said that happened when you were dying. You passed through a dark tunnel until you got to the light. Go toward that brightness I told myself. Go. Just go. The light seemed to be getting closer when I thought I heard a voice. God must be calling me. Good, I thought. I had a lot I wanted to say to Him.

"Are you all right?" a male voice asked.

I opened my eyes wide and looked into a big flashlight.

"God? Is that you, God?" I asked.

"Huh? What's that?"

"Where am I?"

The figure in the dark didn't answer. When he pulled the blinding light away from my face and flashed it over my body, I could make out a bulky, bearded man looking out from under a baseball cap, his long hair tied back in a ponytail. In the dim light, he looked like a bum. He turned away from me and walked toward my car. He's probably going after my purse. Once he robs me, he'll leave me here to die—or worse. I was easy pickings for him. I closed my eyes and moaned. They flew open again when I felt him touching my leg. He had set the lantern-like light down on the ground, so I could see him crouching over me. My God! He's going to rape me. My heart pounded in my throat. I was defenseless.

His hand had reached my knee. "That hurts!" I cried. "Please don't hurt me."

"Try and move it," he said. When I obliged, he seemed relieved. "You have a bad sprain there." He moved the light closer to my face, and he wiped blood from my forehead with a corner of his shirt.

As he helped me sit up, I could see the spider veins on his nose and gray hair in his beard and at his temples. I groaned; my whole body felt bruised.

"Good, good," he muttered. At least things are movin'. I've gotta camp just back a ways. We need to get you outta here, so we can take a closer look. Hang on." He lifted me and carried me up the embankment. He smelled musty, like a mixture of onions and tobacco.

He set me down when we reached the road. I hobbled on one foot, clutching him for support.

"I feel woozy."

"Easy does it." He picked me up again and carried me the rest of the way.

We reached his camp under a small bridge that appeared to cross a dry gulley. He had a fire going there, and he placed me on a worn sleeping bag next to it. I rested my back against a large boulder. The warmth from the fire felt good, but I couldn't stop shivering. He turned away, fished a tin cup from his backpack, and poured a cup of coffee from the blackened aluminum pot he had warming in the embers.

"Drink this slowly. It'll take the chill off." He handed it to me.

My first thought was about cleanliness, but the cup warmed my hands and the strong, black coffee smelled good. With each swallow, I could feel the warmth surging through my body. I was grateful for the caffeine. There wasn't much to his camp. He had a hatchet, rain gear, an old transistor radio, some blankets, a large backpack, a small row of canned goods lined up on top of a pile of weathered newspapers, and a roll of toilet paper. I didn't even want to think about where his latrine might be.

His thick hand reached for what looked like a hunting knife. I shuddered. He's going to slit my throat. Instead, he used it to cut up a T-shirt he pulled from his backpack. He dampened a portion with water from a plastic bottle and bathed the wound on my forehead. Every time he came near me, I caught a whiff of his musty body odor.

"Head wounds always bleed a lot, but it's not too bad. More of a scrape, I'd say. You're gonna have a lot of bruisin' there." He used a piece of the T-shirt to make a bandage and then took the red bandana from around his neck and tied it tightly around my forehead.

He picked up the knife again and came toward me. I set down the coffee cup and braced myself.

"What do you think you're doing?" I yelled.

"I'm gonna cut your pant leg a bit, so I can get to that knee—unless you'd rather take them off." His dark, wild eyes looked amused.

He knows I'm afraid of him. I watched helplessly as he slit the right leg of my jeans just past my knee. I noticed he had a rose tattoo on the top of his right hand. "Who are you?" I demanded.

"John," he said. "And who are you?"

"Helen."

"Well Helen, I don't think your leg is broken, but you gotta terrible sprain there."

"How would you know?"

"I was a medic in the army. Viet Nam. You probably don't remember that one."

He was right. I didn't. "That was my father's war," I said. He didn't answer.

"See here, how swollen it is."

I looked at my knee, which was not only puffy and twice its size, but turning an ugly purple. "It hurts, it really hurts. Please don't press on it anymore."

"Tell me about it," he grumbled. "It's startin' to discolor. What we need is ice, but we don't have none. So-o-o, we'll do what we can." He took the strips of the T-shirt and started wrapping them around my knee. "It's not much, but compression helps, and it will give you some support." He pushed his backpack under my leg and covered me with a heavy blanket. "It helps if you keep it elevated."

I wondered where that blanket had been. Lice could be crawling all over my body. "I...I really need to be going," I said.

"Ha!" He laughed loudly and shook his head. "That car of yers is totaled. You can't walk and, in case you haven't noticed, we don't have limousine service out here. Get real. You won't be goin' no place for a while."

I sunk back against the boulder. "Maybe you could flag down a car—"

"How many cars have ya heard pass over the bridge lately, huh?" He grinned.

He was right. The night was totally still.

"We're off the main road, ya know."

Actually I didn't. I didn't remember turning, but I could hardly see the yellow line through the thick fog.

He opened a can of baked beans and dumped the contents into a cast iron frying pan. In the firelight, his skin looked leathery. He was dressed for the cold weather with a heavy brown jacket over layers of other clothing, jeans, and heavy boots. The ends of his flannel shirt, with my blood on them, hung below the jacket. He wasn't fat or thin; his bulkiness came from the layers of clothing he wore. He stirred the beans in the pan with a big, tarnished spoon until they started to bubble. He dished up a serving in a dented tin bowl and passed it to me along with a spoon and slice of white bread.

"No thank you. I'm really not hungry." My stomach was in knots, and I couldn't help wondering when he last scrubbed that bowl or anything else.

"Suit yourself." He set the food down next to me and poured more coffee. "It's not much, but it's what I got."

I decided it would be okay to eat the bread, since it came from a wrapped loaf. As soon as I took a bite, I couldn't stop, even though it tasted like cardboard. I didn't realize I was famished. Before long, I gobbled the beans and drank more coffee. John just watched me and then passed the loaf of bread; I took another slice and swallowed that, too.

My eyes teared up. "I haven't had anything to eat since this morning," I said, trying to apologize for the way I bolted down his food. John just smiled. He used the empty bean can for his coffee and wrapped a piece of the T-shirt around it to keep the hot can from burning his hand. He ate his portion of beans right out of the frying pan. If I get out of here alive, I thought, I'll probably die from trench mouth or some other dreadful bacterial infection.

"What are you doin' out here on a night like this," he asked between bites, "all *alone?*"

"I...I was on my way to visit relatives," I lied. "They're probably out looking for me as we speak." I didn't want him to know I was alone in the world and totally vulnerable. "I must have gotten lost."

"You came barrelin' over the bridge like a bat outta hell." He shook his head and laughed. "In fog as thick as soup. When your car left the road, it sounded like a crash of thunder."

"What are *you* doing here?" I asked eager to change the subject.

"I'm heading toward Tillamook. An old army buddy owns a dairy over there. I'm hopin' to stay in his barn for a while...once the holidays are over. His wife don't like it none, so I can't stay forever; but I'd like ta winter over there, at least during the worst of the weather. Help out with things while I'm there." He looked at me and grinned, "Sleep with the cows." He started to chuckle. "When the ol' lady goes into town ta play bingo, I get to use the shower. Yes siree, God bless bingo." He toasted the foggy air with his steaming tin can.

"You're a homeless man?"

He didn't answer, but looked amused as he took his piece of bread, cleaned the rest of the beans from the frying pan, and washed them down with a hearty swig of coffee.

"I've been on the road now for a little over ten years," he finally said.

"But why out here? Wouldn't it be better to stay at a mission or someplace like that where you'd be warm and have some shelter?"

"I used to hang around those places at least long enough to eat Christmas dinner; but when the weather turns cold, those places fill up. It gets crazy. There's lots of stealin' and drinkin'." He shot me a glance. "And more. You haffta watch your back."

"I would think that would be better than living under a bridge—at least the mission is *clean*." As soon as I said it, I realized it was the wrong thing to say. He gave me a hard look.

"Christmas in the city with all those people millin' around buyin' whatever they want—sort of leaves me feelin' empty—'specially when I barely make it by." He stared at my neck. I was wearing the small diamond pendant necklace Bill gave me on our last anniversary. Here it comes. He's probably going to want that.

"Out here, Christmas is just another damned day. A nice, respectable lady like you probably never thought she'd be spending Christmas Eve with a bum."

I looked away. I didn't know what to say. Suddenly he jumped up. My body stiffened in self-defense, but he didn't come toward me. Instead, he stoked the fire and put on more wood. I was grateful for the warmth.

"I borrowed the wood from a church camp up the road." He laughed again. "They won't miss it none, since they're closed for the winter."

I took that to mean he stole it.

"At the shelter, they give each man a gift of socks, candy, razors, and a bandana. I know a guy there, and he slipped me mine early. You got the bandana wrapped around your head, and we're havin' the candy for dessert." He handed me a peppermint disk and eyed my necklace again. "Probably not the kind of treat a nice lady like you is used to." He pulled a cigarette from his coat pocket and lit it by holding it against a twig from the fire. When he diverted his eyes to light the cigarette, I pulled my jacket up around my neck.

"Isn't there anyone...I mean family...that could help?"

"What family I have don't welcome me. Even at Christmas."

"How did you get here? I mean this place is miles from anywhere."

"I walk a lot, hitch rides, jump a railroad car when I can. Sleep in makeshift places beside rivers and roads. Spent a couple nights in a junk yard sleepin' in one of the old cars there."

"But you're able-bodied. I mean you could work. Don't you ever work?"

"Oh, that's a great idea." He slapped his knee and hooted. "And how is some nice boss supposed to get in touch with me? We not only don't have a limousine service out here, we don't have a telephone, neither." He took a long drag from his cigarette and looked out toward the heavy brush surrounding the bridge.

"I just thought if you could it...it would make things easier."

"When I was a kid, I did okay in high school and even did a term at the community college, but I flunked out and then got drafted. After the war, I came back to the States but nobody seemed to care. It was like I didn't exist. Finally landed some work on assembly lines and in warehouses. Got married. Did a little weed. Got fired. Had a baby boy. Did some heroine. Got divorced. Then it was on-and-off at gas stations, packing plants, even washed dishes in a hotel. Got fired some more. Well, that's my story."

"I see," I said. I didn't really, but I felt like I had to say something after hearing his life story which was so different from mine and mostly downhill.

"The best job I ever had was workin' in a grocery store, because I could steal the food. Problem was I got into the wine. Then they nabbed me." He paused and looked directly at me. "Ended up in the slammer after that."

I gasped. John was a thief and a substance abuser. Who knows, maybe he wasn't just a homeless man; maybe he did worse things. He could be an escaped convict. A murderer. He had a tattoo didn't he? That would explain what he was doing under a bridge miles from civilization, hiding out in the backcountry. I shuddered, thinking I'd be spending the night here trapped in his web.

"On top of everything else, I have...had a drinkin' problem...which is why I like to get out to the country when the holidays roll around. There's lotsa that stuff around then. Most guys will give you a swig, a smoke, or worse."

"Did you steal this food?" I suddenly blurted.

"Would it not taste as good if I did?"

I lowered my eyes. For heaven's sakes, don't get him riled up. Who knows what's in those cigarettes he's smoking. John kept talking. It probably had been a very long time since anyone listened.

"I get by using food stamps, collectin' bottles and cans for the deposit money, and goin' through dumpsters. You'd be surprised at the neat stuff you *good* people throw out."

"Dumpsters! Good God. How can you trust what you find? I mean it's in there with God knows what else." John had that big grin on his face again. I think he enjoyed making me uncomfortable. Maybe it was his last chance to get even with a society he believed dumped on him.

"That's the hell of it." For a brief moment, the wild look in his eyes morphed into a strange sadness. "After all these years, folks still don't know I exist."

"You said you had a son. He must be grown up by now. Couldn't he...help?"

"After the wife walked out, she took the kid. She wouldn't let me see him. I have no idea where he is. Never did." John winced when he talked about his boy, the same way I did when I thought of mine.

"That woman was a piece of work, let me tell ya. This wasn't the way it was supposed to turn out." John tossed his cigarette butt into the fire and then lit up again. "Actually, now I'm old enough to collect Social Security, but it's not much since I didn't work much. But those beans and the bread you ate were honestly arrived by. Out here a man doesn't need much—a little food, a warm fire, a bar of soap."

I was glad he mentioned soap. He put out the cigarette and swiftly picked up his knife. I cringed, but then he started whistling while whittling on a tree limb. I guess he was done talking with me. I sat there staring at the fire wishing I were home in my warm bed and wondering if I'd ever see it again. What a mess I'd made of things.

Suddenly, John stood up and seemed to be listening for something. "Okay," he said. "It's time."

"Time? Time for what?" How stupid I was. He's going to finish me off now and who would ever know. Thoughts about Bill and his new friend raced through my mind. They were probably huddled in front of the fire in some nice living room—safe and warm, drinking hot buttered rum, opening presents. I was the last to know about her, but everyone else seemed to know all the details. The most crushing blow came when I heard she was pregnant. Those words echoed in my ears again: *I don't love you anymore.* I couldn't help myself. I felt like something was going to explode inside me.

"How could you!" I cried out and burst into tears.

"Could I what?" John was on his feet in a flash standing over me. I stared at the lacings on his leather, mud-caked boots. "What's the matter? Huh?"

"He left me after fifteen years...just like that. Love isn't some switch you turn off. He should be here now protecting me, but he's there...with her. If you're going to kill me, just do it. I don't even care anymore. I'd be better off dead."

"Kill you?" He looked hurt; then angry. "If I was gonna kill you, I wouldn't have wasted a can of beans on you for Christ sakes." He threw the knife down and it stuck in the ground, the exposed blade gleaming in the firelight. I wiped my eyes on my sleeve. I couldn't look at him.

"Look, lady."

"Helen," I corrected.

"Helen, then. There's a small church up the road a ways. They should be havin' their services about now. I think I heard the singin'. There will be people there that can help you." He handed me the walking stick he'd whittled, and he helped me up.

Between leaning on him and using the stick, we made our way up the road through the dense fog. He never said another word to me. Still, I had to wonder if he was telling me the truth. I didn't remember passing a church, but then it was so dark and foggy I wasn't sure. And, didn't he say a while back when I asked about cars, that we were off the main road? I couldn't trust my husband; why should I trust a bum? All he'd have to do is shove me down some gulley and that would be the end of me, but what choice did I have? Then again, if there was a church, maybe there would be cars. If one happened to come by, I'd pull away and flag it down. I was trying to decide what else I could do to save myself when I saw it.

It was a small, yet beautiful, white church with a steeple and real candles shining through the windows. A big, green wreath with a red bow hung on the door. As we got closer, I could hear singing. John helped me up the gray, wooden porch steps. "You go ahead now. Just open the doors and make your way in the best you can. If you feel wobbly, lean on that walkin' stick. Now, go." He gave me a little nudge.

I quickly pulled on the door, and then I turned to thank the man that brought me here, but he was gone. That's strange; how quickly he disappeared. I looked down at my feet and saw my purse. John must have put it there. I felt so ashamed for suspecting him. The small congregation stood in the pews and sang, "It Came Upon the Midnight Clear."

I was so happy to see people, I let go of the door and it slammed hard. The people stopped singing and turned to look at me. The minister, a tall, thin older man in a dark suit, sitting next to the pulpit, got up. He held a Bible in his hand. He stood and stared at me through wire-framed glasses. I must have been a sight leaning on a stick in muddied clothes, a red bandana around my forehead, my face bruised, my pant leg ripped up to my knee exposing strips of John's T-shirt.

"My name is Helen Wilson. I've been in an accident. Please help me." I could feel my mouth move, but I couldn't hear the sound of my words. Their faces seemed to be getting closer, and someone called my name.

"Helen. Helen, do you know where you are?"

"At the church," I said. "Please help me. I need to get back home."

"You're in the recovery room. We're going to take you to your room now, Helen."

I opened my eyes and looked into the well-scrubbed face of a young nurse.

"Where am I?" I asked.

"You're in the hospital, Helen."

"Hospital? Did they bring me here, those church people?"

"You're a little hazy right now, Helen, but the doctor says you'll be fine. Your hypothermia is under control, and we did a little surgery on your leg. Just relax now until we get you back to your room."

The next time I awoke, Dr. Green hovered over me. He told me I scraped my forehead, had torn ligaments in my knee, and a hairline fracture in the bone. I would be able to go home in a few days, but I would need to rest. Once they removed the cast from my leg, there would be physical therapy. He assured me I would be as good as new.

"How did I get here?" I asked. Did I faint at the church?"

"Your car went off the embankment at the cemetery, Helen. The groundskeeper found you there and called the ambulance. You should always fasten your seat belt."

"But I drove to the coast," I said. "I drove and drove until the accident. John, a homeless man, saved me. He told me about his life."

Dr. Green smiled. "They found you just outside the cemetery. You probably were laying there for some time. Out in the cold like that your body starts to shut down and you hallucinate. Fortunately, the groundskeeper came along. You're a lucky woman, Helen."

"But it was so real."

"You'll be all right," he said. "You just need some rest. In a few days you'll feel as good as new." Before leaving, he wrote out a prescription for painkillers.

I went home and eventually recovered, but my experience seemed so real that I could not accept that it was all a hallucination. I had to search for John. I wanted to find him and thank him for saving my life. He had done a good thing, and I had not trusted him—insulted him even. I needed to know that he was okay, and I sincerely wanted to help. Most of all, I wanted him to know that I noticed him. I really noticed him.

When spring came, I asked my friend, Susan, a co-worker at the bank, to go with me. Together, we drove down the road I thought I had taken that night. I took as many side roads as I could and looked for signs of a camp located under a bridge, but I could not find one. I drove around and looked for the church, but it was nowhere. I talked to local people and gas station attendants, but nobody seemed to know about a bridge, a church, or a summer camp. I placed ads in various coastal newspapers, hoping someone would know John, but I never got a single response.

Back in the city, I went to the mission, the Salvation Army and even contacted outreach groups. I described John the best I could, but no one had heard of a homeless man with a rose tattoo on his right hand. I started volunteering at soup kitchens and food banks hoping he would show up, but he never did. I even headed up a food drive and led an effort to find winter coats and blankets for the homeless. My friends said I was obsessed, and Dr. Green suggested counseling; but the more work I did in those places, the better I felt.

Still I could not erase John from my mind. Finally, I drove out to the cemetery and talked with the groundskeeper to see if he might have resembled John; but when a young, thin man with short blond hair greeted me, I knew it couldn't be him. He took the time to describe how he found me, and I thanked him for his efforts.

***

Susan, a human resources manager and dear friend, shook her head. She'd been very supportive during my recovery, but now her tone was skeptical. "Helen," she said, her eyes level, "you've got to move on. Maybe this John character was really you speaking to yourself. Maybe the answer to your problems was within you all this time, and that was the way it came to the surface. Who knows what's deep down in our consciousness?"

"Even if it was a hallucination, how could I have created all those details about his life?"

"They didn't find you at some church on the way to the coast out in the middle of nowhere, Helen." Her voice was firm as if she were lecturing some employee in trouble. "They found you at the *cemetery*. Your totaled car was *there*. The ambulance picked you up *there*. Those are the hard facts."

Her sharp tone hurt.

"Look, it was Christmas." She reached over and touched my hand. "Christmas is a magical time. Maybe your guardian angel or spirit guide appeared to you in the form of this man, John. Maybe he took you to another place and time to help you get over a broken marriage."

She patted my hand again and her eyes softened. "Helen, listen to me. You're a smart woman, and you can get that promotion at the bank. In a few years, you'll be making more money than Bill ever did—but you have to put this...this...whatever it is...behind you before it sinks you. You've got your whole life ahead of you."

***

A year had passed and another cold, gray December had come. I was busy preparing for all of the events—not corporate cocktail parties or tinsel-laden celebrations—but fundraisers and food drives. I remembered that Christmas a year ago; how lost I was, and how glad I felt to be alive and well.

I had quit my job at the bank and taken one with a social service agency. At night, I attended college working toward a master's degree in social work. My goal was to work with homeless children.

I'd met George there. He was a wonderful, compassionate man who planned to be a high school counselor. I learned to trust again, and we even talked of doing a stint in the Peace Corps together once we graduated. How far my life had come.

I was in the garage loading canned goods into the car to take to the food bank when I spied the pile of muddy clothes I'd worn that night. The hospital had put everything into a plastic bag and handed it to me when I checked out. I never bothered to clean them. I simply threw the bag on top of some other junk in the corner. I decided to toss the clothes into the trash as a symbol of my old self passing away.

I pulled out the muddy sneakers and pitched them one by one into the garbage can with great satisfaction. I reached for the jeans with the cut leg and the rumpled sweater I'd worn and hurled them. It didn't matter if John was real or not—that was the irony of the whole sordid episode. What mattered is that meeting him changed the direction of my life. I pulled out the jacket still caked with mud and happily gave it a final, triumphant shake.

Then I saw *it*. The bloodied, red bandana shook loose and lay at my feet.

# Reading Lillie

The day Lillie and her friend, Bunny, caught the Greyhound bus in the Burger King parking lot, they told their parents they were going to a movie.

Once the bus roared off toward Portland, Lillie opened her red vinyl purse and pulled out a tube of cherry lipstick, which she carefully applied using a tiny mirror. She clipped white, plastic earrings shaped like giant lifesavers to her lobes.

"What are you doing?" asked Bunny. "I thought you weren't allowed to wear lipstick, and where did you get those earrings?"

"I don't want the psychic to think I'm just some country hick. Besides, I'm thirteen, now."

Lillie ran a comb through her brown hair and pulled it back into a ponytail to resemble the style of a movie star she'd seen on the cover of a magazine. There wasn't much she could do about the zits on her chin, her flat chest, or the dark-rimmed glasses that rested on her nose.

"Those earrings look dorky." Bunny had a chunky figure and two prominent front teeth, which earned her the nickname.

"I got them off Mom's dresser. As soon as I can, I'm going to get my ears pierced."

"You're such a dreamer," Bunny said.

Lillie and Bunny had been friends since the first grade. Bunny was good at playing the piano; Lillie sang in the youth choir, which she considered training for Broadway. It dumbfounded her that Bunny was content entertaining her mother's church friends.

"All the actresses have pierced ears," Lillie said.

"You've *never* been in a play," Bunny snickered. "Don't you think you should start soon?"

Bunny's words stung. Lillie had showed up to audition for a lead role in the class play, but the drama coach, assumed she wanted to be a stagehand. "Lillie, you're so dependable," he said, checking his clipboard.

"I uh...came to...try...to try..." The words stuck in her throat. She didn't trust herself to say more. He didn't even look at her. Maybe she should get a tattoo.

The bus chugged into the transit mall. They walked fifteen blocks to a dingy, brick apartment building and made their way down a dim hallway. There was no sign on the door, so Lillie knocked. A dark-complected man peeked out. She hadn't expected a man.

"What do you want?" he growled.

"We're here to see the psychic." Lillie held out the small newspaper ad.

"Is that *all* you want?" He had a gold earring in his right ear and huge teeth.

Lillie nodded.

"Have a seat." He motioned toward a small sofa. His eyes roamed from Lillie's red lips to Bunny's ample body. He seemed to be staring at her budding breasts. He smirked; then disappeared behind two heavy gold curtains.

"That guy is weird. What if there is no psychic?" Bunny whimpered. "What if he's a serial killer? No one knows we're here."

"Shhh," said Lillie. "He might hear you."

Bunny sniffed the air. "It smells like sweaty gym socks in here, kind of skunky."

"I think it's some kind of sage. Psychics always burn incense," Lillie assured Bunny. They could hear the man talking with a woman.

"Two young girls…kids. They just want a reading," the man said.

"No stuff?" the woman asked.

"Just a reading," he said.

"You sure?" she asked. "No stuff?"

"Didn't I just say they were kids? *Nunca escuche.*" He sounded angry.

"*Ay dios mio!*" she said. "Give me a few minutes. I get ready."

The girls heard shuffling behind the curtains. "This place is creepy," Bunny said.

"Jeez Bunny, get over it. Psychics need to be a little weird. That's what makes them psychic." Lillie tried to sound confident, but her stomach felt like it did when she sat in the dentist's chair.

"Madam A will see you now," the man said.

Bunny looked at Lillie. "Madam A?" She giggled.

Lillie nudged her, and they followed him through the curtains into a room lit only by candles.

Madam A, a brown-skinned, heavyset woman, in a low-cut blouse, sat at a round table covered with a gold damask cloth. A huge crystal ball gleamed from the table's center. "How can I help you?" she asked. She wore her black hair pulled straight back from her face.

"I want a reading," said Lillie. "This is my friend, Bunny." Bunny smiled.

"You got fifty dollars?" Madam A asked.

"I only have twenty-five." The small ad never mentioned the fee. Lillie opened her purse and pulled out an envelope. She had emptied the jar from her underwear drawer. It was money she had earned picking berries for new school clothes.

"Fifty dollars." Madam A rubbed her two fingers against her thumb indicating she wanted cash.

"Couldn't you do it for twenty-five? We came all this way," Lillie pleaded.

Madam A's small eyes darted from Lillie to Bunny; then back to Lillie. "Okay, I do for twenty-five. You sit over there," she motioned to Bunny, who moved to a chair in the far corner. Madam A stuffed the cash in her brassiere. Then she pulled out a pink cigarette lighter and lit a candle on the table. She looked at Lillie's left palm with a magnifying glass and traced the lines in it with one finger. "Hmmm," she said as she worked. "Close your eyes and concentrate very hard. We must tune our minds to that which is above."

After a few minutes, she ordered Lillie to open her eyes. When she did, it seemed like a little waft of smoke came from the crystal ball, which suddenly brightened.

"What would you like to know?" Madam A asked.

"I want to know my future...I mean, when I'm grown. I want to be an actress, or a singer...a famous ice skater...or a dancer, maybe. Will I? Who will I marry? I don't want to marry a farmer. I want to live in Paris...or London. I don't want to can pears." The words tumbled from Lillie's too red lips. She gripped the side of the table like a defendant waiting for a jury verdict.

"Whoa," said Madam A. "That's a lot for twenty-five dollars."

"I don't want to be like them..."

"Like who?" asked Madam A.

"The women back home. Nothing happens there. They get fat...never go anywhere...they work in the cannery in the summer and their hands are rough. I...I need to know."

"Come closer." Madam A smelled like cigarettes. She removed Lillie's dark-rimmed glasses and pulled off the elastic clip holding her ponytail. She pulled a tissue from her bosom and wiped Lillie's lips.

"Ah," she smiled. "Much better. Do you know the story of the ugly duckling?"

"You mean the fairy tale?"

"Whatever. One day you will turn into majestic swan."

"Will I be an actress...a famous actress...?"

"A swan...you will swim many places."

"But an actress?"

The psychic squinted and looked into the ball again. "I see a swan swimming."

"What about an ice skater or..."

"You gotta a ice rink in that tiny town of yours?" Madam A sounded irritated. Lillie thought she heard Bunny's stomach growl.

"No, but..."

"I see swan swimming in water. There is no ice."

"A singer then? Please, I need to know." Lillie moved to the edge of her chair.

Madam A pursed her lips, leaned forward, and looked directly into Lillie's eyes. Lillie looked away.

"You have pretty gray eyes. One day you blossom...fill out...become lovely, young lady."

Lillie lifted her face. She felt like a flower opening to sunshine on a spring day. She had never thought of her eyes as anything but ordinary. And did she say *lovely*?

"Many things will happen." Madam A looked into her globe. "I am seeing swan...a pretty swan. Oh wait, she's swimming with a handsome dark swan."

"Marriage!" squealed Bunny.

"Shhhh," Madam A hissed. "Not another word. You break the spell."

"*Where* am I swimming? New York? Los Angeles?" Just then, a bell rang. It sounded like the timer on her mother's oven.

"The ball is getting cloudy. The spirit is leaving," said the psychic.

"But..." Lillie said.

"Just keep doing what you are doing," said Madam A. "You will find the way."

"Which way?"

The psychic stood up. "I can tell you no more." The man came back into the room.

"Show these young ladies out," Madam A said. She threw up her hands. "*Tengo tanto que hacer.*"

Lillie and Bunny followed him to the door.

"It must be over ninety degrees out here," Bunny said when they reached the street.

Lillie didn't notice the August heat, the tall buildings, or all the people on the sidewalk rushing somewhere. Her eyes sparkled and her face was radiant. No one had ever told her she was pretty. She took off her glasses and stuffed them into her small purse. Her fingers found the elastic clip she had used to pull her hair into a ponytail. She tossed it into the street. Maybe she didn't need a tattoo.

# Secrets

Keith awoke early that morning after sleeping in his gray Taurus by remote Quarry Lake. It had been a long, muddy drive. The sky was overcast and dull, making the water on the lake appear dreary. He liked it when the lake looked like that. A murky lake knew how to keep secrets.

The sun, trying to break through ominous purple and gray clouds, was not having much luck. Keith ate the last piece of cold pizza, hoping for rain, heavy rain that would rile up the algae. Leaning against the headrest, he tipped his bottle of Jack Daniels and sucked the last few drops needing more, but it was all gone. He wiped his mouth on his sleeve.

Fishing the key fob from his pants pocket, he switched on the car ignition to roll down the window and tossed the empty pizza carton and a half-bitten crust to the ground. The damp air felt cool on his face, but smelled like rotten eggs. He could hear the rhythm of the water lapping against the shore. The comforting sound calmed him enough so his mind could work on his story. *I went to Leslie's apartment, but she wasn't there. No wait, we had dinner at Luigi's and I dropped her off. That was the last time I saw her...*

A large black crow in the tall fir next to his car made shrieking sounds, urging him to leave, so it could claim the pizza crust. *Caw, caw,* it rasped, over and over again. Keith covered his ears, but the continual screeching made his blinding, white anger return. He quickly rolled up the window and rested his head against the steering wheel, grateful for the green apple scent coming from the car air freshener. *Why couldn't Leslie keep her mouth shut? Why did she always have to be on his case? Caw, Caw. Caw.* He repeatedly stabbed at the dashboard with his clenched fist. *Shut up! Shut up!*

He stretched his neck and stared at himself in the rearview mirror—itchy eyes, puffed, and bloodshot; whiskers sprouting on his cheeks. He ran his hand over his brown, close-cropped hair. At least that wasn't messy. He scratched his chest and sniffed his armpits. He needed a warm shower, but didn't dare go back to his apartment. Not now. He tried to swallow the metallic taste in his mouth, but it lingered.

*What was that?* A pinging noise hit the roof of the Taurus, turning into a rushing, torrential downpour. The heavy rain had come, washing away the grime on the car's hood. *Remember to make eye contact. Be sure to vacuum the trunk.* He cracked the window. The crow had disappeared. The air smelled sweeter. Innocent even.

# Epiphany

As soon as I entered the doors of True Light Christian Church in the small town of Ricksdale for G. Ellen's memorial service, a chubby young woman approached. "Thank you for coming," she said, handing me a program. She stared at my fashionable gray pantsuit and Stuart Weitzman heels.

I extended my hand. "I'm Beth Terryjack. I used to work with Ellen at Braddock and Burdick Financial up at the Portland headquarters."

She tucked the programs under the arm of her cotton blouse and clasped my hand with both of hers. "Ah yes," she said. A warm smile lit her face. "Aunt Gwen was a shrewd business woman."

*Shrewd?*

G. Ellen sat a few cubicles away from my windowed office in the Marketing Division. The G stood for Gwen, but she used the lone initial followed by her middle name at work. I guess she thought it made her sound more corporate, even though her physical appearance never matched the image she apparently had of herself.

She was a short, middle-aged, rosy-cheeked beach ball of a woman with chin-length brown hair streaked with gray. I knew from office scuttlebutt that G. Ellen suffered from diabetes, knee problems and, at times, hard-core depression. Climbing stairs left her winded. She never married.

She had landed in the maze of cubicles on the fifth floor of our company four years ago. The then new management relieved her of the marketing manager position she held in one of our branch offices and reassigned her. The big boss, the full-of-himself CEO, totally disregarded Ellen's solid track record, her years of service, and her very likeable personality. In his mind, heavy-set people made poor company representatives. He made no bones about how he felt. Mr. Big would strut around the boardroom and make derisive comments about "land whales," his term for obese women. People from accounting were "pencil necks," janitors were "losers," and some poor bloke from human resources "a pisser and moaner who couldn't wipe his own butt." I guess he never noticed his own jowls, his bald head, or the way his ample gut obscured his belt.

G. Ellen passed her days presenting canned training programs to the sales force and recording their continuing ed hours, so they could retain their licenses. Food became her opiate as she piled on more pounds.

A spray of white lilies and mums stood by the pulpit at the front of the church. I took a seat near the rear. There were no pews. We all sat on gray padded church chairs, which made the sanctuary seem more like a meeting room. I glanced around the half-filled room of ordinary folks—family, church people, a couple of crying babies, a lot of jeans, and no corporate suits. I didn't see anyone else from work except Val, the friendly copy center gal, and Stella, the division secretary, who remembered everyone's birthday and organized the anticipated "treat day" celebrations. I hadn't known G. Ellen that well, but I considered her a worthy colleague. So where was Eric, her immediate supervisor, or the rest of her team—all those folks she interacted with on a daily basis?

The minister was a pleasant woman, somewhere in her fifties I'd guess, with dark-rimmed glasses and short, overly-permed auburn hair who punctuated her speech with distracting "ums." From her, I learned, "Gwen's parents...um...are no longer living. She... um...is survived by two sisters, a brother and several nieces and...um...nephews. She lived her last days alone in the cute house on Elm Street with her beloved cat, Groucho, and was supported by an adoring family who helped with the yard and housework, especially after her health started to decline. She...um...was sixty-two years old."

Once the minister concluded her welcoming remarks and Ellen's brief bio, she read scripture, and offered a prayer. She finished with, "Amen and Amen. Gwen wasn't able to enjoy a long retirement, but she's in God's hands now." After that, she introduced a young man from the church choir who sang "How Great Thou Art."

Finally, it was time for open sharing. A somber nephew told how Aunt Gwen had read to him as a child and helped pay his college tuition. "Thank you, Auntie," he said, looking up at the ceiling. He wiped away a tear. "I know you're in heaven with Jesus."

Friends from her high school class remembered her as a shining star, only they all referred to her as Gwen or Gwennie, never as G. Ellen. A ruddy-faced, heavy-browed man in baggy jeans told about the time they had all piled into Gwen's old Falcon on senior skip day, chugged off to the coast, and got stuck in the sand. "It was a bucket of bolts," he said, "but Gwen loved that car. We all got grounded for being late." His story brought a low hum of laughter from the crowd.

A bent, gray-haired grandma-type shuffled to the microphone. She introduced herself as Gwen's home ec teacher and described the fancy purple dress Gwen had made in her class. "Let me tell you, it was real pretty. It won a blue ribbon at the county fair."

Choking back tears, other family members filled in more of her history. After graduating from college, Gwen traveled to Europe, taught high school English, became an expert on Chaucer, and then left teaching in her twenties to work for the corporation.

The *Corporation*.

They said that word with such pride, as if Ellen had reached the Promised Land. "She was so organized," her niece told the audience, pausing to swallow. "Aunt Gwennie used to paste those little sticky notes all over the place, including the fridge and the bathroom mirror. If you messed with one of Gwennie's stickies, she knew it. Even when she quit work, she was a dyed-in-wool business woman."

Odd. Maybe she was at one time, but that wasn't the Ellen I knew. I recalled a meeting we'd had to plan the annual marketing convention—a big corporate deal. She came with a folder, which she accidentally dropped on the floor. When the papers scattered, she became discombobulated. I tried to help her put things back in order, but we were pressed for time, and I have to admit I'd left shaking my head. I wished now I had reached out to her.

In a quavering voice, her sister, a stocky but taller version of G. Ellen, presented a slide show of memories. Gwen's mother had been a stay-at-home mom, and her father pulled green chain in a mill outside Ricksdale where they all grew up. Gwen was valedictorian for her graduating class, was elected president of this and that, and even sported a crown as a May Day princess, wearing what else—the award-winning purple dress.

Back then, she was chubby, but in the flush of youth, it looked more like baby fat minus the rolls and thick calves that came later. Her brown hair was shoulder length, and she had this radiant, young smile. That smile gleamed in the photo of her receiving a scholarship to Oregon State. Ellen was the first one in her family to complete college. They were darned proud of that, too.

Such bright hope, I thought, such a promising start for a young woman any parent would be honored to claim and any company would be proud to hire. Sadly, like a wounded songbird falling from the sky, it all ended in a downward spiral. I dabbed my eyes.

After becoming pigeonholed at work, G. Ellen never smiled much, and she was sick a lot. Maybe that happens when one minute you're a star, the next an also-ran, when you're undervalued, putting in time, and your unchallenged mind sprouts weeds.

"What happened to Ellen?" I'd asked Charlotte, a marketing research analyst, and the company "knower-of-all-things." I'd suddenly realized G. Ellen's cubicle had been empty for some time and looked "picked over"—an unseemly practice of co-workers descending like buzzards on a former employee's office space in search of a better chair, stapler, or calculator.

After twenty-five years with the company, I knew Ellen was eligible for early retirement, but I didn't remember a party.

Charlotte constantly checked new employee directories against old ones, so she could keep track of people who mysteriously "went missing" from the corporation. She reached for the small three-ring binder on her desk, flipped it open, and announced, "Ellen's not in *it* anymore," as if quoting scripture.

"So, she actually did retire then," I said. "Was it because of the diabetes?"

"Who knows?" Charlotte said. "Stuff like that is confidential. She had a lot of problems."

"You'd think there would've been a card, a farewell lunch...something. I mean after all those years."

Charlotte stared at me over the blue-framed reading glasses resting on the tip of her large, hooked nose, making her look like an educated parrot. "You should check with Stella about that. She's the party queen."

"I already did. She was clueless."

"Look, whenever there's a regime change, everything shifts. They're always looking for new blood or have cronies that need jobs. It's best to keep your ears open and your head down. Wait for the next czar to make things better."

"I'm fifty-eight. That's not going to happen in my lifetime." My shoulders drooped.

She waved me off. "Just sayin'."

When the slide show finished, the minister announced a "celebration of life" reception. "It will be in the church social hall, following our closing prayer. There...um...will be coffee, punch, snacks and...um...Gwen's favorite blueberry cheesecake."

While waiting for the service to wind down, my mind shifted to an ending of my own. In fact, it wasn't long after Ellen had "disappeared" from the corporation, that Hastings, the marketing veep, called me into his office and showed me a draft of his new "reorganization" plan, all the time checking his watch. I had taken in my notepad expecting to get an assignment, but instead, he drew a line through my management position on the Marketing Division organization chart, claiming the department had to downsize. "You do a great job, okay?" he said, his beefy face reddening. "It's just that with this economy, well...the big boss wants to flatten the organization, okay?"

"So, you're flattening me?" I set the notepad on my lap, so he wouldn't see my shaking hands.

"Not exactly. We're...uh...moving you over to special projects." He forced a smile exposing the small gap between his two front teeth. "You'll still be reporting to me," he said, as if that were some prize. He penciled in another awkward box for me somewhere off to the side and down, but with a dotted line. He checked our meeting off his "to do" list, ran his hand through his thinning, see-through hair, and ushered me out, never looking me in the eye.

I stood for a moment in the hallway stunned, my armpits wet. *What had just happened? Who was I now? Being pushed out and down was tough news for anyone, but especially for me—a middle-aged woman. The world wasn't exactly waiting for us. Special projects? That was the corporate graveyard.*

Six months later, the CEO's snappy, *young* son-in-law, Richard, (slicked back hair, three-piece suits, methodical brain, brown-nosing ass kisser) showed up to do my "old" job; only it had a different title, so how could it have been mine?

"You're still in the directory," Charlotte had said, trying her best to console me. "That's something."

*Something.*

The congregation sang, "When We All Get to Heaven." I sat there like a sack of flour unable to join in. Afterward, the minister offered a prayer.

As people slowly filed out to attend G. Ellen's reception, I saw Stella and Val slip out a side door. I followed the crowd to the church basement, but not knowing anyone, stood in the corner sipping a glass of tasteless red punch from a Styrofoam cup.

"That's something," I heard a male voice in the distance say.

*Something.* I had no idea what he was talking about, but hearing that word triggered memories of my awful meeting with Hastings. A queasy feeling crept into my gut. My face flushed. The crowded room seemed to close in like I was wrapped in a giant rug. I crushed the empty cup in my hand and tossed it into the trash. Before leaving, I glanced at the photos of Ellen's life displayed on a memory table near the entrance. Off to one side was a colorful bouquet of paper roses made out of Post-it Notes, a final tribute to a much loved aunt and sister. I mouthed, "Goodbye G. Ellen, I never knew the real you." I fingered the edge of one of the roses. "I truly wish I had."

Outside in the cool air, I took several deep breaths, glad I'd come and pleased to have represented the employment side of G. Ellen's life to her family. But as I hurried toward my car, it became clear to me—I had to leave the corporation before it killed me, too.

# Smart This, Smart That

T racy plopped down on her sofa, pleased with the great deal she got on a new Smart-Tek furnace and air conditioning system. Sure it was expensive, but after enjoying cooled air for the last few days of a too hot summer, she was ready for the blustery weather that would follow.

Not only was Bret, the HVAC installer cute—jet black curly hair, muscles popping out of his tight-fitting T-shirt, Johnny Depp eyes, and gold chain adorning his neck—but her new system had a programmable thermostat. The house would automatically heat before she got up and be toasty by the time she returned from work. How good was that? Tracy was like a delighted child with the latest electronic toy.

A couple months later, a cold north wind sculpted ice crystals on her windows, but Tracy was cozy. Sitting in her chenille robe, she sipped a cup of freshly brewed coffee, savoring the aroma, letting fragrant steam open her sinuses, when she noticed the furnace thermostat lit up. The touch screen said: *You have an alert.*

Ah, clever. Tracy tapped the message button.

*You are no longer connected to the Internet.*

Tracy grabbed her user guide, tapped the settings button, and followed the instructions. She selected Wi-Fi, entered her network password, and hit connect.

*You did it!* the message screen said.

Yay! Technology was wonderful, and s-o-o-o convenient.

The next day granite clouds dropped three inches of snow. The thermostat touch screen lit up. *You have an alert.*

The message said: *Turn me up. It's too cold in here.*

How cool, Tracy thought—a furnace that talks to you. Bret, the HVAC man, was right. Smart-Tek systems were cutting-edge, not to mention bold, reliable, and fun.

Each day, while her furnace cheerfully hummed, she checked for another message.

*Turn me down when you leave.* How thoughtful.

*I love warming you.* Sweet.

*You're so cute when you wake up.* Wait. What?

Was she losing it or was the furnace getting too personal? Unfortunately, there was no way to type a response, so how could she tell it to back off?

The messages continued.

*You're hot*, it said one morning. *Just sayin'.*

How could this be? And, who could you talk to about a cheeky furnace?

The next message was the last straw. *Let's meet. Be at the Court Street Coffee Shop at three p.m. I know you like coffee, and you turn me on. No pun intended. Heh. Heh.*

Tracy's hand trembled. She immediately set down her cup. Maybe she should have gotten a space heater. She jerked out her cell phone and dialed the HVAC man. "Come and fix this thing," she screamed. "I think it's watching me!"

Handsome Bret, in slim-fit jeans and blue work shirt, was at her door in a New York minute. "What seems to be the problem?" he asked, his face innocent.

"It's after me," she exclaimed.

"What is?" the startled man asked.

"The furnace—it's, uh, coming on to me."

Bret's dark eyes widened.

Tracy's hands held her forehead. "I just want warmth. I don't want to date it."

He laughed. "Were you flirting with it?"

Not funny. Had the whole world gone crazy?

Bret approached the thermostat. "Let's take a look." He removed the cover. Touch. Touch. Zip. Zip. After he finished, he stood there staring at the tiny screen. "Huh." He scratched his head. "I'll be darned."

"Well?" She tapped her foot and folded her arms.

He smiled. "I disconnected your device from the Internet."

"You disconnected me? But what about all that convenience I paid for?"

"You've been hacked."

Her hands cupped her cheeks. "Hacked?"

"Yeah. You know, someone used a computer to gain unauthorized access to your system here."

Tracy twisted the ends of her blond hair between her fingers. "Who would hack a furnace? I mean like it's not a bank."

"It's happening a lot," Bret said knowingly. "Technology. It's everywhere. Think about it. Those new-fangled garage door openers folks buy track every time they enter or leave. Those automatic light thingies know when a person goes to bed or does almost anything else."

"Everything?" Tracy gasped.

Bret continued. "Then there are smart clocks, speakers, doorbells, coffee pots, window blinds, hot water heaters, and garbage cans that monitor what you throw away and generate online orders for replacements. Did I even mention smart phones? They all take your commands, but they also know things about you...personal things. Yep, smart homes, they're the new frontier for hackers."

Tracy pushed a curl from her face and shuddered. She reached into her pocket and fingered her cell phone. What did it know about her, and how could a poor defenseless girl protect herself from a world that was becoming overly technical and too invasive? Bret was a furnace ninja, a sun in a bleak night, and s-o-o-o-o knowledgeable. "Now what?" she asked, her demeanor like a wilting bouquet of violets.

At the Court Street Coffee Shop at about three p.m., Bret gazed into her soulful blue eyes. "My best advice when it comes to the Internet of Things and the sprawl of smart devices," he said, "is to stick to the good ol' *on* and *off* switch."

# Cliff Hanger

Cliff gunned the engine of his '07 Ford Focus and headed to the big city on Valentine's Day. He wasn't looking for anyone or anything special. It's just that Ramona with a shrug of her shoulder and flip of her stringy brown hair had walked out on him.

"Look," she'd said, with a sly smile on her thin lips. "It's not working out. Look, some people are meant for each other. Look, we're not." She removed her dark-framed glasses, blew on the lenses, and wiped them with her napkin. "There's more to life than pizza and beer every Friday night, Cliff." She placed the glasses back on her nose and waddled off leaving a rumpled paper napkin and a pile of pizza crusts.

Cliff, two months shy of turning forty, stroked his short-cropped sandy hair and tugged at the whiskers jutting from his chin. Look, he thought, mimicking Ramona, I need to get away and clear my head. I'll show her, by god. With that, he dusted off his little-used credit card and pulled a Ball jar from the cupboard containing extra cash.

He chugged his car into the parking structure off Sixth Avenue and carried his duffle bag into the Royal Ritz Hotel. Ha! Wait till Ramona hears what she missed.

He gawked at the lobby with its giant vases of dusty-pink roses, its polished floors, glitzy chandelier, and red couch. Ladies' heels clicked on the luxury vinyl tile as they smoothed their locks and rushed about perfuming the air. Men in suits, clutching briefcases, scurried past him like he was a fence post. The place dripped with money. Not the kind of pad a forklift driver usually chooses, and he hadn't thought about dressing up. No, he stood there in his favorite outfit, a floppy blue sweatshirt over khaki cargo pants with bulging pockets which did nothing for his pudgy doughboy body. At least his shoes were new. He wiggled his toes in his gray Skechers, the ones he got last week at Walmart. Maybe he should have changed his socks.

When he glanced back at the hotel desk, he couldn't believe what he was reading, but there it was in black and white. The small sign said: ***Don't be lonely. Let our fish companion keep you company during your stay. Ask for details.***

Well, he was and he did.

His finned friend came in a stylish fish bowl with a hood that featured a convenient feeding hole, a built-in LED light with an on/off switch, and colorful aquarium marbles. Cliff boarded the elevator to a room on the third floor, carrying the fish and his duffle bag.

She was a marvelous creature. Definitely upper scale. Gold fins, a trim body with a tail that swished, and big adorable fish eyes. Cliff called her Goldie, and he told her everything. How Ramona dumped him, how selfish she was, how she talked over him, always picked the pepperoni off her pizza slices, made a little pile, and ate it separately. He threw up his hands. "For god's sake, who does that?" he asked, exasperated. "She snores like a motor boat, and she's read *Gone Girl* three times. He pressed his fist against his heart. "Still, I loved her."

Goldie listened to his every word. She blew magnificent bubbles and her full lips made beautiful O shapes in the water.

Cliff took Goldie everywhere. At dinner at the quaint café down the street, he ordered a small table for two. People stared when he set Goldie next to him and told her how good it was to finally be away from Ramona.

A wide-eyed waitress approached to take his order. "Nice fish you have there. Are you waiting for someone, or are you ready to order?"

"What's the special tonight?" Cliff asked.

"Pan-seared salmon," the waitress said, her pen poised over her order book.

"Jesus." Cliff gasped and clutched the bowl with both hands, hoping Goldie didn't hear. "We've got to leave," he said to the baffled waitress.

Out on the street, he muttered, "Sorry about that. I didn't know they were cannibals!"

At Cinema 58, a theatre that featured old movies, he bought a huge bag of salty popcorn, set Goldie on the seat next to him, and placed his arm around the bowl. Amid the stale odor of recycled buttery air, they watched *A Perfect World,* an emotional crime drama starring Kevin Costner, as an escaped convict who kidnaps a young boy.

After their movie date, one blissful day blended into another. Come Friday, he was over Ramona, and he'd never been happier. Still, his stomach clenched when he realized his stay at the hotel was up. He couldn't bear to return to his drab apartment without Goldie. What to do? What to do? He could sneak out in the middle of the night, but wouldn't that be fishnapping? He cringed remembering how in the movie Costner got shot once police caught up with him.

Cliff scratched his head until an idea popped up. Aha! Out on walks with Goldie in the crisp February air, they often passed a pet store two blocks over. Now, he had a plan. He'd buy another goldfish and return the newbie to the front desk. The clerk would never know, and he and Goldie could ride off into the sunset together.

"I know how it is," said the understanding clerk, at Wiggly 'n Wags pet store after Cliff showed her a picture of Goldie on his cell phone. She was an older woman with bent shoulders and a kind face. "I'm so sorry you lost her. The animal-human bond is a powerful one."

"I need another fish just like her," Cliff said, pretending to choke up.

"Now, now." She patted his shoulder and led him past bags of cat and dog food, rawhide chews, rubber balls, and bird and hamster cages to a large tank where they stood together watching dozens of fish dart by. "How about that one?" she asked.

He narrowed his eyes as he checked it against Goldie's photo. *Close enough. That hotel clerk will never notice.* Cliff left smiling with a goldfish swimming in a plastic bag and a new fish bowl. He snuck in using the hotel's back entrance and took the stairs to his room.

The next morning, after swapping the fish, he covered Goldie's bowl with his jacket and slipped down the elevator to the parking garage where he lovingly stuck her in the trunk next to his spare tire, empty beer cans, and his collection of back scratchers.

"It won't be long," he whispered. "As soon as I check out and the coast is clear, I'll move you to the front." He kissed the bowl and lowered the lid.

Back in his room, he hurriedly showered and hummed while he shaved. This was serious stuff—fishnapping—and he had to pull it off like Kevin Costner in that movie, except Cliff would not get caught.

In the mirror, he practiced one last Costner imitation—a nonchalant nice guy with a mild stare—before confidently approaching the front desk with the new fish in Goldie's bowl.

"Look," he said to the young woman ringing up his credit card, "all good things have to end. I'm returning your fish. Thank you. She was such a comfort."

"You're very welcome." She gave him a toothy smile and tossed her long blond hair. "And we're so glad to have Charlie back."

"Charlie?" Cliff blurted. "You mean the fish I checked out was a guy?"

"Yep" she said, handing back the credit card. "All boy."

"But," he stammered. "How do you know? I mean for sure. She...it has such lovely eyes."

"Males have a longer, more streamlined body shape, and females are rounder and thicker." Her eyes blinked. "Well, that's what the guys at the aquarium told us. Basically, we take their word for it." She cooed at the bowl and tapped it with long red nails. "So how's my little guy. Did you have a good time?" She looked up.

Cliff was rushing away, clutching his duffel bag to his chest.

"Sir," she called after him, waving a piece of paper. "You forgot your receipt."

No answer. Just a high-pitched wailing sound as the revolving hotel door spit Cliff out onto the street.

## Have You Ever Been In Love?

Woo-ho-o-o-o! Valentine's Day. Randy twisted the key in the ignition and revved the van's engine. He'd been out of work for six months. Now he'd landed a job, a real one, as the delivery man for Mrs. Benedetti's Flower Peddler. It was nothing like the sorta, part-time one cleaning stalls at that dairy. What could be better than spending the entire day handing off dozens of red roses to people in love? Especially in the middle of the pandemic which brought loneliness and daily announcements of deaths. People were lost and the hits just kept coming. It was exhausting. But Valentine's Day—it was like a big helping of hope.

He thought of Junie... A slight girl, with straight, sleek brown hair and those gorgeous gray eyes. It almost made the veins in his head burst. "Junie, Junie, Junie." He whispered her name softly as he drove.

He'd met her working at Sheila's Place, a small lunch spot off Second Street, where he'd once bussed tables, washed dishes, and did janitorial work. He loved watching Junie direct the people to tables, how she walked with such confidence and recited the day's specials as if she were quoting scripture: "Mac and cheese, you'll eat it with gladness," she'd say. "Our grilled chicken with green salad will fill you with joy. Breakfast a-l-l-l day. It's a good thing." He couldn't take his eyes off her. He almost spilled a whole tray of dirty dishes sneaking peeks.

Oh, he knew Gus, the line cook, was hot on Junie, too, but he was older, twice divorced, had a gut pressing his belt, and in Randy's opinion, obnoxious. Okay, so he was tall, had a head full of curly black locks and a tattoo on his arm which said: *Make it happen.* So what?

Randy was tall enough and wiry, with smattering of dark facial hair that he thought added to his masculinity.

Gus earned more than Randy, but Junie was above all that, wasn't she? He knew she'd had lunch with Gus one time at Nathen's, a bistro in that new strip mall, but the guy probably pushed his way into that. Pushy was Gus's middle name.

With Randy, Junie talked about dreams. She'd get that longing look in her eyes Randy loved, as if it came from deep within and took her to another realm. It was like the one his mother got when she spoke of better times before his father ducked out on them.

Junie insisted she wasn't going to waitress forever. She hoped to go to business college and get an office job with Wormdahl's Insurance Agency or First Bank. "You can work your way up, if they let you in."

Randy just hoped. Maybe hire on at the steel plant. The guys there made good dough and got paid time-and-a-half for extra hours.

Ah, life seemed filled with possibilities, until the COVID virus snuck up on them like that treacherous fog he'd seen in a movie once, creeping under doors, through key holes and cracks in walls until it got inside and smothered people to death.

At Sheila's, they had to mask up and move tables around to make sure people were six-feet apart which meant fewer customers. Confusion hung over them like an about-to-burst cloud. The requirements the authorities issued changed weekly. First this; then that. The café closed and reopened. He and Gus erected a tent outside for sidewalk seating, but things only worsened. There was a race on to develop a vaccine. Was it safe? Should he get the shot when it was available?

Gus definitely wasn't. "Ah, you're a wimp," he said to Randy. "Living in fear ain't gonna buy you a bag of groceries. Besides those vaccines can change your DNA, and God knows what else."

Randy always thought a change in Gus's genetics might improve him. His bigger worry, though, was infecting his family, especially his mother, but kids his age, just out of high school, weren't a priority for shots. The government wanted to vaccinate health care workers, school employees, and old people first.

Randy's mother worked at the Suds Laundry and his two sisters, Casey and little Lorrae, were still in school, except now, the virus kept them home alone all day. His family lived in a sagging one bedroom rental east of town over by the railroad tracks. His sisters shared the bedroom. His room was a cubbyhole in the enclosed back porch which also housed the washer and dryer. His mother slept on the couch. Then she started having heart problems which seemed to worsen when the landlord raised their rent. The doctor told her to quit smoking and lose weight. She struggled with it each morning, swallowing a pill, checking her pulse, while puffing on an unfiltered Camel. "If something happens to me, it's up to you to look after the girls," she'd said enough times to worry him.

All kinds of people came into the café. Sheila and Junie were probably at greater risk for the virus, since they had more contact with the public. It wasn't too long before things came to a head. Customers stayed away, afraid to be in crowds. Finally, Sheila announced she was going out of business.

There used to be a world out there; now it was COVID crazy. The steel plant wasn't hiring—hardly anyone was. Junie hunkered down at home, waiting. At least she had a home. He was out there struggling, shoveling shit at that big dairy when they needed him. He didn't have to wear a mask there, but sometimes with the odor, he wished he did.

On the last day at the café, Junie had said, "Keep in touch. I like having you in my life." She reached out, squeezed his hand with her small, soft fingers. Electricity shot through him.

That meant something didn't it? "Course. Of Course," he managed to say. He knew where she lived—in that yellow house over by the high school.

Enough of the past. Focus on the present. He slowed the delivery van and stopped at a red light. "There's nothing like a dozen red roses to turn a girl's head to love," Mrs. Benedetti, a chunky Italian, with full eyebrows, graying dark hair, and a mole on her chin, had said, as she helped him load vases of flowers. She sighed. "That's how it all started for Albert and me. I was just a kid at the time. God rest his soul. My family didn't have a pot to pee in or a window to throw it out of." She smiled. "I was wandering the streets, looking for work, having a bad day. It was raining something awful. I happened to seek shelter under an awning next to a flower peddler cart, so I could eat the cheese sandwich I carried in my pocket. Albert, he handed me a bright red rose. A simple flower. It changed everything."

It was hard for Randy to imagine such a scene. It all worked out for them. It seemed simple and easy, but in the life he'd been born into everything was a struggle.

"After our marriage, we scraped and saved, and started our florist business, worked hard, and built it together. Your eagerness reminds me of my Albert. When he was young, I mean."

"Oh, Mrs. Benedetti," was all Randy could say at the time. But, she was right. There was something about roses. Wasn't that Junie's birth flower? He remembered the time, Sheila asked her to set a vase with a fresh rose on each of the tables. How Junie glowed and bragged that it was her flower. She sniffed and kissed each bloom like a butterfly bussing flowers in a garden.

Roses that was it. A way to win Junie over for good. But he couldn't afford a dozen of them. They could cost over fifty dollars a bunch, depending on the order and where you got them. At the Flower Peddler, a basic arrangement was fifty-five dollars. That was a lot of groceries. You'd never throw money around like that at home. His mother pinched every penny, except when it came to cigarettes.

He parked in front of a white house, slipped on his mask, grabbed a vase of roses, and rang the bell. The delivery was for Mrs. Ottoman. A short squat woman with silver hair answered, wearing a cotton dress, a sweater, and a paper mask.

"For you," Randy said, thrusting the flowers toward her.

Her gnarled fingers opened the attached card. "Oh, Arnie," she cooed. "He never forgets his mother." She hugged the bouquet to her chest. "Happy Valentine's Day, young man. Thank you."

"Yeah, sure," Randy said. Such a good feeling, but he knew he had nothing to do with it. Mrs. Benedetti's customers ordered the flowers and paid the bills.

And so it went, he made several more deliveries to offices, stores, apartments. Girlfriends, wives, mothers, daughters—thin, wide, pretty, plain—came to the door or lobby. For Bethel, Joan, Sandra, and on and on. Each woman, her eyes glowing, her face melting, grabbed the bouquets. Mrs. Benedetti had such a knack for arranging the flowers in clear vases with white Baby's Breath. Some of the deliveries even came with chocolates.

On his way back to the florist shop to load his second round of deliveries, he drove by Junie's house. Junie, Junie, Junie. Wait a minute. Oh my God, was that Gus leaving? And there was Junie waving goodbye. Gus had a big smile on his face. Why was he there? Where was his mask? Did he bring her something? How could that be? The last he'd heard, Gus still didn't have a job, but was sucking up unemployment. Randy ducked down in the van to avoid discovery and drove away.

***

Back at the florist shop, Mrs. Benedetti was all aglow. "Crazy virus out there," she said through her floral mask, "but people are still caring for each other. Thank goodness for the love." Hmm, she thought, this Randy reminded her so much of Albert—the way he smiled, the way his shoulders slumped, his fervent desire to learn the business, and those soulful brown eyes.

Out back, she helped him load vases into the van, watching as he sniffed each bouquet, almost seeming to kiss the flowers before carefully setting them in the rear compartment. Funny, her Albert always did the same thing, like he had a relationship with the blooms, and they were sacred. They never had children, but if they did, this kid could definitely fill the bill. She was getting on in years and could really use his help. Maybe this Randy was a gift from the universe.

He tapped the van horn, and she waved as he drove away. Sometimes, she thought, amidst all the calamity out there, the world hands you a small gem.

***

Randy gunned the engine; his heart heavy. All he could think of was Junie, Junie, Junie. Hmmm. But wait. Maybe there's a way. Of course, *sharing*. That was it. Especially in these times. Look after yourself and each other. Wasn't that the day's mantra? Oh, there were some bad eggs out there hoarding, buying up all the toilet paper and hand sanitizer. He'd even caught Gus, pilfering toilet paper and paper towels from the café john. The guy almost jumped through the ceiling when he realized Randy spotted him stuffing the loot into his backpack.

He also remembered seeing the Italians on TV coming out on balconies singing to each other in a bleak night. It was like Mrs. Benedetti had said—people sharing love during dreadful times was a touching thing.

At his next stop, Randy carefully plucked a rose from the bouquet, cuddled it in his hands, and let it touch his nose as he imagined Junie. He gave it a kiss and stuck it in the extra vase he found in the back of the van which he filled with water from his plastic bottle. Junie, Junie, Junie. He did that each time he made a delivery.

People would still get their bouquets. Oh, those expressions of delight; how enthralled the women were, delighted that the sender thought of them. One little flower wasn't going to matter. It was still a bouquet. There was no law about how many blooms you needed to fill a vase. Besides, these people had everything.

Junie wouldn't need a dozen. Six would do it, and he could use one of those white plastic vases his mother kept under the kitchen sink and maybe cut some greenery from that camellia shrub by the back porch. He pictured Junie's face as she reached for the flowers, charmed like the women on his route. And then, after kissing the roses, she would kiss him. He was sure of that.

He grinned. Gloated even. Take that, Gus. He smiled again. Oh my God, roses. Lush, velvety, and that sweet, fruity smell.

Randy happily delivered the bouquets until his shift was over. "Junie, Junie, Junie," he sang on his way back to the shop. "Flowers for my Junie."

He parked the van and went inside. Mrs. Benedetti was standing there, arms folded, foot tapping the floor, her mouth like a steel vice.

"Randy!" she shouted. "What have you done? Already, three people have called me...complaining they ordered a dozen roses and only got eleven." She counted on her fingers, Collette Newsome, the banker's wife; Rinnie Whitlock who works at the hardware store, and now Sybil Chambers' son.

Randy's head hung. He didn't think people who got those roses counted them. Why would they? Eleven roses still made a fine bouquet and then some. How much was enough?

"Jesu-me!" Mrs. Benedetti exclaimed through her gritted dentures, her hands gyrating through the air. "I gave you a chance, and you, you stole from me. Worse yet, you stole from my customers. What have you got to say for yourself?"

He didn't know. His armpits were wet; his dark eyes wide open. Scared. Junie, Junie, Junie, say it soft and it's like a summer breeze. Say it loud and it's— Suddenly Junie seemed to evaporate. He saw the desperate looks on the faces of his mother and two sisters. He heard his mother's plea, "If something happens to me..."

"How many did you take?" Mrs. Benedetti's demanding voice broke through his thoughts.

"What? Uh, Six, I think, six."

"Santa Maria Giuseppe!" Her hands held her head.

Randy cleared his throat, his eyes teared. "Mrs. Benedetti," he pleaded. "Have you ever been in love?"

Her arms relaxed. She got that faraway look. The one she always got when she spoke of her Albert. *The flowers started it all. This boy seems so like my Albert. Sensitive. A little foolish at times.*

"You have a girlfriend?" she asked, amazed.

"Sorta. Junie. We met at the café where I used to work. She...she loves roses. It's her birth flower, and I thought...I didn't think it was stealing. I thought it was sharing."

*The expression on his face. That look, like the time her Albert forgot their anniversary, or when he bet their savings on the horses thinking he could win and buy a florist shop.*

"Deceit doesn't bloom love. That's what, six people?"

"I'll work free until I make up the amount. I...I can go back and return the roses. I..."

"You bet you will...along with an apology and a discounted bill." Mrs. Benedetti plunked six fresh roses in individual white vases.

Each time she set a vase down hard on the counter, it made him flinch.

She hurriedly added a sprig of Baby's Breath, and threw in a few wrapped chocolates. "Roses aren't cheap."

Did that mean he still had his job? He didn't dare ask. His knees were shaking. How would he explain this to his mother? He saw his sisters cowering in the corner as his mother exploded. "You lost your job? What are we gonna do?" And, that worst cut of all, 'You're just like your father."

Mrs. Benedetti's small eyes moved back and forth, like she was calculating. *Have you ever been in love? Love. Sometimes it could make a person's good intentions take a left turn.*

Randy grasped the foam box holding the vases, swallowed hard, and headed to the door.

"Randy."

He turned to face her. "Yeah?"

She massaged the back of her neck. "Those roses you took…"

"They're in the van. I'll go get them."

She gave him a level look. "Give them to your girlfriend."

"You don't want them back?" He could hardly say it.

"We'll work something out, Randy. We'll work something out."

He couldn't help it. Tears spilled over his mask. All the pangs of shame gnawed at his gut.

Mrs. Benedetti came toward him and pulled him to her. "There, there," she said, patting his back. "And yes, I have been in love."

# The Lie

Spring had come to the campus of Riley Institute, a small Lutheran college tucked safely in the blue foothills of the Pacific Northwest. Cream-colored spikes covered the huge chestnut trees that lined the sidewalk to the commons area and the gigantic rhododendron by the library was again ablaze in bright peach-colored blooms. The staid little campus bustled with the sounds of singing birds, humming insects, student chatter, and campaign speeches. Awkward election signs spouted alongside purple lilacs and white, fluffy trees. Together they swayed in the fragrant air.

Mary, a junior, rehearsed a speech that she hoped would get her elected student body president. She'd taken a public speaking class her sophomore year and had gotten that part in a play last semester. After that, she headed a campus food drive, which set a collection record. These accomplishments surprised even her. Who'd of ever thought a quiet, small town girl, once so afraid to talk in class, could not only stand up before a group, but could also move it to action.

Once Mary learned the power of words and tasted success in the limelight, she could not step back into the shadows. Winning the presidential election could open all kinds of doors. She saw herself working on some local politician's campaign or maybe heading off to Washington D.C.

Mary's right hand jabbed the air as she practiced her speech in front of her dorm room mirror. She turned to the stuffed animals piled on the end of her bed and emphatically convinced them that she favored open meetings with the college president, an online class evaluation system, and a student-run bistro.

A little on the chunky side, with brown eyes, straight brown hair and dark-rimmed glasses, Mary was never considered pretty, but she was smart and reliable. She'd been valedictorian of her class of eighty-nine in her small, rural high school.

The daughter of a wheat farmer, she was the first child in the family to go away to college, even if it was just Riley and her being there meant repair of a leaky roof and new fencing had to wait.

During the summer, she helped with expenses by waiting tables at Wayne's Place, the town's only restaurant, which was adjacent to Wayne's Gas and Garage. Wayne usually didn't hire young girls, but her pastor highly recommended her. A grateful Mary never missed a day of work, never mixed up an order, and became a favorite with the regulars.

At Riley, spring semester was an odd blur of endings and beginnings. While students looked forward to summer vacation, they worried about finals and next year's class schedules. Seniors tried on caps and gowns and fretted about finding jobs or the right graduate school. In the midst of the flurry, they heard the awful news—a former student had died in the Iraq war—someone named Paul, whose vehicle hit a roadside bomb. Mary hadn't known him, but vaguely remembered his head of curly, brown hair and that he graduated two years ago.

Caitlin, a pretty blond from California with big plans and Mary's major opponent for student body president, marched into the President's Office and suggested that the school hold a vigil. Tall and willowy Caitlin planned to attend law school once she graduated from Riley. At least that's what she said. Mary hoped to teach the second grade, unless winning the student body election led to more exciting things.

The vigil took placed on a chilly May evening on the front steps of the library. Students huddled close, held candles, and sang songs. The chaplain, suffering from a cold and still a bit hoarse, gave a speech during which he talked mostly about peace. After a bad coughing spell, he opened the mike and invited others to speak. Caitlin immediately stepped up, but unlike the chaplain, she'd done her homework. Paul, she said, was a history major. He was an only child and had worked in the library reference room.

"He was quiet, studious, and always helpful...very helpful to so many of us, and we didn't even notice." She paused to clear her throat; her voice quivered. "Paul made the supreme sacrifice...for us. He was a hero. That's why I took action and thought we should have this vigil."

The crowd applauded. No one from Riley had ever gone as far away as Iraq, let alone died a hero. The breeze caught Caitlin's blond hair and her blue eyes gleamed. She looked directly at Mary and flashed a big grin as if to say, "Take that."

"She'll make a great student body president," someone whispered.

What could Mary do? She couldn't just stand there and let Caitlin have the last word. When the crowd quieted down, she made her way toward the mike, nervously adjusting it to accommodate her shorter stature. She looked into the crowd and into those lighted candles that seemed like footlights. It was as if she were back on stage in that play, and this was just another audience. She cleared her throat. She spoke slowly at first, searching for the right words. Suddenly, her voice took on an emotional pitch.

"I know how it feels," she heard herself say. "It's so very sad how someone could have so much promise one minute and be gone the next. I know. I know because I also lost someone very dear to me in war." She paused and swallowed as if it was difficult to go on. "You know, I miss him every day of my life. After he died, it felt like a part of me had died, too." Her hand automatically touched her heart.

"Death seems so wrong in a season of new beginnings." She gestured toward the peachy blossoms on the rhododendron bush softly glowing in the candlelight. Then she removed her dark-rimmed glasses and let the tears come.

"I can see his parents sitting in their living room...just like we did...in that small living room, holding his picture, remembering the curly-haired child they loved and protected, asking why...why did it have to be our Paul."

The students cried, too, and they applauded hard and long. When it grew quiet again, Mary asked them to join hands and sing *Amazing Grace*. After that, Mary knew. She knew her speech was better than Caitlin's.

The next morning on her way to the cafeteria for an early breakfast, she picked up a copy of the *Clarion*, the student newspaper. As she nibbled on scrambled eggs and toast, she saw a teary-eyed picture of herself on the front page, her glasses in hand, and this caption: *Candidate for student body president remembers.*

The election was held that Friday and Mary won by nine votes. A real squeaker the *Clarion* said. In a large photo, Mary smiled in front of a huge banner while a long-faced Caitlin, in a tiny shot, thanked supporters.

"It was that speech for Paul that swayed me," Martin, a sophomore biology major said in a quote. "I thought Mary really understood how we feel about that war—especially since she lost someone in it herself."

Amy, a freshman, said: "She's so compassionate. We could use a lot more of that around here. I hope she comes to terms with her own grief."

Mary smiled to herself. She took a deep breath. It was so easy, like running a hot knife through butter, as her mother would say. She folded the newspaper carefully and put it into her backpack. It would make a perfect attachment to a resume someday.

She never expected the questions.

Who was this dear person Mary had lost? Where in Iraq did it happen? Was he army or air force? Was it recently? What was this poor chap's name?

Mary stammered. "Fred," she said. "His name was Fred, and it was the army. But I don't know that much about the service, you know. It's kind of a guy thing. He, uh...was a cousin." Mary looked down at the floor; she could feel the color rising from her neck to the roots of her hair. She hadn't meant to lie. In fact, she believed that she really hadn't. She had lost a relative in war. She thought maybe it was Korea or it could have been Viet Nam. Well, it was something her father had said at dinner one time...a distant cousin's son or something. She never said it was Iraq.

Mary didn't realize a lie needed all those details. And, she had forgotten about Angela the girl from her home town who also attended Riley. Caitlin had pressed Angela, the plain, big-boned daughter of a mill worker, for more information. Angela, Caitlin announced in the lunch line as she filled her plate with salad, could not remember hearing anything about a cousin of Mary's who died in Iraq.

"You'd think it would have been in the *Herald* if it had happened," Angela had said, happy to be getting attention from someone as important as Caitlin. "Everything in our town gets in the *Herald,* but there wasn't anything in it that I know about."

Mary welcomed finals week. She hid out in the back of the library for hours, just waiting for the cousin incident to fade into the background. She'd gotten a call from a *Clarion* reporter, whom she suspected was one of Caitlin's friends, but didn't return the call. Thankfully, the paper's final edition was Thursday.

At last, the semester ended. In her dorm room, a tired but happy Mary cleared away half-eaten pizza and a mug of stale coffee from the night before. She was glad to be alone and grateful that her roommate had already gone home. She looked forward to summer, hoping to put even more distance between herself and the cousin story. Fall would bring a new year filled with exciting challenges. She took a deep breath and instantly felt better. President Mary. She liked the sound of that. She pictured herself addressing the student body and leading meetings, until she heard a loud knock on her door.

Caitlin stood there with that chilly smile of hers. She handed Mary a small, blue note-sized envelope.

"What's this?" Mary asked.

"Have a great summer," Caitlin said. She stared at her with those cold, blue eyes and a smile so wide Mary could see her fillings. "I gotta run."

Alone again, Mary slowly opened the note. It was handwritten and from Miss Bramrose, the Dean of Women. It said she wished to speak with Mary before she left the campus. *Please call my office.*

Mary felt her shoulders tighten as a chill made its way of up her spine. Maybe it was nothing. Maybe Dean Bramrose wanted to talk about next year and student body affairs. On the other hand, maybe she *knew.* Of course, that was it. The note offered no congratulations, and why would Caitlin be the one to deliver such a message? She imagined Caitlin marching into the Dean's office insisting she look into this *thing.* She saw Miss Bramrose crossing her thick legs, the stern gray eyes looking at her through those rimless glasses that always rested on the end of her nose. "Now tell me more about this cousin of yours," she'd say.

Any time now, Mary's father would arrive in his battered, dark green pickup to take her home. She always wished he'd park that truck blocks away from the dorm, but now yearned to see it pull up right outside. Together, they would drive back to the farm. Her mother would be in the kitchen with a pitcher of cold milk and a freshly baked yellow cake covered with swirls of chocolate frosting. She always baked that cake to welcome Mary home for the summer. Her younger sister also would be there—anxious to hear all about life at college, fueling her own dreams.

Then there would be Angela.

She, too, would be in Mary's summer. Angela would ask her mother about the cousin story, and her mother would call Mary's mother just to inquire and to offer condolences.

Then there would be *talk.*

There was always talk in her small town and sometime whispers. Whispers that would float on the air and probably find their way into Wayne's Place.

Mary picked up her dictionary, the one her co-workers at Wayne's had given her at the end of that first summer. "Here's to a great future," it said in blue ink on the inside cover. Everyone, including the garage mechanic, had signed it. She tossed it into the box she packed and swallowed hard, as if she already had a hunk of that yellow cake stuck in her throat. She looked at her open suitcase sitting on the bare mattress, the empty walls and bookcases; the room stripped bare waiting for another occupant. From her window, she could see the library and the gently fading peach blossoms ebbing away on the rhododendron bush. She remembered that night and how in just an instant everything had changed. How was she, a dean's list student, going to explain *this*—to everyone? Why did the chaplain have to lose his voice? This was all just a misunderstanding wasn't it? She never said it was Iraq. Her stomach felt like she had swallowed a handful of fencing nails.

She read the note from Miss Bramrose again. Her eyes locked on that final sentence. *Please call my office.* She had to decide. She could meet with Miss Bramrose. Try to explain. No, Confess. Face the music.

Then what? Eventually, there would be a front-page story in the *Clarion* and maybe even the local daily. *Oh, God.*

She saw President Caitlin's smirk and the disapproving faces of all her fellow students. They shook their heads and whispered. Pointed and *whispered.* Mary looked out her window. The dark green pickup had arrived. She could see her father waiting inside the cab. *Please call my office.* Those words echoed and bounced off the empty walls. Blinking away tears, Mary crumpled the note hard and tossed it into the wastebasket. As soon as it made a soft thud in the empty can, she knew. She would not return to Riley in the fall.

# Strange Heart

For the most part, Dave kept his mother in his closet except on her birthday when he would set her on the fireplace mantel so she could get some sun.

Now Miriam, his sister, was going to spoil all that.

For Dave, a mild-mannered, bespectacled high school history teacher, life was going along at an even pace. Then, he met Sharon. Last month, he turned forty and planned to marry her in December.

That's when Miriam had jumped in. "It's *time*," she announced in her matter-of-fact way via a telephone call from her condo in the Deep South. "No bride in her right mind wants her mother-in-law's ashes hanging around, especially at Christmas."

Dave's brain told him his mother needed a final resting place, but his heart objected to her floating around out there. Dave was happy keeping her in his closet, next to his last two cats.

Okay, so his closet wasn't the perfect location; but at least it was safe and warm, and it felt like he was taking care of her. Dispose of her. Wasn't that what Miriam had said. *We need to dispose of the ashes.* You disposed of garbage, but not people. Why couldn't they keep things simple and simply get a space at a mausoleum?

"It's been two long years, Dave. We have to get this done." Miriam was unwavering. She announced she was taking time off from her job as an account executive for a Savannah, Georgia advertising agency and flying out to Oregon.

"We have to think about what's best for Mother," she said, when she arrived on that cold December day with two suitcases, a clipboard, and a pencil behind her ear. She tweaked his cheek. "You always were Mother's little dear."

Miriam, who was pushing fifty, had been in Dave's apartment for a long, agonizing week and already he felt like he was on a long hike wearing boots three sizes too small. She parked her pudgy body in front of his computer, researched Oregon's landscape, made numerous phone calls, endless lists, and plastered the wall with yellow sticky notes.

"Why don't we spread the ashes at that park where she took us camping?" Dave asked. "She cherished that spot."

"We need something with more pizzazz," she replied, as if searching for a location to shoot a toothpaste commercial.

"How about those rolling hills that had beautiful sunsets? She loved going there—"

"We can't just dump ashes anywhere." She took a long sip from her Coke. "We'd need a permit. We want a setting with a little bling."

Dave's slight body tensed. "*Dump*. Did you say dump?" He felt a deep stab in his gut. It didn't seem right to dump Mother, particularly during the holidays.

Miriam, brown eyes blazing, fleshy face flushing, kept talking. "A place where there's water—maybe off Astoria where the mighty Columbia meets the ocean." She ran her hand through her short, efficient blond hair.

Dave struggled to understand Miriam's need to be in charge. She and Mother had never been close. Every time they'd been in the same room together, it was like someone curdled milk with vinegar. It had been that way as long as he could remember. Mother never liked Miriam's flamboyant clothing or her choice of men.

"Miriam always goes for the money instead of the man," Mother would say. "And she dresses like a tank on steroids."

As an adult, Miriam didn't approve of Mother's tasteless garage sale art, how she styled her thinning hair, the clutter in her house, or her penchant for hanging onto things like empty coffee cans, plastic cottage cheese containers, or that big wad of rubber bands in her kitchen drawer.

Most of all, Miriam couldn't fathom her mother's decision to suddenly marry her eighty-year old boyfriend, Ross, a quiet man, who was hard of hearing. "He's *just* a retired mailman, Mother, a milquetoast, and why for God's sake, now?"

"He's a good man," Mother had snarled through gritted dentures. "He likes me the way I am, and he wants to take care of me."

Following her second divorce, Miriam moved to Savannah. Things got more peaceful, until they learned Mother had cancer. Two months later, she was gone. Once she passed, Ross, with Dave's help, sold the house and moved to Sunflower Haven, an assisted living community.

"You just don't open the urn and spread the ashes," Miriam said for the umpteenth time bringing Dave back to the situation at hand. "There has to be a ceremony." Miriam checked her clipboard. "We need to get a wreath...one that floats...with red roses and white carnations. Mother so loved that combination. She had those colors at all her dinner parties."

"Miriam, Mother didn't have dinner parties—"

She waved her hand. "I mean the times she had people over." She looked at Dave over turquoise-rimmed glasses that rested on the edge of her bold nose.

Dave swallowed. "Those were gladiolas...red and white glads from her yard."

Miriam wasn't listening.

***

Finally, the day arrived. Miriam had made *her* decision: they should scatter Mother's ashes at sea.

Dave downed coffee and paced waiting for Miriam. After what seemed like hours, she emerged from the bathroom with every hair in place, wearing a navy blue pants suit, green eye shadow that made the skin above her lids look like crepe paper, and dangling snowflake earrings.

Once she grabbed her clipboard, Dave refilled his cup. He gently tapped Ross's shoulder. "It's time," he said. The old man nodded and quietly folded his newspaper.

"I'll get Mother," Dave said, retrieving the plain white ceramic urn from his closet. He placed it on the back seat of his car, carefully securing it with a seat belt. Ross sat in the back squeezed between the urn and the Christmas wreath of variegated holly dotted with red roses and white carnations.

As soon as the car reach the highway, Miriam started in on Dave's driving. "You're going too slow. I have to get back and pack, so I can fly out in the morning."

"What's that?" Ross asked from the rear. "There's no fly back here."

"Sheesh," Miriam blurted.

Dave pressed his foot down on the accelerator. He fought off the urge to push Miriam out the door. Instead, he reached for his coffee cup.

***

They arrived at the coast at 11 a.m. sharp—exactly as Miriam planned. The early morning fog had cleared, and balmy sunlight made the blue waves glisten. Dave took a deep breath, relieved that it was going to be a beautiful day. Hearing waves crash against the beach and seeing gulls flying overhead calmed him even more.

They met Pastor Eldon and Captain Bill at the dock. The captain, sporting a Santa hat, welcomed them to the *Neptune*, a white vessel with blue trim. When he wasn't assisting with ash ceremonies, Captain Bill chartered fishing excursions for salmon and halibut.

Ross carried the wreath, Dave hugged the urn, and Miriam clutched her clipboard. Soon, the dock and buildings became a dark line in the distance. At sea, the crisp winter wind picked up, and choppy water rocked the boat. The acid from that strong morning coffee churned in Dave's stomach. The *Neptune's* fishy smell didn't help either.

Finally, the skipper cut the engines. The sound system crackled and played *Amazing Grace*. Afterward, Pastor Eldon opened his Bible to the twenty-third Psalm. "The Lord is my shepherd: I shall not want..." He licked his lips as if he could taste the words.

Perspiration beaded on Dave's forehead. His gut was about to explode.

"Yea, though I walk through the shadow of death..."

Dave, still clutching the urn, made a mad dash to the side of the boat. *Eeeaugghh*. He heaved, tasting the oatmeal and banana he had for breakfast. A rope of saliva hung from his chin.

Miriam looked horrified. "Jesus Christ, Dave!"

"What's that?" Ross asked.

Pastor Eldon stopped for a moment. His eyes moved from Dave to Miriam. "Thy rod and staff comfort me..."

Dave wiped his mouth with a wad of tissue and returned to his spot.

"...and I will dwell in the house of the Lord forever. Let's bow our heads for a moment of silent prayer," Pastor Eldon said.

The prayer over, Miriam reached for the urn. "I'll release the ashes, Dave. You toss the wreath."

"Dave," she whispered, "for Christ's sake let go." Miriam pried the urn from his hands.

Dave hung his head.

Ross stood there, a wistful look on his face.

The minister nodded to Miriam.

"I just wanted to say I love you, Mother," Miriam said to the urn, "You went so fast, and I was so busy..." Her voice quavered. "Oh, I know we had our differences, but...but you were a saint. You know, to put up with it...and all."

Dave couldn't believe his ears. *Really? Who was she talking about?* He stared at his sister whose eyes were glistening. Miriam was not someone who cried easily.

Miriam twisted and pulled the lid as if she was trying to open a stubborn jar of pickles. "Mother, this is no time to be difficult!" She shook the urn. "You're spoiling our event."

"Here we go again," Dave mumbled. He smoothed what was left of his sparse hair.

"What's that you say?" Ross asked.

Pastor Eldon raised an eyebrow. He looked at Dave, over at Miriam, and finally up at the sky.

Dave checked his watch. In twenty-two hours, ten minutes, and three seconds Miriam would be boarding her plane. He couldn't wait. He yearned for a stiff shot of bourbon.

*Uhhhhhguh.* Miriam, grunting like a tennis player returning a volley, gave the urn another mighty twist. The lid popped off, and she pitched the cremains over the boat rail. Suddenly, the sea breeze shifted. Some of the ashes blasted back into Miriam's face.

"Shit!" She gasped.

Pastor Eldon again tilted his glance heavenward. When he lowered his eyes, he calmly nodded at Dave.

Dave tossed the wreath into the sea. "Goodbye Mother. Merry Christmas." He choked back tears. "We love you."

"Was I supposed to say something?" Ross asked, as they watched the festive wreath float away. His voice sounded tired, and he looked more frail than usual.

"It's okay, Ross. We took care of it," Dave assured him. He put his arm around the old man's stooped shoulders.

"When I go, I want to be out there with her," Ross said, his lower lip quivering like a lost child.

"Sure Ross. Sure," Dave whispered. His throat tightened.

Captain Bill rang the ship's bell eight times to signify the "End of Watch." Pastor Eldon stood quietly at the railing looking out at the ocean, as if he wanted nothing more to do with this peculiar family.

Dave patted Ross on the back and shook his hand. He snuck a peek at Miriam who was still trying to recover from the flurry of ashes.

"They got all over my new coat," she wailed, vigorously stroking her face and brushing her shoulders. Her mascara smeared below her lower lids, making her look like a raccoon. The wind had not been kind to her hair.

For the first time, Dave put his arm around his sister's wide body and cautiously drew her closer. Surprisingly, she didn't explode. He had spent the entire week and most of his life resenting her annoying intrusions. Maybe this wasn't just another event for her, he thought. Maybe it was a journey of sorts—a last chance to make peace with Mother in her own exasperating way. Maybe, somewhere deep inside, Miriam, actually had a heart—however strange it was.

"You're okay," Dave managed to say. "We're all okay."

"Quit squeezing me," she grumbled, pulling away. "We're done here. Let's go."

The corners of Dave's lips twitched before breaking into a smug grin. At least Mother had had the last word.

# Be In Your Own Shoes

Sue had been thinking a lot about dying lately. How could she avoid it? That damn virus could kill. Whenever she turned on the TV news, Lester Holt was counting bodies or showing footage of endless healthcare workers dressed like Martians, wearing face shields and masks, scampering about, or hovering over some gasping older person while relatives clustered around an outside window, not able to say goodbye in person.

The whole world had gone into hiding. People cocooned in their own pods, hoarding toilet paper, mumbling under masks, dousing their hands with sanitizer, not daring to get close. Others, refusing to be cloistered, rioted in the streets, protesting the mask mandate and lots more. No one was going to take away their freedoms by golly. This was America after all. Sue stiffened and drew a deep breath. Every time you stopped at a stop sign, or wore clothes instead of walking around stark naked, wasn't that the government telling you what to do?

"Be in your own shoes." Sue's mother used to say when she was a fretting young teen and times got confusing. "Do what's right for you."

Sue wasn't a kid anymore, but God, she needed to heed her mother's words now more than ever. Especially since it was Thanksgiving, and she was alone. She couldn't remember ever being by herself on this day. Wait, there was that time when she was six, had the mumps and got quarantined to her upstairs bedroom.

But Thanksgiving, for God's sake—a time for gratitude and family.

Sue was seventy-two with two grown kids who were afraid to visit and didn't plan to come and pick her up. "We don't want to kill you," her son said over the phone. "This stuff's so contagious, and there's no vaccine yet."

"Sorry, Gram," thirteen-year-old Eddie, back from tossing basketballs, huffed into the receiver. "Love you."

"If you need toilet paper, I can leave some on your porch." Lil, her daughter, assured her when she called. "I won't come in." Her voice quivered. "I don't want you to die."

Die?

Sue had planned to make her famous pumpkin marshmallow pie, her crowning glory. There wasn't another one like it in the entire county. Everyone said so. But then the dang rug got yanked away. That Dr. Fauci came on TV and told the entire planet to stay home.

So that was that. Endgame.

She sat at her kitchen table, still in her rose-sprigged pajamas not caring that it was noon, her white hair uncombed, her face unwashed. A basket of laundry, begging to be folded, occupied the opposite chair. She stared at the tuna sandwich in front of her. Who eats a cold sandwich on a holiday when you should be celebrating the year's blessings with your family? She took a bite, chewed, and swallowed. It tasted like cardboard. Could be the mayonnaise had gone bad. She nibbled on marshmallows pulled right from the plastic bag. Well, what was she supposed to do with all the dang things? Divorced from the pie, they were reduced to mere gelatinous orbs. Heck, eating alone even made the coffee taste bitter. "Probably should throw that can out," she muttered aloud. "Can't remember when I bought it."

Hmmm. What would she turn into if the virus did kill her? She wasn't thinking about heaven or hell. No, those were *places* people go. Her knobby fingers tapped the table. But here on earth, all old people turned into something after they died. They worked hard all their lives, watched their pennies, and then left everything to the kids. Harrumph. That's when they *convert* you. There was plenty of evidence of that. Just look around.

Last spring, when her longtime friend, Ellen, passed at seventy-six, after years of grappling with heart trouble, her son took his inheritance and bought a flashy neon-green Ford pickup with the body jacked up on huge tires so high off the ground it could be an airplane. How on earth would you step out of that thing without breaking your neck?

Every time he roared by, gunning the engine, Sue would think, well, there goes Ellen. Not to mention, its garish color. Ellen was such a modest, proper woman. It didn't seem right.

Poor ol' Masie from down at the church. Eighty-something and a genuine God-fearing woman until Alzheimer's took her. Not long after, her daughter Judy turned her into a new washer and dryer. She didn't even buy a stellar brand—not as far as Sue could tell.

She'd run into Judy at Brownstein's Grocery in the detergents aisle where the artificial fragrance of soaps and cleaners always triggered her allergies.

"I've never tried these laundry pod things," Judy lamented as she reached for a box. "Think I'll feed them to my new Whirlpool twins."

Not a word about her mother. If you had to turn into appliances by God, you'd think they'd be front-loading Maytags. Now every time Sue did her own wash, she thought of Masie, tumbling around in Judy's dryer with her sheets and towels. Sheesh.

So what would her own kids do when she kicked the bucket?

Ronnie, her son, would probably spring for a new computer. He was always messing with some kind of electronics. Who'd want to own a dang computer let alone become one? Those things crashed, and when they weren't doing that, they spied on you. She heard that on the radio. Yeah, there was a pandemic, but this Internet thing with its hacking and scams was going to be the end of all of us. Staring at a screen all day. Didn't people matter anymore?

Becoming a computer, though, was probably better than being a set of Michelin tires, another thing Ronnie was hankering for. That, and a showy set of hub caps.

And what about Lil, her daughter? No question, she'd turn Sue into a trip to France. Then what? Trips don't last. When they're over, all you got is photos which meant you'd be over, too. Yep. A trip or that fandangled Cuisinart Food Processor she keeps talking about. These days, folks have an appliance for every little thing—air fryers, instant pressure cookers, fancy coffee makers, and digital toaster ovens. Gadgets that made kitchen counters more crowded than bus terminals. When Sue first got married, she was grateful to have a set of pots and pans and really, they were enough.

Eddie, her grandson? Threw his thumbs out of joint working a silly cell phone blabbing about something called 5G. Pulls that dang phone out even when we're all sitting around the table for Sunday dinner, like we weren't even there. Tweeting. People used to talk. Now they tweet. When she was Eddie's age, tweeting was something birds did. Still is, and that's the way it should stay.

Thud.

That was the paperboy tossing her newspaper on her porch. She checked the clock on her kitchen stove—12:45. He's late, but heck it's a holiday. At least somebody's moving out there.

She shuffled to the front door in her felt slippers, ventured out, and picked up the paper which was heavier than usual, loaded with holiday advertisements. What a waste. Who's going shopping in the middle of a pandemic?

Back at her kitchen table, Sue popped two more marshmallows into her mouth, chewed, and washed them down with a swig of now cold coffee. She pulled the newspaper out of its plastic wrap and settled back to glean the day's news. My goodness, even the new president is staying home. What's this? A major story about a vaccine—a vaccine for crying out loud with first doses expected next month. Not to mention, Dr. Fauci is very excited about it.

That's something.

Outside her window, the sun spilled through a cluster of gray clouds. A group of chickadees gathered in her leafless hawthorn tree. Cute little things. Alive. Unafraid. Tweeting. Not insults, but real bird sounds. Maybe, just maybe, hope was edging its way into the world again. She smiled, her mother's words echoing like chimes. Thoughts about her impending death and her conversion into some god-forsaken thingamajig gave way to an idea. She'd wash up, get dressed, comb her hair, add a dab of lipstick, put on her clip earrings, and make her famous pumpkin marshmallow pie anyway. Even if, over the next few days, she had to eat the whole damn thing by herself.

# What Good Is Sorry

Ed had signed up for the seven-day Zen retreat in the woodsy Oregon countryside because he didn't want to be alone on *that day,* and he couldn't bring himself to talk about it anymore.

He sat on his cushion in the meditation hall, legs crossed, eyes closed. After the soothing tones of the three opening bells, an image of a little hand came out of the darkness in his mind and wrapped its tiny fingers tightly around his index finger. *Timmy.* For a moment, his mind slipped back in time, and he smiled into the quiet face of his newborn son. He concentrated on his breath to quell the spasm in his throat until the fingers loosened and the face dissolved into space.

At the monastery, each day was the same. Silent. Thank God for the silence. A group of twenty retreatants got up at 5 a.m., sat for an hour, did walking meditation in the Zendo, before eating a simple breakfast in silence. After that, it was back to more sitting, a longer walking meditation outside in the monastery's idyllic setting, before heading to the dining hall for a mindful vegetarian lunch. In the afternoon, they had two hours of free time to rest or walk through acres of unspoiled countryside.

Ed lived for the free time. After three days of sitting on a cushion, his body screamed for relief. He sat on the floor and laced his shoes, eager to take a long walk along the pond and into the woods.

Outside, bright sunshine accented the enormous rhododendron bush of cream-colored flowers with dark purple centers that resembled hundreds of staring eyes. Ed couldn't resist touching the fragile blooms as he hurried down the stairs. Around the meditation hall, red and purple azaleas added vibrant splashes of color. Plantings of ajuga covered the ground with tiny blue blossoms. Bees hummed over the petals. He noticed so much more when his world went silent. *Tim*. He could almost feel him looking over his shoulder.

Ed meandered down the gravel path that surrounded a big, gray-green pond—the centerpiece of the monastery grounds. Blue sky replaced the clouds that threatened rain earlier in the morning. On the bank, two mallard ducks had their bills tucked into their wings for a nap. Bullfrogs hid in gauzy debris that casually floated near the water's edge. They sang to each other, their throats forming yellow bubbles as amorous croaks boomed across the pond. Ed found them especially comforting because Tim had once said those primordial sounds were among the first the earth knew. He stepped off onto the grass, so the crunch of the gravel would not startle the frogs. Still, they sensed his approach. As he neared, they gave a single high-pitched squeak and then a brownish-green blur dove into the water with a splash.

Ed squatted by the bank and watched tiny fish dart back and forth. Tim would have loved this pond teeming with life. Every summer they took at least one extended hike into the wilderness where they camped under the trees, watched the sun dip behind the mountains and the sky darken into amazing starry splendor. Ed braced himself for that familiar wrenching twinge deep in his gut.

Timothy Edward Baines Jr. He was just twenty-four-years-old. Ed shook his head. That kid had everything going for him.

Ed headed up a trail leading into the surrounding forest of towering Douglas fir, large poplars, stately cottonwoods, sprawling oaks, and many other leafy trees he couldn't identify. Together they made a symphony of green shades, from yellow to blue to gray to true green. White lichen wrapped the branches and trunks of some trees; others dripped with moss. Heavy blossoms covered the wild apple trees, while thick clumps of bare blackberry vines banked the trail. Tiny birds twittered in the trees. A squirrel darted across the trail.

"I'm very sorry you lost your son. I can't even imagine how that feels," Winslow, the managing partner at Ed's law firm, had said after Ed had consumed too many martinis and passed out in court. Winslow's face turned beefy red when he was agitated. He ran his hand through the thin strands of hair struggling to cover his baldness. "But you can't go on like this." He sighed heavily. "You've got to get it together, man."

Two weeks later—after Ed downed what he thought were only a few whiskey sours—he overshot a curve and totaled his car. The judge suspended his license.

Ed had agreed to take a break from the practice. The firm paid for counseling, and Ed spent three long months talking with a therapist. He learned all about the stages of grief, and he quit trying to drown his pain in alcohol. But, alone at night, he tossed, turned, and struggled with continual bouts of anxiety welling in a shadowy pit of guilt. When sleep finally came, there were those strange dreams. He heard the lulling sound of a train in the distance that suddenly got closer and louder. He saw Tim standing on the tracks. "Run," Ed screamed.

"For God's sakes, run!" Instead, Tim froze and Ed couldn't move. The wheels hammered on metal track. Tim's shoes flew through the air. Ed bolted straight up in bed, his T-shirt drenched with sweat, realizing the pounding sound was his own heart. After his doctor wrote out several prescriptions, Ed traded alcohol for pills. They didn't help.

Finally, something good happened.

While waiting for the bus on a cold, rainy day, he ducked into a busy Starbucks to wait out the downpour. The crowd pressed Ed into a corner. He stood there, his shaky hands gripping the warmth of his paper coffee cup. A young, frizzy-haired blond looked up from her latte. A string of wooden beads with an agate pendant hung from her neck. Her inviting smile beckoned him, so when she motioned for him to share her table, he eagerly took a seat.

"You look lost," she'd said. After a bit of small talk, she told him she was on her way to meditate. "You should come sit with us."

Maybe it was her calm demeanor, her kind, dark eyes, or Ed's desperate need to be with people that made him follow her out the door like a lost puppy. He expected a meeting with the counter culture, but instead found a group of young business professionals, several college professors, students, and middle-aged folks seeking a peaceful start to their mornings. Although trying to sit cross-legged was awkward, and at times downright painful, his experiences meditating with such a welcoming group soon felt like the fit of comfortable old jeans.

Ed didn't consider himself a Buddhist, and he didn't always understand the ritual—the bowing, the chanting, or the odd stories they told, but meditation helped to quell the anxiety that stretched from his chest to his stomach and lingered there long after his tears dried up. Breathe. Count your breath. Be mindful. Stay in the present moment. Don't dwell on the past and don't worry about the future. It sounded easy, but it was hard to do. At least the practice had gotten him off the prescription drugs he'd gulped like M&M's.

He'd signed up for the retreat to avoid being alone on the anniversary of Tim's death. He was grateful for the silence, but struggled to clear his mind. He'd sit quietly on his cushion, counting his breath, his mind silently repeating *peace, peace*, but he couldn't stop the mental slide show that crept in and tortured him—the day Timmy was born, Timmy dressed in a Halloween costume, Timmy learning to ride a bike, the Little League games, the nature hikes, and *that day*.

It wasn't like he had other children to think about. Tim was it. Now he was gone. Ed had always felt guilty about the divorce when Timmy was thirteen, but that didn't even compare to the despair gripping him now. He still heard those tormenting echoes from the sessions with his grief counselor: *Many young people who commit suicide give some type of warning. Parents often miss the signs.*

Why didn't he notice something? Why didn't Tim come to him? The answer fluttered in his stomach. He knew the awful truth: *Tim had tried.*

While meditating, Ed saw images of the funeral. Mary accompanied by her second husband with his ruddy face, bad haircut, and layer of fat hanging over his belt. She clung to Melanie, Tim's half-sister—a chubby girl with stringy brown hair who constantly dabbed her eyes with a tissue.

He saw the long line of people, felt the handshakes and the hugs. He even thought he could smell the flowers and hear the music. Now, it all passed before him in fragments like tattered shreds.

"We are sorry. We are very sorry. We can't imagine how you feel. Sorry...sorry...sorry." It didn't change a damn thing.

Tall like his dad with a shock of blond hair and the bluest of eyes, Tim had gotten up early every morning to run. He lived for the next hike. Native flora and fauna intrigued him. He could identify all of the birds and most of the plants, spouting their names like old friends.

Ed, on the other hand, liked the challenge of the hike itself. He constantly logged the miles they walked and bragged about the peaks they'd conquered. That Christmas they'd planned their next trek—the Strawberry Mountain Wilderness area in Eastern Oregon.

At his small liberal arts college in California, Tim had gone from a shy youth to a daunting pacesetter. He involved himself in many activities, easily made friends, and was a star on the track team. In his senior year, he was elected student body president, winning with seventy-five percent of the vote. In spite of the activities, he managed to keep a straight-A average. At graduation, his fellow classmates voted him the most likely to succeed.

When Ed was Tim's age, he'd worked his way through college as a waiter, a tutor, and even a janitor. He didn't have time to join clubs, and he wasn't a popular kid. During the summer, he worked hard on the farm and later in the canneries. He'd graduated with a degree in English and began teaching high school in a small town where he met Mary Linden. Getting married seemed like the next logical step.

He came to realize teaching was not his cup of tea. After ten years of grading papers, he studied law at night school, eventually passing the bar. He landed a job with a large law firm, moved to Portland, and found himself working long hours to succeed, and even longer hours to avoid going home. Mary's provincial ways no longer fit his highball lifestyle. In fact, she didn't seem to fit into his life at all. After a steamy affair with vivacious Toni, the young, red-haired personal trainer he met at the athletic club, his marriage hit the rocks. He didn't want his son to make the same mistakes.

Where was Tim now? Some people assured Ed that his son was in heaven, but Ed never thought there was a heaven. So where did that leave him? At times, he could sense Tim's presence in the trees, the breeze, the ripples of the pond, the way the clouds moved in the sky. It was comforting in a strange way and far more consoling than the idea of heaven or hell.

A tiny, gray bird with a black head tittered in a tree. Its beady eyes sized Ed up as he walked deeper into the woods. When Tim was ten, he and Ed would go on short nature hikes at Cascade Head on the Oregon coast or to Eight Dollar Mountain near the state's southern border.

"If you could be any animal, what would it be?" Ed teased.

Tim always giggled and clapped his hands. "I'd be a bird because I could fly anywhere and no one could catch me."

The bird chirped again.

"I'm sorry," Ed said to the bird as if speaking to a reincarnated Tim. "I'm so very sorry." It flapped its wings and flew away.

After Tim went off to the University of Chicago law school, every-one said he was a chip off the old block. And, he looked so much like the old block, except Ed's once blond hair had darkened and thinned. He was heavier, gray at the temples and wire-framed glasses covered his blue squint. Ed even envisioned Tim joining his firm—the two of them working on cases together. Ed would see to it that he met the right people, joined the right clubs, and yes, married the right woman.

Then something changed.

While Ed talked excitedly about their future together, Tim gazed off into the distance like he was withdrawing into another world and shutting Ed out.

At law school, Tim lived in a small studio apartment by himself and studied long hours alone for average grades. There wasn't time for sports or hikes or other school activities. He no longer was a big fish in a small pond. He was close to finishing his second year when he came home that day in late spring, a few days before finals. Haggard and unshaven, he stopped in at Ed's law office and announced he was thinking of dropping out. "I need to find myself," he'd said.

Ed tried to tell him. No, it was more like he totally lost it. "Find yourself?" His voice rose. "What the hell are you talking about? You're going to be a lawyer and a damned good one."

"I...I just want to take some time off," Tim had stammered, "to...uh...spend the summer in California with my old friends. Hang out for a while. I'm thinking I'd like to teach high school. Maybe coach track."

Ed never liked Tim's laid-back California friends, and he thought teaching was too bourgeois for a kid with Tim's talents. "Listen man, I've been there. You don't want to do that. The pay is rotten. Kids these days are challenging. Law school is only three years for Christ's sake. You're two-thirds of the way there. If you leave now, you'll hate yourself for the rest of your life. Law school makes everything possible. Sure, it's a struggle. Welcome to life."

In a second, the conversation turned ugly. Ed struggled to remember, although his mind didn't want to go there. Okay, so he was under tremendous stress, working long hours on a difficult case that wasn't going anywhere. He'd spent the whole morning in court, and he needed to prepare for a one o'clock meeting. Winslow kept breathing down his neck, not to mention the billing problems. Bellamy, his chief rival at the firm, planted the idea that Ed over-billed some clients. After much angst and a lot of checking, it turned out to be a computer glitch.

All the stress wore Ed down and brought on a virus. His head ached, his nose dripped, and his throat burned. He downed several over-the-counter cold pills, which made him woozy. He tried to choke down a tasteless egg salad sandwich with help from a cup of bland coffee from the office pot when Tim had shown up unannounced and plopped himself down in one of the leather chairs in front of his desk. His decision to drop out of school was the final straw.

"I don't have time for your whiney nonsense. If you drop out, don't come crying to me." He stared at Tim's wrinkled shirt and unkempt hair. "And for god's sake, clean yourself up. You don't want *them* to see you like that. Get some sleep."

"I want to do something more creative." Tim's hand motioned toward Ed. "Than just vegetating behind a desk."

"Vegetating? Listen, I've talked to them. They're thinking about hiring you for the summer. It's a great way to get hands-on experience." Ed paused. His lips widened into a smile, exposing a row of white teeth. "Winslow's daughter—the cute brunette? She was in the other day asking about you." He gave Tim a knowing wink, the kind men give when they talk about women. "She's a ten, and she's smart, too."

"I don't want to be a lawyer."

"What?" Ed's jaw dropped. He slammed the file he held in his hand against his desk.

"I want to work with kids. Maybe teach botany." Tim had one leg crossed over his lap; that foot jiggled nervously. "Lawyers are assholes."

"You're going to finish law school," Ed ordered.

"I'm not going back, Dad."

"If you leave school, our summer hike is off. You understand?"

Tim flinched. "I don't want to be *you*."

That comment hit Ed like a brick. His mind flashed back to his own father lying in a drunken stupor on the sofa. Those had once been his own words, but his father had deserved them.

"You ungrateful little bastard," Ed pushed back his chair, abruptly standing up, his hand gripping the file on the desk. Ed's last image of his son was the sole of Tim's sneaker kicking back as he ran for the door and slammed it hard. Ed threw the file, hitting the door just as it closed. "You drop out and you're dead to me."

That night. My God, that *very* night. He couldn't shake the memory, it was so ominous. The smoke detector in his condo beeped. Ed thought the battery must be waning, and he remembered being angry because it was supposed to last ten years. He struggled to sleep, his throat raw, his cold moving to his bronchial tubes. He had just nodded off when the damn thing started beeping again. He reached down next to his bed, found a shoe, and flung it with all his might. It missed the smoke detector but knocked loose a picture of him and Tim hiking in the wilderness. He flicked on the bedside lamp and saw the picture lying on the floor, its frame split and the glass shattered. "Story of my life," he croaked, his voice compromised by laryngitis. The smoke detector never beeped again. Was there something in the air? Was that Tim's spirit or something else trying to warn him?

Ed paused on the trail and sucked in the spring air. He'd thought about packing up and leaving the retreat but hesitated because he'd be back in his condo.

Alone.

He remembered his one-on-one meeting with the Zendo's Buddhist nun. "Leaving won't stop your thoughts," Sensei Heiwa, a pleasant woman in a golden robe and close-cropped hair, advised.

Ed had confessed some of his story, but not all of it—not the part that gnawed at his gut.

"In our tradition," she said, "there is the story of a peasant man who was cutting reeds to make a hut for his family, so they would be warm and dry in the winter. He worked long and hard and was very tired. It was getting late. He had only a few more reeds to cut when he tripped over a large rock and fell on his knife. The knife stuck him in the middle of his heart. He lay on the ground screaming about the pain, cursing himself for being clumsy, and damning the stone for causing his injury."

Ed stared at the floor. It was almost as if she could peer into his mind and see all his twisted thoughts.

There was an awkward silence.

"That man suffered a lot of physical pain," Ed finally said in his lawyerly way. "What I'm feeling is different." He instinctively placed his hand over his heart.

Her smile was kind, her blue eyes calm. The silence made Ed uncomfortable. He wanted to say something profound, but he didn't know what that would be, and he didn't understand what a clumsy peasant had to do with him.

"I wanted Tim's life to be so perfect," he blurted. "I wanted him to have everything I didn't. I was just trying to get through the day. I didn't mean to...to ..." He couldn't say the dark thing.

Her eyes turned sad. The silent awkwardness returned.

"Ed," she said finally, "what our peasant friend needed to do was to *pull* the knife out."

Ed looked away. "There's so much I want to say to him, but...but I'll never have the chance."

"Your agony runs deep inside you, but your subconscious is very wise. Let your thoughts come, watch them pass by, and pay attention to what they are telling you. Over time, they will give you peace."

Ed bowed awkwardly and backed out of the room. She didn't understand. She couldn't understand. How could someone who lived in a monastery understand? The robes, the cropped hair, it wasn't the real world. She...It wasn't that simple. It just wasn't.

At first, Ed had refused to believe Tim had taken his own life. It made no sense. It was a tragic accident. He thought Tim was staying with his mother, but later learned he'd rented a hotel room. He'd gone out with friends, had a few drinks. Afterward, he went back to his room and took the sleeping pills. He was young and inexperienced. Tim probably was tipsy and didn't realize how many pills he'd taken. It was a tragic accident—but then the coroner said he downed most of the bottle. Eventually, his friends reported receiving a bizarre text message: *I can't take it anymore. I just want to be free.*

What the hell kind of note was that? Take what—being handed a top-notch education on a silver platter? Having many friends? A great future? Why Timmy? For God's sake, why?

He remembered Mary's desperate, haggard face when they met at the funeral parlor, her eyes puffy from crying and lack of sleep. He had not seen her for several years. Time had not been kind. Her hair, which had gone gray, was pulled straight back into a bun. She'd gained a lot of weight and her dumpy figure made her appear older. She wore a loose-fitting print dress with an uneven hem and brown oxfords. He couldn't help thinking that except for Tim, their marriage had been all wrong.

"You never think you're going to outlive your children," she'd managed to say. She twisted the handle on her purse with her plump hands. "I knew he was a little despondent—"

"You knew?"

"I thought it was a phase. Why didn't he come to me? Mothers are supposed to fix things for their children."

"Did he say anything about our…When did you talk last?" Ed asked.

"I didn't even know he was in town."

"Oh."

She cleared her throat and swallowed. "I just don't understand why he didn't talk to you first? You two were always so close. He was looking forward to the summer hike to…where was it now?"

"Strawberry Mountain."

Her eyes searched Ed's face. "What could have pushed him over the edge?"

Ed's eyes watered. A fist tightened in his chest. He patted Mary's hand. It was the least he could do because he knew what that thing was, and he would have to live with it for the rest of his life.

Ed came to a clearing. A few puffy clouds lingered in the blue sky and thousands of tiny yellow wildflowers covered the field. He sat on a fallen tree. Tim would know the name of those flowers and probably the kind of the tree he was sitting on.

He'd tried so hard to be a good father and in those last few moments, totally blew it. He prayed to God that Tim didn't hear those final words—*You drop out and you're dead to me.* How could he be sure that he didn't? Tim said he had to find himself, but why? Was it the stress? Why didn't Tim talk to him? Of course, that's what he was trying to do. The divorce. Maybe that's where it all started. Maybe it threw his son off-kilter. Ed didn't know. When he was a kid, things were tough. His family never had much money. In fact, they never had much of anything, but he never, ever thought of... taking his...killing himself.

Today was the *exact* day Tim died. Is that the way to say it? No, the truth was his son took his own life. Ed got up from the log. High up in a Douglas fir, a crow broke the silence with caws. He took a final look at the sea of yellow flowers swaying in the soft breeze and headed toward the pond. Spring is a beautiful time. No one should think about dying in spring.

Ed heard the bell ringing in the distance. That was the call to return to the Zendo. He hurriedly made his way down the trail, until he reached the gravel path around the pond. His pace slowed. The late afternoon sun angled in the westward sky, causing the trees to cast soft shadows on the seemingly opaque green water. The air was calm, tinged with a sweet fragrance.  Ed stopped.

A blue heron stood at the pond's edge directly in front of him. He'd heard that herons occasionally visited, but it was the first time he'd come across one. Ed watched it carefully, trying to see it through Tim's eyes. What a fascinating creature. It had a long, yellow bill and the black stripes above each eye extended to the back of its neck like a thin plume, which reminded Ed of a bad haircut. It stood like a blue-gray statue on two long legs that turned reddish at the thighs, its eyes alert yellow buttons.

In the distance, the bell rang again, but Ed didn't move. He didn't want to disturb this magnificent bird, and he didn't want to leave this place. This moment. It was so peaceful, so perfect, so *safe*.

The sun warmed his back. The light breeze swaddled him like a blanket. Gnat-like bugs danced in swarms over the banks to the music of the wondrous, croaking frogs.

Whoosh! The heron's neck lunged forward. Its long, sharp bill pierced the surface of the pond and speared a squirming frog.

*Timmy*!

# Tangle

B rian rolled his wheelchair into the High Ground coffee shop on Blaine Street every Friday to order a tall vanilla latte but mostly to escape from his cocoon and experience what he called the swarm of life—the low hum of laughter, cups coming and going, the rich aroma of coffee, the faint smell of cinnamon, the eclectic background music, and snatches of conversation: "My mother makes a killer cheesecake." "Sure, I could give in, but hey, I've got my pride." "Would you buy that car?" "He's seeing someone else."

He loved everything about the coffee shop because it was such a welcome break from working alone in his tiny apartment as an online corporate banking analyst. This throng of distant souls, as he called them, not only fueled his passion for people watching but helped quench his angst about his past which, like lions lurking in his mind, stalked and snarled attacking his very being.

High Ground also had Merrilee. The young barista intrigued him with her engaging smile, curvaceous body, and blond good looks. Once he placed his order, she happily brought his coffee to the table where he parked his wheelchair and scribbled poetic starts in a notebook. He prized the way she said, "Hey, Brian," as she handed him his cup with a latte art heart in the center. "How are you, today?" She smelled like lilacs and had sparkling jade eyes that seemed wild, yet caring.

"What are you writing about?" she'd ask lingering to chat.

"Poetry. I write poetry."

"Awe-some. Poetry's always been way over my head."

"That's what I used to think. Actually, I happened onto it by, uh, accident." He stopped there. That word pinched. Best not to say too much. After his long recovery, his therapist, Emma Whitfield, encouraged him to write his thoughts in a notebook. When the two discussed what he'd written, she marveled at his word choice, his observations, his imagery, his turns.

"I...I'm not a writer," he'd protested, but then Mrs. Whitfield assured him that anyone who writes is a writer. She gave him books by Mary Oliver, Billy Collins, Kim Stafford, and Charles Goodrich. Good bards all, whose verse touched a common nerve. He especially liked Goodrich who wrote a whole collection on bugs. It was just amazing how the man could elevate the common to poetic elegance. Brian signed up for a poetry workshop at the counseling center. Wow. It was addictive. Once he started, he couldn't stop. In fact, it was evening poetry readings at the High Ground that first introduced him to the coffee shop.

"I've got some poetry books I bet you'd like. I could lend you one."

Merrilee wasn't going there. She seemed more interested in how he could drive his two-door Nissan. "I saw you unfold and assemble your wheelchair from the window. I mean that's just awe-some."

Those lips, those luscious lips formed a dazzling smile, and he loved the way she said *awesome,* lingering on the first syllable. He could only manage a shy grin, "The car's equipped with hand controls. I can go just about anywhere and not have to depend on anyone else."

While she had never asked directly, she hinted at what had crippled him. "I don't see your injury." She pushed back a blond curl and beamed. "You're always so cheerful, capable, too."

Those words made his heart swell. Still, he knew she was curious. Most people were, but he didn't like to talk about it, and for the longest time, he couldn't. When she finally did flat out ask, he cringed, but she stood there like a firmly rooted tree. He hesitated, making small talk about the weather, hoping the conversation would move on.

She didn't budge. "So, I mean, what happened?"

*Careful. Don't scare her away.* His lips formed words and he heard himself say, "I...uh...had just graduated high school." He stared at his cup and lied. "A bunch of us guys had gone to the river, you know, roasted hot dogs and had a few beers. We started climbing nearby fir trees and sliding down the branches. The higher you climbed, the bigger the thrill. I was outdoing everyone." His hands cut through the air. "You guessed it. A branch I rode snapped. It threw me off balance, and I couldn't stop the momentum." He choked. "I hadn't counted on that. I hit the ground hard. It changed everything." He looked up. *"Everything."*

Her green eyes brimmed with empathy, as if she were staring at a version of himself that he'd thought was long lost.

He wanted to linger in that moment, but the *real* memory crowded it out—that April morning, daffodils, a soft, sparse rain, his mother already planning Easter, two months to graduation and then what? He was seventeen on his way to school, a kid with a future, driving his father's precious old pickup. Wham! In seconds, it all changed. He shivered. Colleen's father called him a murderer. The judge called it involuntary manslaughter.

"Just like that." He swallowed hard and went on with his lie. "Those guys, my friends, they moved on with their lives and I was alone. When you can't run and jump, well, you know." He sipped his vanilla latte, swallowing his fib, clinging to every nuance in her expression.

"You came through it. You're okay. That's what matters." She patted his arm, giving it a little squeeze. "Awe-some. Just awe-some."

That touch sent electricity through his body. Each Friday, he came and ordered his latte, studying her, recording descriptions in his note-book—the way she gave shape to her bibbed tan barista apron, how her legs moved with such confidence, her infectious laugh. Little pieces that he gleaned and later spun into poems. Who was she? He wanted to know more.

Sometimes, he brought her small gifts—a flower, pieces of Dove chocolate candy with the little quotes inside. She especially liked those, carefully unwrapping the candy and reading the messages aloud: "Today, something special will happen." "We are the author of our dreams." He liked watching her stuff the candy past her full lips, savoring the small bites, and carefully chewing. Afterwards, she smoothed and folded the foil, tucking it in her apron pocket like it was precious. She always took his offerings and held them against her heart. "You're so thoughtful."

He smiled to himself, constantly thinking of her, seeing her small, soft hands with the short, square-tipped red nails setting his latte on the table. How gratifying to feel the cup's warmth, drink in its comforting scent, and hold something she'd touched. Being near her made him feel whole again, a bubbling up of something. Love? What was that exactly? He'd always shied away from intimacy, keeping to life's perimeter.

Colleen had small hands, too, only he'd never touched them, just remembered her fingers clutching a pencil in Algebra class, rapidly jotting equations. He'd been in a hurry, trying to get to school early, so he could read his paper over once more before turning it in. Mr. Springstone thought his writing showed promise and wanted to talk to him about college. He'd never thought about it before, thinking he'd graduate and get a job, maybe work in the sawmill with his dad, but there was Mr. Springstone, talking about scholarships and his future. This time he'd written about Addie Bundren, a character in Faulkner's *As I Lay Dying*, arguing she had existential tendencies. It would blow Springstone's mind. Future? After school there'd be baseball practice. At the last game, he hit a home run. Jesus, the cheering. He was going to do that again before the season ended. College English major? Really? Could he play baseball at college? Why was that SUV in front of him moving like a snail? Get out of my way. Here I come. He stepped on the throttle powering his dad's pickup, hearing the engine growl as it picked up speed. The world was his and he wasn't letting go. He steered into the oncoming lane to pass the snail.

Kapow!

The loud crash of metal sounded like an explosion, the pickup on its side, blood trickling down his face. He wiggled his toes, his legs, his shoulders, his neck. His whole body worked. He was okay, but what did he hit?

He lifted his head to see.

The other car, a small black sedan, was mashed and on its side. He heard sirens. Police cars and ambulances had wasted no time.

While an EMT checked him out, others were tending to Millie, Colleen Peterson's younger sister.

Colleen's younger sister?

She was sobbing. Where was Colleen?

Colleen was dead. Killed instantly in the head-on collision—a collision so ferocious, rescuers had to cut the metal away to retrieve...the body...Colleen.

He didn't even really know her. She'd been his classmate over the years. There, but distant. She was a straight-A student, a cheerleader, with a cute figure and long reddish, brown hair. So popular, she didn't know he was alive.

*Alive* that word. But she wasn't. And Millie, now walked with a limp and had a scar on her face. Her life reduced. The judge was sorry, his parents were mortified, his older brother Ron was quiet, so quiet. A pall hung over his high school, grieving for her, but not him.

He remembered Colleen's father, his scowl, and anger, speaking at his sentencing. "Every time I look at Millie and see her limp, every time I look into her face, it tears at my heart. And Colleen. I will never *ever* see my precious Colleen again. Ever." He sniffed and dabbed his eyes. "They were on their way to school, but turned around and headed home because they forgot their lunches...their mother's meatloaf sandwiches. Meatloaf, for Christ sakes. If they'd only kept going." Then he sobbed. People in the courtroom cried with him.

Brian closed his eyes and saw red blood dripping on his English paper, the one he'd been so proud of, the one that pointed to a future. He could still smell burning rubber and hear the sirens. Of course, he was sorry, he was very sorry. Sorry. Sorry. But what good was sorry? It wouldn't bring Colleen back; it wouldn't fix Millie's leg or her face.

At the end of the day, he got hit with involuntary manslaughter, criminally negligent homicide, fourth-degree assault, and reckless driving. His eyes opened when he heard the judge commit him to a youth facility until age twenty-five. In one ugly second, just one, his whole life imploded.

***

His psychiatrist, Dr. Reiner, encouraged him. "Give yourself a chance. You've been through hell, but you've already accomplished more than most people ever do. You finished college, have a good job. You're independent and out in the world. If this Merrilee that you speak of likes you, don't run away. Just take one step at a time."

Out in the world. Out. What good was that? Colleen was in a cold grave. Dead. Killed instantly in a head-on collision he *caused*.

"I still get that depression. Sometimes, I close my eyes and see this huge black spider pouncing on me, covering me with its hairy legs until I can't breathe, and I feel a wave of hopelessness of being smothered in a dark tunnel. I—it kills me to think about it, I mean, what happened afterward. Why I chose to ..." Brian gripped the arms of his wheelchair so tightly his knuckles turned white. His eyes locked on the painting on Dr. Reiner's office wall, an abstract of a leafless tree with dark branches reaching out like eerie tentacles touching the black frame. *Did I choose what I did to myself?*

Dr. Reiner leaned back in his chair and steepled his hands. "You've struggled with guilt and depression for a long time, and you're still going to have those bouts, but you've made so much progress. Keep taking the medication I prescribed and doing what you're doing—showing up for work, staying engaged with others, expressing yourself through poetry." He winked. "You're still a handsome guy, Brian. And talented, too. People make mistakes. Sometimes they make several of them. You're *not* your mistakes. Looking backward is only for time travelers. Life is always out there waiting for you."

Waiting. Waiting. Just waiting.

Dr. Reiner introduced Brian to Ron, who'd also suffered a spinal cord injury. Ron worked as an emergency dispatcher, was married, and expecting his second child. "We're just like everyone else. We can do anything," Ron said. "We just do it sitting down. Look at the Governor of Texas."

Brian did a Google search. Yes, Governor Greg Abbott. At age twenty-six, Abbott was paralyzed  below the waist when an oak tree cracked and fell on him while he was jogging following a storm. It never stopped him. He finished law school and went on to achieve many things. People looked up to him, listened to him. While, Brian didn't particularly agree with Abbott's politics, he certainly proved he didn't have to walk to make his mark. Then there was Franklin Roosevelt and George Wallace who didn't let disabilities hold them back, either.

Maybe Merrilee would consider going somewhere with him, like to sit in the park and watch the ducks on the pond. Eventually, he'd have to tell her the truth about his injury, but he was becoming more confident she'd understand. Last week, she'd rescued a tiny gray kitten who wandered the street outside the coffee shop—wide, frightened eyes, skinny, and limping. Merrilee wiped its face, cleaned its little body with a wet paper towel, and massaged its sore leg. When she touched that leg, Brian could feel it under his skin. She wouldn't set the kitty down, until a customer offered to take the stray to the humane society, much to the coffee shop manager's relief.

Friday-after-Friday he relished his visits to the High Ground, gleaning little snippets of lives:  "How can you believe that?" "Yeah, well that fly you were trying to swat wants to live as much as you do." "No one has the corner on the truth." Spoken shards that were great prompts for his writing. And Merrilee. She was so kind, so refreshing, so full of life.

"You should perform your poems at the weekend poetry slam this Saturday night," she said, setting his latte in front of him. "They always have an open mic."

He'd never actually done a reading before, and someone would have to lower the mic. Was he good enough? He didn't want to make a fool of himself. But, ah, Merrilee's suggestion gave him the opening he'd been waiting for. "I wrote one about that little kitten you rescued."

"Awe-some," she said.

He'd hoped she'd pull up a chair, lean in, hang onto his every word.

Instead, she said, "How sweet. I'd like to hear that one sometime, but there's a line of customers at the counter." She turned and scurried off.

***

He worked on his courage, practicing in front of the bathroom mirror at home, the one lowered for his convenience. "Would you like to go for a stroll?" No wait. "The park is so lovely in spring. Maybe you could join me after your shift? I could drive us there." That was better.

He stared at his reflection. Blinked his small gray eyes, cocked his head, and flashed a smile. The doc was right, he was okay looking. The "accident" had done no damage to his face. He ran a comb through his rust-colored hair, smiled, and flexed his shoulder muscles, kept firm from working with weights. The ol' Brian he knew was still in there. He shivered. *Who exactly was the old Brian?*

He read, "Lifesaver," the poem about the kitten rescue over and over aloud. He read it while he cooked himself a hamburger. He read it outside on his balcony to a cool breeze. He read it after he brushed his teeth and again before he killed the light and hit the sack. In the darkened room, his mind lingered on the last lines: *In all of us there's a bit of a stray./A part that cannot mesh, making us fear who we really are.*

It had to be perfect.

That night he dreamed of his deceased mother, vague and blurred, a filmy image, her face becoming the photo he kept by his bedside. A smell like vanilla teased his nostrils. That scent. Her scent. "It's okay. It's okay, baby," she seemed to say giving him a pat. "It's your time. Let it come."

On Friday, the High Ground was busier than normal. Why were all these people here? Maybe it was the ad they ran in Thursday's paper—thirty percent off for first-time customers. Hmmm. Merrilee wasn't behind the counter. Instead, that skinny kid, the one they called Matt with a splatter of acne on his chin, took his order and brought him his latte.

"Where's Merrilee?" Brian asked. The kid nudged his shoulder toward a table by the windows. Merrilee had seated herself with a group gathered there. She seemed to be staring into the eyes of a dark-haired man with a high forehead wearing a green fisherman's sweater. *Who could that be? Some visiting relative?*

Brian craned his neck and sat taller hoping he could catch her eye. The espresso machine wheezed like an annoying asthmatic. Noisy, boisterous laughter and loud talk came from the group by the windows. He tried to hear what they were saying, but the volume of the coffee shop chatter made his head throb. Even the bell that jingled every time someone opened the door, which he'd once found intriguing, went flat.

Merrilee held up her hand, showing a ring to the others. What was she saying? Then he heard it, *awe-some.* The group at her table laughed and applauded. "Congratulations." "Have you set a date?"

Those words thundered over the din. Merrilee giggled, leaned forward, and kissed the dark-haired man on the lips.

"No!" Brian blurted. Two middle-aged women at the table next to him turned and exchanged glances before resuming their conversation and nibbling pastries. Brian winced. His whole life spilled in front of him. *It was an accident, wasn't it? Why couldn't they turn the music down?* "I didn't really want ...I didn't think I had...She was dead. Millie couldn't walk straight. People shunned me." *Why was I alive with barely a scratch?* The two women were gaping at him again. *Did they have to do that?*

He swallowed, but it didn't stop the bile inching into his throat. His mind wouldn't let go. It had a grip on him like a wild animal, jerking him back to that awful winter night years ago, not long after they released him from that youth facility. His time served had made no difference. He was still a pariah in his hometown. Guilt ripped his insides.

He sensed that familiar veil of depression choking him and saw his hand leaving the bridge railing as he slipped over the side. Everything blurred. He didn't remember hitting the water. *Justice for Colleen.*

If back then, he could've connected with someone like Merrilee, if he could've felt forgiveness and all of the possibilities of life. Maybe then...he would not have jumped.

# Mildred's Secret

The gingerbread men lay in a line on the kitchen counter like a class of uniformed schoolchildren ready to march to an assembly. Some had jerky smiles; others looked like they needed eye muscle surgery.

Mildred squeezed strips of white frosting onto the last row. "You know it's the arthritis in my hands that makes things bumpy," she said to her friend Edna, "but at least they're all smiling."

Edna laughed. "That last one looks a little drunk."

In spite of her arthritis and seventy-some years, Mildred—tall, slim with a full head of silver curly hair—was still an attractive woman. Her lips formed a natural smile, giving her face a pleasant, peaceful look.

She set the final batch of awkwardly decorated gingerbread men on the counter next to a luscious assortment of her other sweet delicacies: peanut butter, chocolate chip, star-shaped sugar cookies with colored sprinkles, and her specialty—decadent, chocolate-frosted brownies.

The coffee maker gurgled, adding its aroma to the buttery air, making Mildred's small kitchen in the apartment complex for seniors seem cheerful against the grip of another cold December day. Outside, morning frost still clung to the stiff grass, and a cold wind continued to nurture leftover ice around the edges of the windows. Sunshine, Mildred's orange-striped cat, huddled in her bed close to the baseboard heater.

Edna pointed to the counter. "What're you gonna do with all those…those…cookies?"

Mildred poured hot coffee into two dark green mugs decorated with rosy-cheeked Santas. "I plan to give them away as gifts. One box is for Nelda. She has no family to speak of, and she hardly gets out anymore. And uh…I have some friends I plan to call on."

Edna felt a twinge of envy. Judging by the number of cookies on Mildred's counter, she must know tons of people. All of Edna's friends had evaporated. Then, again, maybe they were really Gilbert's friends. After he died, she was all alone. Edna reached for a dark chocolate brownie studded with walnuts. "I shouldn't be eating this. I got a touch of the diabetes, you know."

"A touch?" Mildred wiped her hands on a kitchen towel. She lined up boxes on her counter to package the cookies.

Edna sunk her teeth into the brownie and washed it down with a swig of coffee. "The doc said I need to get rid of my stomach, but I'm gonna wait till after the holidays to work on that." Edna was always talking about losing her stomach, but it still bulged there like a tightly inflated beach ball. She was a stocky woman with thinning, mousy gray hair that she parted in the middle and wound into a knot at the base of her skull. Her heavy breasts almost met her stomach under the loose purple dress she wore.

Mildred stopped and filled a green tree-shaped tray with cookies. She stretched clear plastic wrap across the top and handed it to Edna.

"Put these in the freezer. When you feel like you need energy, just take *one* and eat it slowly."

A widow, Mildred had moved into Pleasant Point Villa in the fall. Each apartment had one bedroom, a small bath and a combined kitchen, dining and living area. She'd met Edna one sunny September afternoon in the courtyard.

A dyed-in-the-wool fussbudget, Edna didn't make friends easily. She quit going to church after she got into an argument with the new minister because *she* allowed guitar music at the morning service. Hymns, in Edna's opinion, only sounded spiritual when played on an organ or piano, and she thought ministers should be men. Her apartment was either too hot or too cold, the lounge was drafty, and the mail always came too late. When other tenants heard the tap, tap, tap of Edna's black cane, they quickly disappeared like geese escaping winter. Mildred was her only friend.

"I don't bake anymore," Edna said. "My son sends one of the grandkids to pick me up for Christmas. I usually take my special red Jell-O salad that I make with marshmallows and a can of fruit cocktail." Her lips tightened. "They don't even appreciate it. I bring most of it back with me, eat off it for days, and then toss it out. It gets rubbery sitting in the fridge."

Mildred rinsed the bowl she'd used to mix frosting. "You have family, and they probably send you home with a nice gift."

"Oh yeah—bath salts, a can of mixed nuts, maybe a candle...a lot of tea. I got tea coming out the wazoo. If I get another kitchen towel, I could make a quilt. You got family close-by?"

"No. My siblings are gone, except for a brother that lives clear over in Vermont and a few scattered nieces and nephews. Ed and I never had children, but being a teacher, I was always around youngsters."

"So what're you gonna do tomorrow? Spend Christmas with your *friends*?" Edna stared at the cookies.

"I'm going to stay right here with Sunshine."

"That's sad that you don't have some place to go...and lonely."

"No. I get up early, take my walk, weather permitting, make something special for Sunshine, and cook myself a nice meal. Afterward, we just curl up with a good book. People try to lump this wonderful season into one day, when what we really need to do is spread it out over the year. Don't you think?"

"Harrumph," Edna muttered. She'd already had enough of the holiday. The artificial tree in the lounge blocked the sunlight, and she had to dodge that stupid, grinning bell ringer down at the shopping center who was just after her money. She'd had enough of those damn Christmas carols—why did she have to listen to *Jingle Bells* at the grocery store when all she wanted was a carton of cottage cheese?

Sure, she had family, a place to go, but it made her feel like a nut without its bolt. Most of the other guests were from her snooty daughter-in-law's side. The great grandkids ran around like a bunch of wild hoodlums making more noise than her nerves could handle. Edna just sat in the corner and tried to make conversation with her son's father-in-law who was hard of hearing, blew his nose too often, and told the same corny jokes. Last year he even passed gas. It didn't faze him; he just kept talking. "Did ya hear the one about the two men that got lost when they were out huntin'?" he chortled. A frazzled Edna looked away but she wanted to yell, "Yeah at least a hundred times, and did ya think I didn't smell that?" She was grateful when they drove her home to her cold, dark apartment carrying the gifts she didn't need and her bowl of barely eaten Jell-O.

Mildred lined the gift boxes on her counter with parchment paper and filled each with an assortment of cookies. All of the boxes were the same size, except for one.

Edna eyed the big box. "That sure is a lot of cookies for Nelda."

"Oh, this one isn't for Nelda. It's for a special friend."

"Special friend? Someone you've known for a long time?" Edna studied Mildred's face.

"Not really, but I'm sure he'll enjoy them."

"*He?*" Edna gasped. She sat up like she'd been pricked with a hat pin.

"Now, where did I put that ribbon?"

"Where did you meet *him*?" Edna leaned forward anxiously awaiting details.

Mildred counted cookies. "I don't want anybody to get too much of one thing." She smiled.

Edna winced. She set down her coffee mug. Maybe Mildred had a secret beau. If that were true, she might move away, and then she'd lose her one friend. Mildred must've been quite a looker when she was young. Intelligent, too—her tiny apartment was crammed with books, and she always had her nose in one of them. "You better watch yourself in Nelda's neighborhood. There's lotsa crime in the north part of town. There's stealing, drugs, and graffiti everywhere."

While Mildred wrapped her packages of cookies in red paper, Edna continued her tirade. "There's lotsa mixed what-nots over there and way too many of them Mexicans. Why, I bet most of 'em came in the back door. All my people went through the right channels and waited their turn to get into this country."

Mildred carefully topped each wrapped box with an elegant white bow, except for the larger package. That one got a special silver one. "That's just about perfect," she said, admiring the special loops and curls she made with the shiny ribbon. "I didn't think my hands could do that anymore."

Edna stared at the big box and then at Mildred. "You're sure goin' through lots of trouble for your *gentleman* friend."

"Everybody needs to feel special at Christmas." Mildred offered no other information, so Edna started in on Nelda's neighborhood again.

"And those street kids that hang out at that park across from her place. I don't know how Nelda handles it."

"Nicky, one of those boys, helped me that time Nelda tripped on the sidewalk after we'd gone grocery shopping."

"Nicky! You know his name? I'd be mighty careful who you're chattin' up over there. First thing you know, he'll steal your purse."

"When Nelda went down, her bag of groceries spilled all over the sidewalk. Nicky stayed with me until the ambulance arrived. Then he helped pick things up. He even got a broom and swept up the glass from that jar of pickles we lost."

"Mildred, he's a street kid!" Edna squawked. "Hanging around all day, out for no good, and we're all paying for it with our taxes."

"He seemed like a nice young man down on his luck. I gave him a loaf of bread and a package of sliced cheese."

"You're s-o-o-o naïve."

"He looked thin. At first, he was reluctant to take the stuff. Waved me away, like accepting it embarrassed him. When I insisted, he said 'thank you,' and then ran off. There was just something in his eyes...about the way he looked at me... I can't explain it. I think, maybe, he used to live in that building. He sure knew where to find the broom."

"His eyes! He probably was zonked on drugs. Mildred, he could be a gang member!" Edna's voice went up. "When they're on drugs, they don't care what they do!"

Mildred seemed deep in thought and didn't respond. Instead, she stacked the wrapped cookie boxes in a brown paper shopping bag. Finally, she said, "I think I *get* Nicky."

Edna stood up. "I suppose you better get going if you're gonna get those delivered." She reached for her cane. "I wouldn't want to be in that neighborhood after dark, and it's cold enough to freeze every hair on your head. Maybe you should get that *special* friend of yours to go with you." Edna eyed Mildred, hoping she'd say more about her gentleman, but Mildred just went to the closet and pulled out her coat. She wrapped a red wool scarf around her neck and covered her silver curls with a matching red hat.

***

Edna waited on the sidewalk and watched until Mildred's green Chevrolet disappeared around the corner. A tight, envious twinge crept through her body. She pictured Mildred and her new man-friend laughing over eggnog and having dinner together. Edna slowly tapped her way back to the apartment complex. Maybe this year, she'd bring green Jell-O.

***

Mildred pulled up in front of Nelda's apartment building and luckily found a parking spot on the narrow street. The sky was gray with a few threatening, angry-looking clouds in the distance. The neighborhood seemed unusually quiet, the street deserted, as if all the people had gone inside to avoid the cold. She got out of her car and grabbed a package of cookies for Nelda. A wide smile covered her face as she stepped over bits of paper, an empty beer can, and other trash that littered the street. She rang the apartment building bell, waited, and then headed up the stairs.

She never looked back.

***

Nicky poked his head around a tree in the park. He'd been watching the grandmother lady arrange something in the back seat. When she disappeared into the building, he tossed his cigarette down, mashed it on the sidewalk, and pulled his black wool cap over his ears.

Like a cat closing in on its prey, he quickly crossed the street, peered into the window and spotted the wrapped packages. He stared at the big box with the fancy silver bow that Mildred had left close to the door. He walked by again, looked over his shoulder, and tried the door handle. It was unlocked! He glanced up and down the street.

It wasn't like he was stealing. No. She'd be giving these things away and to people that had more than he did. In one fast swoop, he snatched up the big package and the shopping bag. He'd done it so many times before in those convenience stores—waited until the lone attendant turned his head, grabbed something, and ran like hell.

He didn't stop running until he was safely in the alley. Gasping, he could see the clouds his breath made in the air. God it was cold. He crouched behind a dumpster that smelled like vomit. Then he reached for that big box. Hopefully, it held something he could trade for a joint. He tore off the beautiful silver bow, ripped the red paper like a little kid on Christmas morning, and pulled the lid off the box.

"Cookies," he muttered. "Shit! Well, what the hell." He couldn't resist. Man he was hungry, and he could feel the December chill deep in his spine. He reached for one of Mildred's silly gingerbread men. "Sorry fellow," he said and bit off its head. Next, he grabbed a peanut butter cookie, then a chocolate chip and swallowed them fast. He fumbled with the shopping bag, found a second box and tore off the wrapping. "More shit ass cookies!"

He wiped his mouth on his already soiled jacket and devoured a chocolate brownie. A knot welled up inside. In a flash of memory, he suddenly saw his grandmother. She was standing by the door of their apartment handing him a brown bag. "*Escúchame.* Don't lose your lunch. I put in two of my special cinnamon cookies."

"*Mi Abuela,*" he said to the empty, cold alley. She always saw to it that he and his little sister got a Christmas gift, even if it was just a small plastic toy or something she knitted. They couldn't afford a tree, so his Lita would make little decorations and hang them on that discarded palm tree plant she rescued from the hallway. She could nurse anything back to health, except herself. Now, his Lita was gone, and his sister was living with some guy in Albuquerque.

Once his grandmother died, everything fell apart. They got kicked out of their apartment, his mother moved in with one of her endless boyfriends, and Nicky found himself on the street. It seemed like he'd been out there forever, sleeping in a friend's damp basement one night and under a bridge the next. Now, he and two other guys usually bedded down in a decaying building, but they had to wait until it got really dark before they made their way over that chain link fence.

The sweet smell of chocolate and spices kept taking him back to the little dingy apartment—his last secure place. He felt his grandmother's brown hands covering him with a warm quilt and patting his shoulder before turning out the light. Where had all that gone? Tears glistened in his eyes, but it did no good to cry on the street. If guys thought you were weak, they just beat on you...or worse.

"Make me proud," his abuela would say whenever he screwed up. "Make me proud." She even said it that time he "borrowed" a bike and a cop knocked on their door. Only then, his Lita was the one in tears. How the hell was he supposed to do that now? Maybe he should just end it, find a bridge and slither over the side into the Willamette River. If he got high enough on some weed, he probably could do it. If he got his hands on enough crank, he was sure he could. He heard of a guy who killed himself by drinking antifreeze, but that seemed messy.

*Make me proud, Nicky. Make me proud.* The words seemed to echo in the alley bouncing off the cold brick walls. He shouldn't have stolen the packages from that grandmother lady. The nice lady who always smiled at him, stopped to say hello, and gave him a loaf of bread that time. Other people glanced away when they saw him, as if he was some slimy reptile, but she always looked right into his face, like he was somebody. Hell, he didn't even know her name.

Maybe he could put the packages back. He stared at the torn pieces of red wrapping paper, the muddied silver bow sullied by the damp, dirty alley, the crumbs on his lap. No, he couldn't fix it, and he'd never make anyone proud. His stomach felt sour; he could hardly swallow. He wanted to cry, but the tears wouldn't come. He was alone, and it never was going to change. He needed to do it. Find that bridge. Jump.

A gust of chilly wind blew pieces of wrapping paper down the alley, and the sky started to spit sleet. Nicky pulled the big box to his lap and reached for the lid. *What's this?* In his haste, he hadn't noticed it. Wedged between rows of cookies was a folded note with his name on it. Was this some kind of a dream? Maybe he was freezing to death and his brain went numb. He held it up to the light and squinted. Sure enough, the note said *Nicky.* He flipped it open. Inside was a message written in the grandmother lady's shaky hand: *I hoped you would take these and open the big box first. Not to worry, I made these cookies especially for you. Please enjoy, and share them with your friends. They are my gift to you. Your gift to me will be to remember this kindness and to never, never give up hope. Merry Christmas—M.*

# About the author

Jean Rover is novelist, short story, and personal essay writer. She is the author of *Touch the Sky*, a heart-rending novel, filled with intrigue, about a missing child in Oregon's backcountry and its sequel, *Ready or Not*. Her writing has received awards or recognition from *Writer's Digest, Short Story America*, Willamette Writers, Oregon Writers Colony, This I Believe, Inc., and the International Association of Business Communicators (IABC). Her work has appeared in various literary magazines and anthologies, including the *Saturday Evening Post's Great American Fiction Contest* anthology. Other stories were performed at Liars' League events in London, England and Portland, Oregon. She has also authored a chapbook, *Beneath the Boughs Unseen*, featuring holiday stories about society's invisible people. She lives and writes in Oregon's lush Willamette Valley.

# Acknowledgments

A special thank you to Dawn Eisler Smith, Lois Rosen, Jane Fernandez, Sandra McDow, and to the current and past members of the Tuesday Night Group for your helpful suggestions and encouragement along the way. You make me a better writer.

Hats off to the Java Quackers, my fun-loving coffee group. You jumpstart my week, cheer me on, and can solve any problem in a New York minute. Your invaluable support is so important to the solidary writing life.

Special hugs to the kids—sweet Tara who barks, nudges me to my computer, and sits patiently by my side until Forester, arches his back, and gives one high-pitched, shrill meow to remind us it's time to eat.

And speaking of eating, short story collections present little nibbles of life, a buffet of ups and downs. As Robert Frost noted, "In three words, I can sum up everything I've learned about life. It goes on."

May all of our lives progress with minimal blips and lots of loving kindness.

***


If you enjoyed reading this collection, please consider posting a review. Just a few words will do. It will make Tara happy, and Forester won't have to come looking for you.  Above all, our sincere appreciation for your support.

9 780099 671305 4